Girls Only!

VOLUME TWO

Books by Beverly Lewis

GIRLS ONLY (GO!)
Youth Fiction

Girls Only! Volume One
Girls Only! Volume Two

SUMMERHILL SECRETS
Youth Fiction

SummerHill Secrets Volume One
SummerHill Secrets Volume Two

HOLLY'S HEART
Youth Fiction

Best Friend, Worst Enemy • *Straight-A Teacher*
Secret Summer Dreams • *No Guys Pact*
Sealed With a Kiss • *Little White Lies*
The Trouble With Weddings • *Freshman Frenzy*
California Crazy • *Mystery Letters*
Second-Best Friend • *Eight Is Enough*
Good-Bye, Dressel Hills • *It's a Girl Thing*

www.BeverlyLewis.com

BEVERLY LEWIS

Girls Only!

VOLUME TWO

◆ BETHANYHOUSE
Minneapolis, Minnesota

Published by Bethany House Publishers
11400 Hampshire Avenue South
Bloomington, Minnesota 55438

Bethany House Publishers is a division of
Baker Publishing Group, Grand Rapids, Michigan.

Printed in the United States of America

Library of Congress Cataloging-in-Publication Data is available for this title.

ISBN 978-0-7642-0462-3

BEVERLY LEWIS is the bestselling author of more than eighty books for adults and children, including the popular CUL-DE-SAC KIDS and SUMMERHILL SECRETS series, several picture books, and numerous adult fiction series. Five of her blockbuster novels have received the Gold Book Award for sales over 500,000 copies, and *The Brethren* won a 2007 Christy Award. Beverly and her husband make their home in Colorado, within miles of the Olympic Training Center, headquarters for the U.S. Olympic Committee.

Girls Only!

Follow the
Dream

AUTHOR'S NOTE

I am grateful to my daughter Janie, who helped with the story line for this book. Big hugs, honey!

As always, I refer (and often) to the skating authorities at the U.S. Figure Skating Association. I am also thrilled to live so close to the World Arena in Colorado Springs, Colorado.

Now, just a personal note to the many readers who've written to me since the GIRLS ONLY series began. Thank you for your amazing enthusiam for these books!

Thanks to my editor, Rochelle Glöege, of Bethany House Publishers, who first got me thinking about this series. Also, I want to thank my husband, Dave, for his recent surprise gift to me—tickets to Stars on Ice. A very special birthday!

To

Amy Meredith,

*one of my most
loyal fans ever!*

Follow the Dream
Chapter One

Olivia Hudson stared at the ice-skater figurine on her bookshelf. She ran her fingers over the delicate work of art. "*This* is my dream," Livvy whispered. "Nothing must keep me from it."

The piece had been chosen by her mother before her death to leukemia. The statuette was the super-coolest birthday present ever. It was a constant reminder of her mother's devotion and love. Not to mention Mom's great encouragement.

"*I believe in you. . . .*" Her mother's words still echoed in Livvy's memory.

Carefully, she placed the skater back on the shelf. Then she turned toward the windows. Through the delicate yellow curtains, she looked out at the Colorado sky. The sun was making its gradual descent behind the ridge of purple mountains. The sky would soon turn blue-black. House lights would light up the windows along the streets of Alpine Lake.

Livvy sighed. *Why'd Grandma have to stick her nose into my life?* she thought. *Dad and I were doing fine on our own.*

Grandma Hudson's recent hovering was making Livvy a little crazy. Constantly, she was reminding Livvy, "There's a very good reason why I'm here, Olivia Kay."

"I know the reason," Livvy muttered to herself. She drew the curtain back, continuing to brood. "She thinks I need a 'good dose of mothering.' " It had become her grandmother's catchphrase, but Livvy was beginning to despise it.

Something had to be done. Very soon. Especially if Livvy was ever to reach her skating goals.

She let go of the curtain and moved away from the window. Falling onto the bed, she thought back to the past months since her father's mother had moved here from Illinois. At first, things were only slightly tense. Now, though, Grandma insisted on driving her to the rink and attending every single practice session. Livvy actually preferred to walk the short distance to the mall skating rink. After all, it was only a few blocks. Walking was one way to get her leg muscles limbered up before her rigorous stretching exercises.

"I have to talk to her," Livvy said into the air. "But

how?" She absolutely dreaded the thought of confronting her aging grandmother.

Oh, she could just imagine the sorry scene. Grandma's eyes would turn misty and wide. Her heart-shaped face would get all pinkish red. Livvy knew this because she'd accidently observed Grandma's reaction one other time when she was terribly upset. Dad had been annoyed with Grandma's choice of laundry detergent. *Very* politely, he'd said it gave him a skin rash.

Grandma's feathers had gotten quite ruffled, and several days passed before things blew over. That was at the beginning of December. Now it was mid-March, coming up on Easter. What a lousy time to be ungrateful.

But Livvy couldn't help it. *Her* gripe with Grandma would never just blow over. She draped her arm down over the side of the bed, groaning. "It's pointless," she said aloud. "Grandma will never understand."

Yet she was determined to do something. She *had* to. Her skating future was at stake!

Across the room, Coco, her parrot, began flying back and forth in his cage. "Livvy . . . Livvy . . ." he called repeatedly.

"That's my name, birdie-boy." She sat up.

"Birdie-boy . . . birdie-boy" came the reply.

Livvy got up and went to his cage. "Aren't you a lively

one!" She watched him preen his feathers. "Must be nice not having a care in the world," she muttered.

"Not a care."

She laughed at the parrot's innocent mockery. Before moving to Alpine Lake, Livvy had actually considered Coco one of the best listening ears around. Now Jenna Song, her closest friend, definitely filled that spot. For always.

Thinking of Jen, Livvy wiggled her fingers good-bye to her beloved pet. "It's time for some people talk. Sorry, birdie."

Coco began cawing, making a general nuisance of himself.

"Oh, calm your feathers." She closed the bedroom door and hurried downstairs.

Coco kept screaming, but Livvy knew he'd cool it eventually. She crept into the kitchen, relieved the portable phone was available. She eyed the small, fragile woman near the sink. Grandma was wearing a bright red apron, making a supper casserole of chicken and noodles. Before Grandma could notice her, Livvy disappeared back upstairs with the phone.

In the privacy of her bedroom, she dialed Jenna's number.

Her friend picked up on the first ring. "Song residence, Jenna speaking."

"Jen! I'm glad you answered. It's Livvy."

"Hey," Jenna said, warm as always. "How's your day going?"

"Okay, but I need some advice." She sighed. "Oh, how can I ever say this . . . without sounding super horrible?"

"Well, try me. How's that?"

Pausing, Livvy remembered the occasions when Grandma had nearly followed her right onto the ice. At practice, no less!

"Liv?" prodded Jen.

"Oh, I'm sorry. . . ."

"Everything all right?"

Livvy couldn't keep it inside any longer. "You know I love my grandmother, but . . ." She bit her lip. "She's making my life totally miserable."

"What's happening between you and her?"

"To begin with, she treats me like a four-year-old," Livvy explained. "She follows me around at home, makes sure I do my homework, make my bed . . . stuff like that. But on the ice, it's even worse. Grandma's starting to act like my coach!"

"You've gotta be joking!"

"She doesn't know the first thing about ice-skating!"

Jenna was quiet for a moment. Then, "Is there something I can do?"

She wouldn't burden her friend with a family problem like this. "I don't know . . . probably not."

"What about our Girls Only club?" suggested Jenna. "Maybe the four of us can help. We could talk it out at the next meeting."

Livvy shook her head at the phone. "That's why I called *you,* Jen. I'd rather not blab it around."

"I understand. But I'm sure Heather and Miranda will keep this quiet," Jenna persisted.

Livvy didn't want to tell the whole world. "Sorry, Jen, I didn't mean to bother you. Besides, I better get ready for supper. Grandma's calling."

"See you at school," Jenna said.

Before Livvy could press the Off button on the phone, Grandma was already calling up the stairs for the second time. "Food's getting cold, Olivia" came the insistent voice. "Hurry, now, and tell your father."

Livvy trudged down the hall to the door leading to the attic art studio. "Dad," she called, leaning her head into the stairwell. "Supper's ready."

"I'll be right down." He sounded distracted. Like he was preoccupied with an important project—something more important than a chicken casserole.

She knew she'd better make herself very clear. "Grandma's called twice already, Dad."

That's when she heard his chair roll back from his sketching table. *He* knew Grandma wasn't kidding.

Grandma had attempted to train them, in only a few months, to come to the table promptly when called.

Turning, Livvy hurried back down the hall. It would be a mistake to delay supper with Grandma in charge of the kitchen. A very *big* mistake!

Follow the Dream
Chapter Two

Their suppertime conversation centered around Livvy's practice schedule and several upcoming skating events. All Grandma's doing, of course.

"Now, Olivia," her grandmother said, "we must discuss your costume for Springtime on Ice. The revue is coming up very soon now."

Livvy's stomach knotted up. "Coach Sterling said it's not necessary to buy a new outfit. Not this time."

"Oh, never mind him." Grandma waved her hand as though Livvy's coach didn't know beans. "Of course you'll have a new outfit."

Never mind him? How could Grandma say such a thing? Coach Sterling was her guide, her mentor. She wanted to follow his instructions to a tee.

Sneaking a peek at her dad, Livvy wondered what

he thought of Grandma's chatter. Looked like he was busying himself with other things, all right. At the head of the table, he was winding up the noodles on his fork. Focusing attention on his plate was *one* way to block out mealtime stress.

Livvy picked up her fork, wishing she could do the same. Sure, she could daydream while Grandma jabbered on and on. That was always an option. . . .

She let her mind wander back to a road trip. She and her mother had been driving home from a skate competition in Michigan. They'd played all sorts of road-trip games—finding as many different states as they could on license plates. And, of course, Twenty Questions. Super-fun stuff.

Between games, Mom had glanced over at Livvy, sitting next to her in the front seat. *"You're star material, honey. I hope you know that."*

Livvy hadn't known what to say at the time. She wanted to believe her mother. She was doing her best; she knew that much. *"I'm glad I have someone to believe in me,"* she'd said at last.

"I know in my heart you'll go far," Mom had said, reaching over and smoothing Livvy's hair. *"I just know it."*

Mom had always understood her dreams to make the Olympics someday. She'd cheered her on at every skating event, competitive or otherwise. She wanted to be there for her daughter, no matter what. Dad, on the other hand, was the introspective artist in the family. Quiet and thoughtful, he preferred to stay home. So Mom and Livvy would fly or drive different places— always together.

Dad had made small strides this school year, Livvy recalled. He'd come out of his shell long enough to be introduced to her new coach. But that was months ago, and her father had slipped back into his own work routine. More than half the day, he hung out in his newly remodeled attic studio. Although it was a fantastic getaway for a master artist, Livvy felt shut out of his life. Again.

"You're awfully quiet, Olivia," Grandma said.

Olivia this . . . Olivia that, thought Livvy. Forcing a smile, she managed to say, "Your casserole's delicious."

Grandma leaned closer, across the table from her. "Tell me, dear, what would you say if *I* made your new springtime skating outfit?"

Please, God, don't let this be happening, she prayed silently.

Grandma continued talking, her hands fluttering about. "How about a pale pink skirt with a delicate lace bodice insert? And just in time for Easter, too. Oh, dear me, you'll look perfect."

"Perfect?" Livvy squeaked. "But, Grandma—"

"Now, don't you go worrying over the cost of materials and such things," the older woman interrupted.

"I've made a good friend down at the Cloth Mill. Mrs. Newton says she'll be glad to help me economize any time at all."

Livvy hadn't realized it, but she'd begun to slip down slowly in her chair. She stared at the salt-and-pepper shakers. They were part of her mother's set of best china. Why were they mixed in with the everyday dishes?

She fumed about it. Everything was off kilter since Mom died. No . . . since Grandma had come to live here. Worse yet, why didn't Dad intervene? Better yet, why couldn't *she* speak up for herself?

She glanced at her dad again. Busy with his green beans now. She wanted to say something. *Do* something! But she felt completely helpless. Next thing, Grandma would have her dressed up all prim and proper for Fifth Avenue's Easter parade, carrying a basketful of dyed eggs!

———

Two hours later, she complained to Jenna by phone. "Grandma's starting to plan my outfits. And, get this, *she* wants to sew my spring costume!"

"Maybe things'll calm down. Just relax."

Livvy couldn't believe her ears! "You want me to forget about this? How can I?"

"It won't hurt to let it go just this once. Let your grandma do whatever."

Livvy wished she'd never brought any of this up with Jen. Her friend was being totally unreasonable. "Let me ask you a question," she shot back. "Would *you* wear a gymnastics leotard sewn by your grandmother?"

Jenna was silent for a moment; then came her apologetic words. "I see what you're saying. You're right, Liv, and I'm sorry."

Livvy leaned back against the headboard of her bed. She thought of her petite friend wearing a hand-sewn leotard. How ridiculous that would be! Jenna was an advanced gymnast—nearly a Level Nine. The highly competitive sport was her life, just as ice-skating was Livvy's. No way would Jen's grandmother think of intruding into *that* part of her granddaughter's life.

Livvy pondered her own predicament. "It's the hardest thing I'll ever have to do. I just know it."

"What is?"

Taking a deep breath, Livvy continued. "Telling Grandma to back off. Somehow, I have to do it."

"Have you thought of asking your dad? Won't he talk to your grandma?"

"Don't I wish," Livvy said softly.

"So your dad's too busy?"

"He's working on a new project. The studio's actually off-limits to both Grandma and me."

"Then you're stuck, right?" asked Jenna.

Livvy imagined her Korean friend holding the phone,

her dark brown eyes narrowing with concern. "I'm going to pray about it. That's all I can do," Livvy said at last.

"Good idea. I will, too."

"I need all the help I can get," Livvy admitted.

"So why don't you bring it up Friday afternoon at Girls Only? It's really ideal."

Twice now Jenna had suggested it. She was a determined friend. She probably wouldn't give up till Livvy gave in.

So . . . what could it hurt? Maybe it would help to talk things out with the other girls in the top-secret club.

"Well, I hope I won't regret it," she said hesitantly.

"Great, Liv. You won't be sorry," her friend said before hanging up the phone. "Things'll work out."

Things'll work out. . . .

Livvy wished with all of her heart it could be true.

Follow the Dream
Chapter Three

Long before the sun arose the next morning, Livvy was dressed and ready for her practice session. She really wanted things to go well with Coach Sterling. And she hoped every jump would be clean and solid. Excellence was her goal—and Coach's, too. *For* her.

She smiled into the mirror, brushing her hair. She pulled her shoulder-length locks back into a ponytail. Coach's nickname for her, Her Grace, came to mind. As if she were of royal blood. The name actually made her want to skate like a princess.

When she thought of the older gentleman, she got grateful goose bumps. Odell Sterling had postponed his plans for retirement because she needed a top-notch coach. And he was the best, all right. He'd coached numerous Olympic stars in his prime but had come to

Alpine Lake to escape the "madness." To settle down and relax a bit. The story of how they'd met was absolutely mind-boggling. Even now as she remembered, Coach was a super cool answer to prayer.

"Olivia Kay! Are you ready to go?" Grandma was calling up the steps, as usual. In fact, Livvy could set her watch to the first call of every morning.

"I want to walk today," she said, as she did every morning. "I really do, Grandma." She added an extra punch to her words. Hoping . . . praying that her grandmother would take the hint.

"Nothing doing" came the reply. "I'll back the car out right after breakfast."

Livvy's anger boiled. "Why is she doing this?" Putting down her hairbrush, she leaned close to the mirror. "I can't live my own life," she whispered at her image. She scowled back at her reflection.

Coco bristled in his cage. Promptly, Livvy turned to greet her pet. "Grandma doesn't listen to me," she cooed. "My life stinks."

The parrot cocked his little yellow head to the side. "Stink . . . stink . . . stink," he cawed.

On any other day she might've laughed out loud. Today, she watched her clown of a bird in silence. His white body seemed extra bright today. "It's not funny," she said, tapping on his cage.

"Livvy stink . . . stink," he replied.

She couldn't help herself. She smiled at Coco. "Did you give yourself a bath, birdie-boy?" she asked, making kissy sounds. "Did you?"

He began to make loud, screeching noises. Obnoxious ones. So noisy Grandma came huffing and puffing upstairs. "What in the world is going on?"

"It's just Coco," Livvy explained. "He does chicken impersonations every so often."

Grandma put both hands on her heaving chest. "Well, in all my days . . ."

"He's a super special bird."

"Super special, my eye," Grandma whispered.

Livvy heard it all the same. "Coco's the best pet anyone could ever have," she said, turning to the cage. "Aren't you, cutie-bird?"

Grandma wagged her head, obviously disgusted. "Come, now, Livvy, it's time for breakfast. We can't be late for your practice."

"I'm not going," Livvy said, surprising herself.

Grandma's eyebrows shot up. "You're not *what?*"

"I'm staying home today."

"Well, I'll be—"

"You go ahead, Grandma."

Gulp. She'd stuck her neck out.

A confused little frown passed over Grandma's brow. "What ever would I want with skating practice, Olivia Kay?"

My point exactly, Livvy thought but knew better than to say it. She wouldn't stoop so low—although she'd already skirted the edge of disrespect.

"I think you'd better come along, dear. Coach Sterling will be waiting. It wouldn't be polite not to show up." Without another word, the woman turned and headed for the stairs.

Livvy gave her bangs a quick brushing. Then she flashed a smirk at Coco. "I almost had her, didn't I?" she whispered.

Then, eyeing him a little closer, she said, "Please . . . no more chicken routines, Coco. At least not till I leave the house." Suddenly, she thought of her dad. He'd be getting up in a couple hours, *after* the sun came up. He worked late at night and slept in a bit in the morning. "On second thought, better not make any racket at all."

Livvy left the room, waiting to hear what Coco might do. She paused at the door. Then, noticing the attic stairway door was ajar, she tiptoed down the hall. She rounded the curve near her father's bedroom, hoping she wouldn't awaken him.

Time to see what's happening upstairs, she thought and sneaked up the narrow stairwell to the art studio. Her father had asked both Grandma and Livvy to stay out of his studio.

"What're you painting?" Livvy had asked.

"Just trust me," he'd said. *"You'll see it soon."*

Since she hadn't promised—neither had Grandma—Livvy figured it was all right to have a peek. Just one little glimpse couldn't hurt. It didn't strike her that she might be disobeying his wishes. Livvy was just so curious.

At the top of the stairs, she reached for the light switch. The recessed and track lighting made the place spring to life. Super cool.

Just then she heard Grandma's voice two flights below. She skimmed the room with her eyes, hoping to spy something without actually walking into the studio. Only one thing caught her attention: a draped canvas. Nothing unusual about that. Dad always covered up his work when he was away from his studio.

"Olivia Kay" came Grandma's voice again.

If she didn't go now, she'd run the risk of waking Dad. That would never do. Especially since he wouldn't be thrilled about a snooper in his studio.

Turning off the lights, she crept back downstairs, grimacing as she stepped on a creaky step. Then, fast as she could, she scurried down the second-floor hallway. "I'm coming, Grandma," she called softly.

Coco could be heard mimicking her in his cage. "Grandma . . . coming, Grandma . . ."

Thankfully, the beloved bird was considerate enough not to squawk this time. At least he wasn't pulling another chicken charade. Not yet, anyway.

Grandma was waiting near the coat closet. She wore her warmest jogging suit, a soft pink fleece. The outfit brought a slight rosy hue to her wrinkled cheeks.

"There you are," Grandma said, smiling. "I'm so relieved. Honestly, I thought you meant for *me* to keep Coach Sterling company this morning."

Livvy hardly knew what to say. "I didn't mean that at all, Grandma." She was astonished at the comment. What a silly thing for Grandma to say. Unless . . . of course, Grandma was attracted to Livvy's Coach. Now, *that* was an interesting possibility!

Follow the Dream
Chapter Four

Triple jumps were the topic of the morning.

Coach Sterling gave Livvy ample time to warm up under Grandma's watchful eye. The gray-haired woman was obviously restless. She couldn't seem to sit down. When she did, it was only for a few seconds at a time. She was like a yo-yo this morning—up and down.

Most of the time, Grandma paced back and forth behind the barrier. No matter where Livvy worked on the ice, there was Grandma Hudson, flitting about.

Coach didn't seem to notice, which surprised Livvy. How could he *not* see that the woman was a major distraction? Was he so totally tuned in to his coaching? Was that it?

"Let's have some flawless landings today," the well-dressed gentleman said with a smile. "Nothing less." He clapped his hands, urging Livvy on from the sidelines.

Grandma clapped, too, calling out, "You can do it, Olivia!"

I'm Livvy . . . not that sophisticated-sounding name, she thought, taking a fast turn around the rink. She attempted to think through her setup for a triple toe loop. Coach Sterling, as well as her previous coach, always prompted her to do this. She must take time and care to envision her every action. Gliding backward on the back inside edge of her skate—knees bent gracefully—she extended her free leg behind her.

Livvy was right-handed, so she almost always jumped off her right foot. Not when performing the loop jump, though. The left leg was the one for this easiest of the toe jumps.

She gained power with a backward crossover, accelerating more quickly. She felt the speed as she pushed and pulled hard with her edges. This jump would take off and land on the exact same skate edge. Livvy could imagine herself giving the extra kick from the toe pick. Yep, she was ready to go for it.

"Give it all you've got, Olivia!" Grandma suddenly called.

Hearing her given name threw Livvy off. Her focus was messed up—*super* messed up. She didn't even try for the jump. She skated out of it, burying her face in her hands. Skimming the ice, she felt like calling it a day. More than anything, she wanted to skate just once without Grandma Hudson.

"Livvy? What is it?" Coach called.

She shook her head. How could she explain to Coach with Grandma standing nearby? Her complaint might come out sounding very bitter. Deep inside—no, right on the surface—she felt as upset as she'd ever been.

Coach stood at attention, waiting. She could see him through her fingers. Then, dropping her hands, she made another pass around the rink, avoiding center ice and the side nearest Coach and Grandma. She was having a horrible time centering herself. Her balance was tottering, too.

"I'll try again," she said.

Another skate around the rink would surely do it. If only Grandma would stop calling out. It was as if Grandma was confused about her role in all this. Like maybe she thought she was the assistant to the coach. Or something other than just a grandmother.

Livvy thought about it. Why did her grandmother bug her so much? Surely she was only trying to help, not wanting to take over every inch of Livvy's life. Surely not.

This time around, Livvy turned into her backward glide, coming faster across the ice. *I, Livvy Hudson, future*

Olympian, can and will do this jump! she psyched herself up. *Please, God, help me.*

One leg trailed the other as she sailed toward the spot where she knew she must jump. There was a slightly prolonged amount of time when it seemed she was merely flying. But then she kicked her toe into the ice and leaped off her skating leg, into the air. Three spins counterclockwise high in the air were flawless. The landing was supposed to happen on the back outside edge of her right foot. Instead, both her feet came down together!

She was furious with herself. Especially because she'd let Grandma get to her.

Again!

But she wouldn't give up. She tried the same jump again. Four more times in a row.

Finally she landed correctly, on only one skate— her right. Her free leg swung around gracefully behind her and up.

"That's it, Her Grace!" Coach was saying, though not loudly. His voice had the most pleasant ring to it. He even applauded several times.

Grandma, on the other hand, waved her skinny little hands like a cheerleader—but a rather dilapidated one. Livvy couldn't begin to imagine her grandmother in a short, pleated skirt and tennis shoes. The best she could do was to think of Grandma Hudson back in Illinois, baking bread in her kitchen. Where she belonged.

Livvy met up with Jenna in P.E., their third-period class. The locker room smelled of hair spray and deodorant. There were a number of girls rushing out, late for their next class.

It was impossible not to notice how happy Jenna Song was. Her face nearly shone with glee.

"What's up with you?" Livvy asked, searching her face.

Jenna rummaged through her book bag and produced the reason for her delight. "It's this!" She showed off an A-plus in math. "Do you have any idea how unbelievable this is?"

Several other girls were grinning, too. In fact, two girls came over to peer at Jenna's math grade.

Livvy opened her gym locker. "Congrats, Jen," she said softly, without turning around.

"Hey, you okay?" Jenna asked.

Livvy did a double take. "What do you mean?"

"You just sound so . . ." Her voice trailed off.

"Ticked off?"

Jenna nodded, her eyes serious. "Did something happen at practice this morning?"

Livvy felt the lump in her throat. Tears clouded her

eyes, and she leaned deep into her locker. She couldn't do this. Not here, not now!

"Oh, Livvy, it's your grandma, isn't it?" Jenna patted her shoulder. "I'm really sorry. I shouldn't have brought it up."

Livvy tried to say, "I'll be okay," but it came out mushy and squeaky. She was sure her best friend had no idea what she was trying to say.

"We'll talk at Girls Only Club," Jenna offered.

Livvy nodded. She watched Jenna walk to her locker. Actually, it was more like floating. But then, gymnasts were known to walk that way. And ice skaters, too, but only when their world wasn't crumbling beneath their feet.

Jenna's graceful walk made Livvy's heart sink. If Grandma Hudson didn't leave her alone—and soon!— she would never be able to float or skate gracefully or do any of the demanding jumps and moves in her repertoire. In short, she would never be able to follow her heart—to the Olympics!

Follow the Dream
Chapter Five

After ballet class at Natalie Johnston's private studio, Livvy, Jenna, Heather, and Manda hurried to Jen's house. Jenna—president of Girls Only—called the meeting to order. She was the prez because her attic bedroom was the location of their Friday meetings. The ideal setting.

Her room was super cool, with hot pink carpet. There was also plenty of space to hang out and relax. The barre and wide mirror Jenna's father had installed stretched across one long wall. A computer desk and large bulletin board behind it filled up one spot at the far end of the room. Posters of Mary Lou Retton, Keri Strug, and the Magnificent Seven of recent Olympic fame decorated the walls near a four-poster bed. One glance around Jen's room, and her athletic obsession reached right out and zapped you.

Actually, all four members of Girls Only were on course for the Olympics: Jenna Song, Heather Bock, Miranda Garcia, and Livvy herself. Heather was an ice dancer with her older brother, Kevin. Manda was an Alpine skier.

"What's up with old business?" Jenna said, giving a nod to Heather. Blond and vivacious, Heather had been both the secretary *and* the treasurer for the club. Now that Manda was one of the foursome, *she* was in charge of the bucks. Not that there was much money to be in charge of. All the same, Manda held the position of treasurer.

"Let's vote on what to do for our springtime activity," Heather spoke up. "It's been months since we've performed anything for our families."

Manda wore a fleeting frown. "Easter's only a few weeks away. Not much time to pull something together."

Livvy wondered about Manda's comment. Was there a downhill event coming up for her? Manda was a first-rate skier. Maybe she didn't want to be distracted. "Are you training for a race?" Livvy asked thoughtfully.

Manda shook her head. "My mom and I are going to visit my grandparents in Kansas over Easter weekend."

"Oh," Jenna said, face drooping. "That'll leave just the three of us."

"Maybe we should skip it," Livvy said, feeling as glum as Jenna looked.

"Why can't we do something anyway?" Heather suggested. "You wouldn't mind, would you, Manda?"

Livvy, Jenna, and Heather turned simultaneously toward the tall, Hispanic skier. Blushing, Manda pursed her lips. "I don't want to be a party pooper," she said comically.

"Oh, don't worry. You're never that," Livvy assured her.

Manda nodded, grinning. "Sure . . . go ahead, plan something for Easter. I'll cheer you on from afar."

Was there still some hesitation in Manda's voice? Livvy kept staring—not to be rude, she just wanted to be sure Manda really didn't mind. "You know, it would be real easy to wait till you get back," she said. "We could put on a program *after* the holy days."

Manda insisted, shaking her head. "Do whatever you like. Honest. I'm cool with it."

So, with Manda's help, the girls put their heads together. They decided to create a pageant-type play. "Complete with our pets," Jenna said, stroking her golden-haired cat, Sasha.

"Who's going to write the play?" Heather asked.

The room was still. The girls eyed one another without speaking. Almost bashfully.

At last, Jenna volunteered. "If no one else wants to, I'll do it."

Applause followed, and Jenna's face lit up. Her jet black hair shone under the ceiling lights. "In case you didn't know it, I have a secret dream." Her eyes squinted nearly shut.

"Let me guess," teased Livvy.

But Jenna volunteered the secret before Livvy could say more. "I've always wanted to be a script writer."

Livvy wasn't surprised. Jenna was known to be quite creative on paper. She loved writing in her leather-bound book. Every day she wrote, no matter what.

"How will you keep up with writing *and* gymnastics?" Manda asked. "When you're an adult, I mean."

Jenna smiled her perky smile. "If God wants me to do it, I'll give everything my best shot."

Livvy said softly, "My mother used to say, 'Your creative strengths will start to narrow down as you grow up.' " She startled herself. It had been months since she'd spoken so openly about her deceased mother.

Heather reached over and squeezed Livvy's arm. "I think your mom was positively right."

There was lots more talk of the pageant—how to bring certain animal pets into the show. "Be sure to include Livvy's talking parrot," Manda piped up. "Coco's a real kick."

"Yeah, we could train him to do the echoes," Jenna said, her eyes blinking.

"What echoes are you talking about?" Livvy asked.

The girls burst out laughing.

"Yeah, what's with the echoes?" Heather said.

Jenna's olive skin turned slightly purple. "Oh, whatever."

"Please, just put lots of action into the show," Heather said, twirling her long golden hair. "Maybe even write in a ballet finale—we could do an encore for a change."

"Yes, an encore!" Jenna said.

"Great idea," said Heather.

Livvy agreed, especially since they were all in ballet class together. The more she thought about it, the more she liked the pageant idea. But they'd have to work hard to pull it off, beginning with Jenna and her script. "How fast can you write the play?" she asked.

"Probably in a couple days," Jen said.

"Wow, that fast?" Heather said. "Are you sure?"

"Oh, she's fast," Manda piped up. "I've seen her do her double salto forward. She's lightning."

"But can she *write* that fast?" Heather asked, teasing.

Jenna pointed to her new computer. "Check it out."

Livvy chuckled. "Does your computer take dictation?"

"Not yet, but someday." Jenna was smiling.

Livvy was excited about the program plan. But she felt terribly unsettled. When should she bring up the subject of her grandmother?

Or should she keep quiet?

———

After refreshments of only healthy snacks—canned V8 juice and celery sticks with peanut butter—Jenna shared Livvy's problem. Jen sat cross-legged on the floor, explaining the predicament. "Liv needs our support," she told the others, eyes serious. "Her grandmother's calling all the shots. On and off the ice."

Livvy fidgeted, then spoke up. "I didn't want Jen to say anything. Not at first. But things are getting worse. And . . . I don't want to be rude to her, but I really don't know what to do."

"We'll help," Heather promised.

"You know who your friends are," Manda said.

"How long has it been going on?" asked Heather.

Livvy explained. "Well, when Grandma first came to live with us, things were pretty much okay. But more and more, her constant attention is suffocating."

"My grandparents are just the opposite," Manda said. "Thank goodness! But if one of them came to live with us, well . . . I don't know how that would work."

"Older people can get stuck in their ways," Jenna

said. "Who knows how *my* grandma would behave if she lived with us."

"Is she trying to be a mother replacement, maybe?" Heather said hesitantly.

Livvy shook her head. "It's hard to say what's going on in Grandma's head."

"Can you gently ask her to mind her own business?" Manda suggested, which brought a big laugh.

"Seriously, though," Livvy said, "I don't want to hurt my grandmother's feelings. She's a big help around the house, cooking and doing other stuff. Besides, I think my dad would be lost without her."

Before the meeting was adjourned, Jenna prayed. She also encouraged each girl to pray for wisdom. "Liv really needs it."

"Yeah," Livvy whispered, "so I won't do the wrong thing."

Jen, Heather, and Manda gathered around and hugged her good-bye. All the way home, Livvy thought of Jenna's prayer. *"Help our Livvy know what to do, Lord. . . ."*

She smiled, remembering it as she walked the short distance home.

"Our Livvy . . ."

It was the sweetest prayer ever.

Things have to get better now, she thought.

Follow the Dream
Chapter Six

Sunday at church, Livvy spotted Kevin Bock in the foyer. He was tall, blond, and very cute. She didn't want to interrupt because he was talking with his sister Heather and two other friends. Secretly, Livvy wished Kevin would notice her. Someday . . .

But Kevin was a teenager, way cuter than most of the boys at church. There was no chance he'd think twice about a girl who was close to turning just *twelve*.

Taking a deep breath, she walked past their group. She waved when Heather caught her eye, but kept going. She wanted to check her hair before Sunday school.

She had been in the ladies' room for less than a minute when Grandma came flying in. "Oh, Olivia, there you are!"

Whirling around, she was startled by her grand-mother's entrance. "What is it?" asked Livvy.

Grandma studied her, eyes unwavering. "I'm glad to know you're still here . . . in the church," she said.

"Dad drove us both, remember?" Livvy wondered if Grandma's mind was slipping. "Are you all right?" she asked softly.

Grandma stood in front of the long mirror. She fluffed her hair with her skinny fingers—getting grayer by the second, it seemed. Then her grandmother freshened her pale pink lipstick. "Well, of course I'm all right. I wondered if you were headed off to Sunday school, that's all."

"Where else would I go?"

Grandma lowered her voice, glancing around a bit. "It's just that I've noticed some of the young people over at the convenience store down the street."

"Oh, they'll be back." Livvy knew who her grand-mother was referring to. A few of the kids liked to sneak off to get gum and candy.

"Don't you be one of them." Grandma shook her finger at Livvy. "Hanging out at the store when the parents are thinking their young people are in church . . . Well, I should say!"

Livvy wanted to say, "Just relax," but bit her tongue. "I'm right here, Grandma. As you can see."

Grandma straightened her tan suit coat, then turned

and tottered away to the sink to wash her hands. Livvy took it to mean the conversation was finished. Eager to be gone, she flew out of the rest room and down the stairs to class. Of all the nerve, being accused of leaving church! She'd never thought of doing such a thing. What was Grandma's problem, following her around *everywhere?*

———

In Sunday school, Livvy slid in beside Heather Bock, who was dressed in a floral skirt and soft green top. "You look pretty today," she said. "New outfit?"

Heather nodded, smiling. "Thanks."

Livvy almost expected Grandma to show up again to harass her further. "I think I must be paranoid," she muttered.

"What?" Heather whispered.

Livvy shook her head. "Oh . . . nothing."

Heather leaned closer. "Your face is turning red."

She sighed audibly. How could she tell Heather? Honestly, she wanted to send Grandma Hudson packing. Back to Illinois.

"Livvy? Since when do you bite your nails?" Heather asked.

Astonished, she pulled her hand away from her mouth. Sure enough, she'd been gnawing away on her fingernails. "My life's in shambles," she said, staring at her hands. "Just like my nails are now."

"Your grandmother, right?" Heather sat up straight. Their Sunday school teacher had just entered the room.

Livvy nodded. She remembered the prayer Jenna had prayed. How long could she possibly wait for an answer?

———

Early Monday morning, Livvy and Grandma drove to the skating rink. As usual, the village mall was deserted. Surrounded by numerous shops, the skating rink was smaller than the Olympic-sized rink in Colorado Springs. On weekends, she was thrilled to be able to practice there. The rest of the week, she made do with the small-town ice rink.

Trees, with twinkling white lights the year round, adorned the sidelines. Several wooden benches were scattered around, making it possible for an occasional audience. There had been numerous times when mall shoppers stopped to watch her practice. They often clapped, whether she performed with or without music backup.

Grandma paced behind the sidelines. "Let's see your loop jumps today," she said.

Livvy ignored her, waiting for Coach to suggest some jumps. Grandma was way too pushy.

She could just see it now. If something didn't happen to stop her grandmother, she'd end up running off Livvy's terrific athletic trainer. But by the look on the gentleman's face, Coach Sterling didn't seem frustrated by Grandma's comments. Not at all.

Livvy just didn't get it. Why didn't Grandma's comments annoy Coach, too? Was Coach interested in Grandma . . . romantically?

Coach was talking now. "I think you should work through your entire spring program, Livvy. Complete with music."

She glanced up, surprised. But Coach was decidedly serious, so she took her center-ice stance. Counting the beats, she listened carefully to the introduction of "Give My Regards to Broadway." It was a rousing version of the song, and Livvy loved every measure and stanza. Today there was one major reason: The music would easily drown out Grandma's voice.

Coach Sterling certainly knew how to handle things! She was beginning to feel encouraged, even jazzed about this small triumph. Maybe things were going to go better, after all.

Toward the end of the session, Mrs. Newton, the fabric shop owner, showed up. Livvy was delighted. Mrs. Newton was one way for her grandmother's attention to be less focused on what was happening on the ice. Spirits soaring, Livvy sailed through her entire program a second time. Near-perfect landings on every jump. She could hardly wait to tell Jenna!

After practice, she was unlacing her skates when Mrs. Newton and Grandma came over. "You were quite stunning, Miss Livvy," Mrs. Newton said. Her red bangle earrings swung back and forth as her head moved.

Grandma poked the younger woman playfully. "Tell Olivia what we've been planning."

"Well," Mrs. Newton began, "it seems your grandmother has an idea for a skating outfit."

Grandma's eyes were shining. "Go on."

"She wants your opinion on the material," Mrs. Newton informed her. "What do you say, Livvy?"

What *could* she say? She held her breath, thinking she'd at least like to have a look at the pattern!

"Olivia Kay, you simply must see the lovely fabric." Grandma looked cunningly at Mrs. Newton. "I think you're going to love it."

"What style is the outfit?" she asked.

"Oh yes, of course! The pattern is very important," Grandma blurted.

Mrs. Newton winked at Livvy. The dear lady was attempting to downplay the situation.

Grandma continued to talk about the material *and* the pattern during the drive back home. Livvy found it both a little comical and extremely frustrating. Two women concocting a plan to create a new costume. An unwanted, unnecessary spring costume!

At home, she showered and dressed for school. All the while, Livvy thought about the morning practice session. She actually felt proud of herself for a change! Yet she also felt tense, worrying about how things would go on Wednesday. What if Coach wanted to work on technical things instead, without music? What if Grandma didn't have Mrs. Newton to chat with?

One thing was super good, for sure. Mrs. Newton was getting involved with the new outfit. Livvy was definitely relieved about that. It wasn't that Grandma couldn't sew. She was a very capable seamstress. It went much deeper. Grandma was so out of touch with what was in vogue for modern-day skaters. In fact, she had no idea about new-millenium preteens at all!

To think she was trapped living with an old relic of a grandmother! Why, Grandma might stay around till Livvy left home and headed off to college. Maybe even longer.

What could be worse?

Follow the Dream
Chapter Seven

Livvy was first to arrive at the school locker she shared with Jenna. She zipped through the combination and opened the locker. The locker was a mess.

"What on earth!" She stared at its interior in disbelief. Someone had ripped out the pink carpet from the locker shelves so that only the bare metal was left. "Who did this?" Livvy muttered.

Suzy Buchanan, perky and plump, stood near the locker next to Livvy's. "I figured you already knew about it. Jenna tore out the carpet last Friday after school," Suzy told her.

Livvy was amazed. "Are you sure?"

Suzy moved back to her own locker. It was covered with super cool green-and-yellow gum wrappers. Even the mirror was trimmed with the colorful wrappers. "I saw her do it," said Suzy.

"And *I* helped her," explained Suzy's tall and blond locker partner, Diane Larson. Diane had come rushing down the hall, like she was late. But then, Diane was always out of breath, going somewhere.

"I can't believe Jenna didn't tell you . . . or *ask* you first," Suzy said, eyes blinking fast.

"She must've wanted a change of scenery," Livvy said, still baffled. "Did she say why?"

Tall Diane spoke up. "Jenna said she was tired of the hot pink carpet. 'It's too bright for a locker,' she said."

Suzy was nodding. "Yeah, she wants something more athletic looking, I think she said."

Just then Jenna came down the hall. She was carrying rolled-up contact paper. "You're gonna love this, Livvy!"

Suzy and Diane waited to see what was up. "We told your locker partner you'd decided to remodel," Diane said.

"And that's the truth," Jenna said; then her eyes went wide. "Oh no, I forgot to tell *you* about it, Liv!"

"Well, thanks a lot," Livvy taunted, stepping aside. She watched her friend unroll the colorful paper.

"Wow, bright stuff," said Suzy.

"But *very* cool," said Diane.

Jenna stepped back to show off the five interlocking

Olympic rings. They represented the union of five original major continents: Africa, America, Australia, Asia, and Europe. And, of course, the meeting of the athletes who participate in Olympic sports. "So . . . what do you think, Liv?"

"It's super. Where on earth did you get it?" She really did love it.

"My dad found it for me on the Web. I want to order even more to line my closet shelves at home." Jenna pulled out a scissors from her backpack.

"Here, let me help you." Livvy held the paper while Jen cut the pieces to fit two shelves. Top and bottom.

"What do you think of decorating the inside of the locker door, too?" Jen asked.

Diane laughed from the next locker. "Just don't cover the mirror."

"Too true," agreed Jenna.

"What should we do about the pink rickrack on the mirror?" Livvy asked. "It'll be messy if we pull it off."

"We'll leave it as is," Jen said. "Okay with you?"

Livvy grinned at her best friend. "It's about time you ask my opinion on something. This is *my* locker, too, in case you forgot."

Jenna's smile faded. "You're ticked off, aren't you?"

Livvy hadn't meant to sound so harsh. "No, I love the Olympic theme. Really."

"Okay, if you're cool with this."

"Super cool," Livvy said. And she meant it.

When they finished, both girls took turns admiring their locker makeover. "I hardly recognize it," Livvy said.

Jenna nodded. "But it's perfect, isn't it? I mean, aren't we both headed for the Olympics . . . someday in the not-too-distant future?"

Livvy was silent. It was easy for Jenna to talk casually of her athletic future. But if Livvy didn't get her life back, and soon, she wasn't sure *where* she was headed!

———

Room 123—Livvy's homeroom—was in a mild upheaval when she arrived. At first glance, there appeared to be a sub. A little gray-haired lady sat with her hands folded atop the teacher's desk. A steady flow of chatter continued as Livvy hurried to her seat.

Opening her book bag, she searched for her homework assignments. English, math, history. Finding everything in its place, she leaned back in her chair. That's when she nearly fell off. She stared ahead at the teacher's desk.

I don't believe this! What on earth is she doing here? Livvy wondered.

The boy in front of her made a wisecrack. "Where're they getting the subs these days?"

"Nursing homes are overcrowded," another boy mouthed off.

Livvy slumped down in her seat. She had to be dreaming. *Had* to be! Pinching herself, she knew she was wide awake. But given the choice, she would've picked having a nightmare over this. Any day.

It was *Grandma Hudson* who sat behind the homeroom teacher's desk. Tiny, pale eyes seemed to squint as Grandma scanned the room. Then, spying Livvy, the older woman's eyes caught hers and held. Grandma's lips were moving, as if to say, "Oh, there you are, Olivia Kay."

While Livvy stared, totally bewildered, Grandma stood up. She pushed the teacher's chair in and moved slowly down the row of desks. "Olivia, dear," she said, standing in the aisle. "You went off without your lunch money." Then she placed several dollar bills on Livvy's desk.

The class burst into riotous laughter. Livvy, mortified, bore a hole in her own lap. She thought she might faint on the spot. Sadly for her, she didn't. She remained fully conscious, aware of the pounding of her heart.

Then, without warning, Grandma Hudson left. Just like that, she exited. Without a good-bye or an "I didn't mean to embarrass you."

Young Mrs. Smith, their homeroom teacher, entered the room just then. The two women nearly collided as

Grandma scurried out the door. The teacher glanced over her shoulder, probably wondering who in the world that was.

Livvy, humiliated beyond belief, knew she would never live this down. Snatching up the money Grandma brought for hot lunch, she shoved the dollar bills deep into her book bag. It was too crazy—Grandma bursting into Livvy's homeroom class, treating her like a two-year-old. Things had gone way too far this time.

Trying to ignore the questioning stares around her, Livvy remained slouched at her desk. No matter what, she had to have a talk with Dad. About *his* mother.

There was no way out!

Follow the Dream
Chapter Eight

Livvy fidgeted with her hair until her knocking brought Dad to the art-studio doorway. Livvy had dashed up the attic steps immediately after school. She couldn't suffer another day. It was time to spill out her woes.

"Hey, kiddo." Her father rambled down the third-floor hallway. His hands were tucked into his pants pockets. "What's on your mind?"

"I have to talk to you."

He glanced over his shoulder as if there was something in the studio he didn't want her to see. "Wait here." He headed back to the studio and closed the door. Returning to her, he said, "Now, what were you saying?"

She studied the lines on his face, especially the deep ones in his brow and around his mouth. Dad had been one of those happy-go-lucky types. But that was many months ago, when Mom was still alive. She remembered how her father used to laugh out loud, even tell jokes around the table till late in the evening. Everyone said it was Mom who brought out the fun-loving side of Dad. Actually, she had a knack for encouraging it in most everyone. But now that Mom was gone, Dad scarcely ever smiled.

"Are you all right, honey?" he asked.

"Not exactly." She sat on a small director's chair in the corner. Dad straddled an old, unpainted chair. "Grandma's going to be the end of me," she stated flatly.

Eyes serious, Dad nodded. "Elderly people can try our patience at times. I understand what you're feeling."

"No, Dad," she whispered. "You couldn't possibly begin to understand."

"Kiddo . . . what is it?"

She looked at him, no longer hesitant. "You weren't there today when Grandma invaded my homeroom." She recounted the dreadful scene, including the part when Grandma slapped down the lunch money. "She treated me like a baby. She called me 'Olivia Kay' in front of the entire class. Oh, Dad, it was horrible!"

He leaned his face into his hands and was silent for a moment. "Grandma means well, honey." He looked up just then. "You may not understand this, but we need your grandmother, Liv. We need her to live with us."

She felt the anger rising in her. "Maybe *you* need her."

"I think in time you'll see how important Grandma is to our lives."

"But for how long?" she asked. "Forever?"

He straightened. "I don't know how long she'll stay. But the three of us belong together."

Belong together? No way! she thought.

"You have no idea what she's put me through, Dad." She felt the hot sting of tears. "She's running my life on the ice . . . and here at home. I can't focus on my jumps. My Olympic dreams are the most important thing to me. And . . . and Grandma's ruining all of that!" A burst of sobbing kept her from saying more.

Dad reached for her hand. "I'm sorry you're upset. I'll talk to Grandma if you'd like."

"You will?"

He smiled briefly, nodding. "I'll see what I can do."

Livvy brushed away her tears, taking several breaths. "I wouldn't want to hurt her feelings."

Dad let go of her hand. "Your grandmother has your best interests at heart. I know she does."

"Then why does she follow me around everywhere?"

Dad frowned hard. "What do you want me to say to her?"

She paused, knowing the first and best thing was for Grandma to go back to Illinois. But seeing the concerned look on her father's face, she knew better than to suggest it. "To start with, ask her to stay home from skating practice."

He raked his hand through his thick, dark hair. "I just don't know, Liv. She has her reasons for going."

"But I don't want her there!"

Standing up, Dad went to the tiny dormer window. He stood there without speaking for the longest time. "Grandma needs us as much as we need her."

Livvy couldn't believe her ears! Dad was turning this whole thing around. How could he?

Her father continued. "She won't understand if I'm too hard on her. I'll have to go easy."

Go ahead, be hard on her . . . send her home, Livvy thought.

Turning around, Dad said, "Let me pray about this, kiddo."

She stood up. "You already said you'd talk to her."

He put his arm around her shoulders. "I may have been hasty. You'll forgive me for that."

"But . . . aren't my skating goals more important than Grandma's feelings?" The bitter words choked out.

"I don't know, Livvy. You tell *me*." Dad's eyes were somber, his face sagged.

She turned away and ran all the way down the attic steps. In her room, she closed the door—even pulled down the shade, blocking out all chance of sunlight.

An overwhelming sadness filled her. She crawled under the covers fully dressed.

The after-school conversation with Dad haunted Livvy all evening. During supper, she replayed his words. While doing her homework, she saw his disappointed face on every page.

No question, she was an ungrateful jerk. And Dad had every right to ignore her request to confront Grandma. Still, she was frantic at the thought of dealing with Grandma at skating practice or showing up at school. And, possibly worst of all, Grandma's plan to create an undesirable spring skating outfit.

She decided not to call Jenna and dump on her. No, she'd just suffer through this trauma. Do her homework. Try not to glance up at the pictures of Michelle Kwan or Tara Lipinski. World-champion skaters. Ice-skating legends.

The words that stuck in her mind now were the strangest thing Dad had said: *"Grandma has her reasons. . . ."*

What possible reason could Grandma have? Except to totally dominate Livvy's life!

Putting her pen down and inhaling deeply, she made a decision. She was *not* going to let Grandma control her any longer. If Dad didn't meet her head on, Livvy wouldn't hesitate to do it. And without a single feeling of regret!

Once her homework was finished, she crept out into the hall. She listened, wondering if Grandma had already gone to bed. Tiptoeing down the hall, she discovered a light under the north bedroom door. *Super,* she thought. Her grandmother was still awake.

"Grandma?" she said softly through the door.

Waiting, she hoped for a reply. She wanted Grandma to be the one to invite her in. Surely the best way to start the conversation was to let Grandma make the first move.

But there was no reply.

So Livvy called again, softly. "Grandma, are you still up?"

More waiting. Still no answer.

Gently, Livvy pushed open the door. She peeked around it, not too surprised to see Grandma asleep, sitting up in bed. Dressed in her white cotton nightgown, her grandmother had fallen asleep with the light on.

Must be those early mornings, she thought. Livvy knew the feeling. She knew exactly why Grandma was so wiped out at the end of the day. Often, she was tired enough to hit the sack at nine o'clock. But she was many years younger than Grandma Hudson. No way could the older woman keep such a grueling schedule. No way should she have to!

Livvy slipped into the room as quietly as possible. She would merely turn off the light. Maybe prop Grandma's pillows around her on either side to make her more comfortable.

On the bed, she noticed an assortment of envelopes scattered around. Some envelopes were empty, the letters lying about. Others had been opened, but the letters were still inside.

She didn't take time to investigate, though. Grandma was making wispy sounds in her sleep as Livvy turned off the light and tiptoed out of the room.

———

Livvy didn't give the letters a second thought. Not till the next morning when Grandma called up the steps, "Time for breakfast, Olivia Kay!"

That's when she began to wonder about the envelopes she'd seen last night. Were they old love letters from Grandpa? Was Grandma reliving her past? Was she remembering the handsome young man who had become her one and only love?

She was eager to know. But at breakfast, Grandma

was abuzz about the spring skating outfit. She talked nonstop till it was time to leave for practice. "Did you take your vitamins?" "Are you ready for your jumps, Olivia?" "Are you focused on your program?" Annoying things like that.

Livvy fumed silently on the way to the mall rink. She dropped the notion of asking about the letters. Grandma was just impossible!

Follow the Dream
Chapter Nine

"It's the first day of spring," Grandma said in the car on the way back from practice. "A very special day."

Livvy didn't respond to her grandmother's announcement. She wasn't a little child. She was coming up on the end of sixth grade. She knew what day it was.

The twenty-first day of March had always been a much-anticipated day, growing up. Back when Mom was living, they would go around the neighborhood—leave baskets of flowers or baked goodies on doorsteps. They treated it almost like May Day. But the day belonged to her and Mom, and their super cool tradition.

So far, today had been anything but super or cool. In fact, the first day of spring had started disastrously. She dreaded the practice session, remembering the chaos Grandma had caused off the ice. Coach Sterling wasn't there, which was usual for a Tuesday. She was coached only three times a week. On the off days, Livvy was totally capable of practicing on her own, minus her coach—the way any other advanced skater might.

So it was a day to solidify her moves and jumps. In general, work out technically. She was to "get the bugs out" by referring back to Coach's suggestions from yesterday's session.

But no. Grandma behaved like a drill sergeant—an obnoxious one, at that. Livvy didn't know what was wrong with Grandma to cause her to act that way. She guessed her grandmother was attempting to make up for Coach's absence. Whatever the reason, Livvy had come uncorked. She'd come close to telling Grandma off.

Only one thing had kept her sane. Natalie Johnston's class of beginning skaters had shown up halfway through Livvy's skating time. Thank goodness they'd come. Otherwise, she was sure she would've blurted every detail that was bugging her. Straight to Grandma's face.

As it was, she did a million and one unnecessary figure eights, just to cool off.

———

At school, she thought of confiding in Jenna and Heather during lunch hour. But the cafeteria was so crowded that it didn't seem like the right time or place.

Most students were indulging in hot lunch on the side where she and her friends always sat. Soon, Manda joined them, too.

"How's our spring play coming?" Livvy asked Jenna.

Jen was super wound up today. She wore her bright blue pants and sweater outfit. "It's already half written," she replied, grinning about it. "Can you believe it?"

"What's it about?" Manda asked, next to Heather.

Jenna's eyes twinkled. "I'm calling it *Resurrection*."

"So . . . it's a Passion play?" Heather said, her blue eyes shining. "What a great idea."

"Yeah, super cool." Livvy could hardly wait to hear more.

"Since only three of us will be acting in it, I'm writing in two characters for each one of us," Jenna explained.

"So there'll be six parts total?" Heather asked.

Jenna nodded. "I think it'll be very exciting. We also need to discuss the kind of music we want to use for the ballet encore."

Livvy had almost forgotten about that. "Something classical or from a Broadway soundtrack?"

"How does the play end?" asked Manda. "When Jesus rises from the dead? Or when He's taken up into heaven?"

Jenna shrugged. "I could go either way. What do the rest of you think?"

"To begin with, we should probably decide how long we want the play to be," Livvy spoke up. "Most Passion plays are long, at least two hours."

"Good point," Heather said, reaching for her soda. "Two hours is probably too long."

"I agree." Jenna turned to Manda for her opinion. "How long do you think it should last?"

Manda, who was eating a hamburger, waved her hand. "Count me out of the discussion. I'll be in Kansas, remember?"

So Jenna, Heather, and Livvy talked out the angles to the play. After a while, it got too noisy in the cafeteria. "Let's go finish our discussion outside," Jenna suggested. So all four girls hurried to their lockers for warm jackets.

The middle-school courtyard was a good place to continue their talk. Small shrubs and low-growing plants were starting to green up, and a few pink crocuses had pushed their heads through the cold ground. The place was largely forsaken due to the chill in the air.

Livvy sat on a stone bench and faced the sun. "I like the idea of concluding the play with the women's discovery."

"You mean when they find the empty tomb?" Jenna said, pacing back and forth. Suddenly, she stopped in her tracks, her face lit up. "That's it! I'll write the story from the women's perspective."

"*Only* the women's," Livvy echoed. "The story of the women closest to Jesus. What a super idea."

So it was settled. And even though Manda would be gone for the play, she voted, too. "Jenna should write the play just the way she described it," she said.

Livvy leaned back, looking at the sky, a mixture of blue with a few fluffy clouds. "Can you imagine how cool it would be to have the play outdoors?"

"Cool is right." Heather laughed. "But this is Colorado, remember?"

"True," Jenna said. "Things don't warm up around here till early June sometimes."

"Because we live near the mountains," Manda complained, getting up. "Let's hear it for the high country!"

They were starting to act silly and cheer for their particular state when the bell rang.

"Guess we better call it quits," Jenna said.

"Probably a good thing," Manda said, laughing.

"Can you believe it?" said Livvy. "We had a Girls Only club meeting at school."

Heather nodded, pushing her hair away from her face. "And Jenna's writing a play based on the Bible . . . with only girls in it."

"*Women,*" Livvy reminded her.

"Well, you know . . ." Jenna added.

Heather and Manda linked arms and headed inside. They laughed as they went. Livvy and Jenna did the same.

Hanging with her girl friends had made Livvy feel better about life in general—at least for now. For some odd reason, she didn't feel the need to dump on her friends about Grandma.

Not anymore.

She breathed in the crisp springtime air. It was the *first* day of spring. . . .

Follow the Dream
Chapter Ten

After school, Livvy took a rare opportunity to skate for the second time in one day. *This time, without Grandma,* she thought. It had been ages since she'd had time to work out after school. Usually, she was buried in homework.

Hurrying into the mall's side entrance, she spied Mrs. Newton having a snack. She was sitting near the rink on one of the wooden benches.

"Hi, Mrs. Newton. I'm glad to see you," she said, sitting down. "Do you mind if I ask you something?"

"That depends on what it is," the woman said, smiling her warm and welcoming smile. "Of course you may. I'm always happy to chat with you, Livvy. You know that."

She certainly didn't want to launch off on Grandma.

Not right away, at least. And she didn't want to sound like a spoiled brat, either. Yet she had a feeling Mrs. Newton might give her some good advice. This was the same woman who'd befriended her last fall—at the beginning of the school year, when she was the new girl in town.

Yep, Mrs. Newton had turned out to be one of the coolest adults around. The jovial woman not only owned the Cloth Mill, she was also the cheerleading coach for the middle school. All the students looked up to her because she was so sunny. Mrs. Newton made you feel good about yourself. Which, right now, was exactly what Livvy needed.

"So . . . how's everything going for you?" Livvy asked, wanting to be polite.

"Is *that* your question?" Mrs. Newton asked.

She should've known the outgoing woman would inquire. Mrs. Newton was like that, eager to hear about others. Good or bad, it never mattered with Mrs. Newton. "Not really, but tell me about *you* first."

"Well, my store's doing well and my duties at school are fun, as always." She turned to Livvy. "Now . . . how are things going for you?"

She knew the woman would keep asking till she leveled with her. "I'm kind of having some trouble focusing these days."

"Oh?" Mrs. Newton fingered the tiny silver charms on her bracelet.

"I hate to say anything, especially because you and my grandmother are becoming good friends."

Mrs. Newton smiled knowingly and touched Livvy's hand briefly. "Whatever you say will remain in complete confidence."

Livvy felt comfortable enough to share her concern. "I think my grandmother means well," she said, using her father's words.

"Yes, I believe she does."

"But she's messing me up on the ice."

Mrs. Newton nodded. "Only on the ice, dear?"

Livvy folded her hands and squeezed. She didn't want to lay into Grandma without her grandmother around to defend herself. It didn't seem quite fair. "Well, it's tough getting used to things . . . the way they are right now."

"With your grandmother in charge?" Mrs. Newton's eyes seemed to look right through her.

"I thought you might be able to help me," Livvy said softly. "I don't know what to do."

"Have you tried talking to her? Woman to woman, so to speak?" The bangles-and-bracelets woman offered a thoughtful smile. "That's what I would do if I were you."

Talk to Grandma? she thought.

"She tells me you used to write the most wonderful letters to her," Mrs. Newton remarked.

"Yeah, back before Dad and I moved here."

"But you also wrote to your grandmother *after* you came to Alpine Lake, as well. In fact, your grandma says you 'poured out your heart' in some of those letters."

Livvy felt a bit sheepish. "Sounds like the two of you have been sharing secrets."

Whose side was Mrs. Newton on, anyway?

The friendly woman winked playfully. "Don't you worry, darlin.' Your grandma and I are *not* conspiring against you, if that's what you're thinking." She took another bite of her peanut-butter cracker.

Livvy wondered about Mrs. Newton's comment. Should she actually try to sit down and discuss things with Grandma? Did she have the courage to talk the way she used to write "her heart"? Did she even want to?

Honestly, she wasn't sure.

Follow the Dream
Chapter Eleven

Livvy walked home from the mall rink, enjoying her freedom, the sky, and the fresh mountain air. Suddenly, behind her, she heard someone cycling fast.

Turning around, she saw Heather's gorgeous older brother. Kevin Bock was headed her way!

Her heart in her throat, she knew this was her chance. Possibly, her one and only opportunity to impress him. But what did she do? She froze in place, gazing at him from the sidewalk.

Less than two feet away, he smiled. "Hi, Livvy," he said.

"Uh . . . hi." She was positively tongue-tied.

Kevin didn't seem to notice. He kept right on, riding his bike up Main Street. His blond hair peeked out from under his blue knit ski cap, and his long, blue-jeaned

legs pumped the bike pedals hard. Then, unexpectedly, he made the turn at the next corner. Gone, just
like that!

The unforeseen encounter left her feeling jumpy.
She couldn't seem to make her legs work. *What's wrong
with me?* Livvy wondered.

Slowly, she put one foot in front of the other, forcing herself to keep moving. Of course, she knew better than to share any of this with Grandma. It wasn't
the kind of heart-to-heart news you just dash into the
house and tell. Nope, not even Jenna Song was going
to hear about this!

———

Three-twenty Main Street—the tall gray Victorian
house where she lived with her father and grandmother—was way too quiet when she arrived.

"Grandma, I'm home," she called.

When no one answered, she was secretly glad to
have the house to herself. Alone! One afternoon in a
thousand.

She took her time removing her jacket and mittens.
Quietly, she went to the closet and hung up her coat,
first stuffing the mittens inside the wide pockets. *Where
is everyone?* she wondered.

Trying her best to enjoy the peaceful moment, she
headed for the kitchen, where she made a snack. A

peanut-butter-and-jelly sandwich was a good idea. After all, she'd watched Mrs. Newton nibble on her peanut-butter-and-cracker snack.

Remembering the conversation, Livvy poured herself a tall glass of milk and sat at the table. But the sound of Kevin's voice—*"Hi, Livvy"*—continued to ring in her ears. He'd smiled at her and called her by name! She still could hardly believe it. She was dying to phone Heather, to find out if he'd ever mentioned her name to his sister. But no, she wouldn't do that. No sense getting her hopes up, anyway.

She took sips of her milk between bites of sandwich. She remembered that Mrs. Newton had encouraged her to talk to Grandma. But Livvy wondered if Grandma would actually hear her out.

Three years ago, she and Mom had spent a whole week with Grandma Hudson. It was early summer, and everything about life was beautiful then. She'd taken first place at regionals and was more than anxious for skating camp to begin. Mom had suggested they spend some time with Grandma, a recent widow. So they drove across town, not far at all.

Mom and Grandma had become much closer that short week together. Livvy didn't know why for sure. Maybe it was because her mother needed to connect with Dad's mother, especially now that Mom's parents were no longer living. It may have been more Grandma

Hudson's need—to reach out in her loneliness. Whatever the reason, Livvy and her mom enjoyed the week, doing lots of "girl" things. Mostly, they hung out at Grandma's big house. They went barefoot, all three of them. And she and Mom listened intently to the stories Grandma told while they sat on the back porch.

Livvy remembered staring out at the enormous shade trees and the surrounding woods. At the time, she wondered why everyone didn't just build tree houses and live high in the branches. Be country bumpkins for the summer, at least.

They sifted through hundreds of black-and-white pictures that week at Grandma's. They baked strawberry-rhubarb pies and banana-nut bread, too. And Livvy "put up" her first ever dill pickles.

Shifting gears back to the present, Livvy was sure her dad would not come through for her. He wouldn't want to approach Grandma, prayer or not. He was too peace-loving for his own good, preferring a stress-free existence. He wouldn't make waves. She was stuck dealing with Grandma on her own.

She sat there, staring at the stove. All at once, she realized the light was on inside the oven. Getting up, she went to peek inside. *What's this?* she wondered.

Grandma was baking a cake. Why hadn't she smelled the sweet aroma when she arrived? Was it possible she'd been so caught up with seeing Kevin Bock?

The more she thought of it, the more she wondered. This was so strange because Grandma was downright funny about cakes. They symbolized a celebration, "only for special occasions," Grandma often said.

No one in the house was having a birthday. And there were no more wedding anniversaries to be celebrated. So what was going on? Why a cake?

Peering through the oven window, she spotted two round layers. It was obvious Grandma had made lemon cake. Livvy's mouth watered, imagining the chocolate frosting.

Because of her skating goals, Livvy rarely allowed herself junk food. She never felt she was missing out because the trade-off was worth it. Feeling good, having plenty of energy on the ice—that was far better than the sluggish feeling sugar-laden foods offered.

She knew something was up for Grandma to bake her all-time favorite cake. There had to be a reason. She washed her hands and dried them, then headed upstairs, eager to find out.

Coco was babbling like crazy when she stepped foot in her room. "Birdie-boy miss Livvy," he was saying.

She went right up to his cage. "I know you missed me, but do you have to be so loud about it?"

"Livvy . . . Livvy . . . Livvy . . ."

"I'm here," she said. "You can quit now."

She wandered out of the room into the hallway.

Looking in both directions, she noticed that her grand-mother's bedroom door was closed. *She must be resting,* Livvy decided.

Feeling a bit lonely, she headed up the attic stairs. "Dad?" she called softly, hoping not to either awaken Grandma or alarm her father. He could be easily startled while intensely concentrating. "Dad?" she said again, reaching the top of the stairs.

She walked down the hallway that led to the arched threshold. It was the entrance to her father's off-limits art studio. Not sure if she should knock softly or call to him again, she stood in the wide hallway. The area was large enough to be considered a foyer, a waiting room for a few choice clients. The multicolored braided rug was one her mother had picked out years before. And the navy blue director's chair had been a birthday present to her dad. From Mom, of course. Her mother was the generous one. Always giving, that was Mom.

Raising her hand to knock, she was surprised when the door opened by itself. "Hi, kiddo," Dad said, look-ing a bit disheveled. "How was school?"

"Good."

He stepped out of the studio and closed the door behind him. "I had a feeling you were sneaking up the steps."

She smiled. "I wasn't sneaking; I just didn't want to wake up Grandma."

"Oh, Grandma's not napping. Last I heard, she was going out to do some shopping."

"Shopping?"

Dad shrugged his shoulders. "I didn't quite get it, either, but she said it was important."

"And she's baking a cake, too. So . . . what's going on?"

Her dad seemed as surprised as she was. "A cake?" He sniffed the air. "Lemon?"

"Yep."

"Must be a significant date that only Grandma knows," he said with a faint smile.

Livvy didn't like the sound of it. Did this mean she'd forgotten something? "Could it be Grandma's wedding anniversary or something?"

Dad chuckled a little. "Are you talking *my* parents' anniversary, Liv? Don't you think I'd remember a thing like that?"

Livvy had to laugh at that. For a moment, she saw a glimpse of the old Dad returning. The before-Mom-died Dad.

The phone rang, interrupting the pleasant moment. "Just a second, Liv." Her dad disappeared into his studio to answer it. Although he left the door slightly ajar, she decided not to spoil his surprise—whatever it was— and didn't peek.

———

Back in the kitchen, the timer ticked away. Livvy was still baffled by the presence of a cake in the oven. And when she opened the freezer, she spied French vanilla ice cream!

"Grandma's definitely got something up her sleeve," Livvy said, roaming the kitchen.

She searched for more clues. What could Grandma possibly be thinking? She racked her brain but came up with absolutely nothing. Could it be that Grandma wanted to celebrate the first day of spring?

Livvy wandered into the laundry-utility room. Grandma often did her mending or a sewing project at this end of the house. Homespun and comfortable, the long room had become Grandma's hideaway. Framed family pictures hung in neat groupings on the wall. A yellow-and-green Tiffany lamp stood near the sewing machine, and a small chair and ottoman filled what had been an empty space in the corner. There was also a rectangular-shaped wicker basket on the desk, where Grandma kept her sewing patterns. Spying the basket, she realized something: The spring skating outfit in question was probably filed away right there.

She began searching, one by one, through the patterns. She noticed a recent skirt pattern of Grandma's. And a long dress her grandmother had sewn for Christmas.

When the phone rang, she almost ignored it. But then she remembered Kevin. Dashing to the kitchen, she hoped the caller might be Heather Bock.

"Hello? Livvy speaking," she answered.

"Liv, I've got to talk to you." It was Jenna.

"What's up?"

"I was wondering . . . can you come over tonight? Just for a little while?"

She glanced at the oven. "I should probably wait till after supper."

"You could eat with us," Jenna urged. "Mom's nodding her head. Can you, Liv? Please? It's very important."

"Why, what's going on?"

"It's this Passion play I'm writing," Jen said. "I need someone to read the parts out loud. I want to hear how they sound."

Livvy wondered why Jenna couldn't ask her mom or dad to read the script. But then, they were the proud *new* parents of an adopted baby boy. They were probably busy with little Jonathan Bryan. "Yeah, sure, I guess so."

"Cool! How soon can you come over?" Jen asked.

"I'll have to let you know. Can I call you back?"

"Sure."

Livvy said good-bye and hung up the phone. Then she hurried back to the attic and knocked on the studio door. "Dad? Jenna Song just called. I need to talk to you." She almost said, "Since Grandma's not home," but caught herself.

He opened the studio door. "I suppose you want to go over to Jenna's?" He seemed tired, distracted.

"I don't know if it's such a good idea, since Grandma made a cake. But I'll come home after supper."

He nodded. "Before dessert, okay?"

"I promise." She turned to go, then stopped. "Tell Grandma where I am, okay? And don't let her freak."

"I can do that," said Dad.

"Tell her I have to help Jen with something very important."

"Something very important," he repeated.

She ran down the steps to the closet, grabbed her jacket, and flew out the door. The light was fading quickly as she rushed down the street. Jenna's house was only two streets away.

She couldn't stop thinking about the lemon cake. Grandma would soon have it iced with smooth and rich chocolate icing. And what about the French vanilla ice cream she'd discovered in the freezer? What was Grandma planning?

Dad had let something slip about Grandma going shopping. Grandma Hudson was one woman who literally despised the national pastime. She stayed as far away from the mall scene as possible. Except, of course, in the wee hours of the morning, during Livvy's skating sessions at the tiny mall. In fact, she scarcely went anywhere except to the grocery store, church, and the post office.

Livvy just didn't get it. She worked her brain—hard. What *was* so special about today?

Follow the Dream
Chapter Twelve

Jenna's front door was propped open slightly. Livvy wondered if Jen expected her to walk in without knocking. "Anybody home?" she called, then pushed the door open cautiously.

Jenna met her with a broad grin, coming into the living room. She offered to take Livvy's jacket, then hung it up. "I'm thrilled you could come." She grabbed Livvy's hand, and they ran off to Jenna's attic retreat.

Every time Livvy visited, she was in awe of her friend's room, tucked under the eaves—away from everything. "I wish my grandma could see this pink carpet," she said, leaning on the barre. "It's so bright and cheerful. It would do her good."

"Almost too bright, don't you think?" Jen was still smiling.

"That's what you said about our locker . . . but—"

"No, don't worry. I'm not ripping the carpet out of my bedroom, too!"

Livvy perched herself on the barre, leaning back against the mirror. She thought of Kevin Bock just then. She didn't know why, but the very special moment drifted back. His adorable smile, his cute knit hat . . .

"Hey, Livvy. You're daydreaming." Jenna was standing in front of her face, waving her petite hands.

"Uh, sorry."

Jenna handed her a bunch of papers. "Here's the script. I'm not sure, but it might be too long. I think it's pretty clean, though."

"Clean?"

"You know, correct grammar . . . spelling. Stuff like that."

"Oh."

Jenna was laughing. "What did you think I meant?"

"Nothing," she said, getting down off the barre. "Where should I stand to do this? Or do you want me to sit?"

Jenna assured her that she didn't have to act it out.

"Just sit somewhere comfortable and read it to me. A little expression would be cool."

"Sure, I can do that." She sat on the high four-poster bed. Sasha promptly came and curled up next to her. "Hello, kitty," she said. "Are you making a cameo appearance anywhere in this play?"

"Read and you'll find out," said Jenna, planting herself on a giant black beanbag.

Livvy began to read. It began with Mary, in the town of Bethany. She anointed and wiped Jesus' feet with her long hair. The writing was exceptionally beautiful. Jenna's words seemed to make the story come to life.

Livvy read on, discovering that she actually wanted to read with even more expression. She could almost see the costumes, the sets, everything. Wow, she could just imagine herself, Heather, and Jenna acting out the parts of the Bible women. She could hardly wait to start rehearsing!

Jesus' ride into Jerusalem, before His crucifixion, was the spot where Jenna's cat was to make her appearance.

Jenna explained. "I thought a cat might've been in the crowd when they were waving the palm branches."

"Could've been. I don't see why not." She reached

over and petted Sasha. "What do you think of that? You're going to be a biblical cat for one day."

The comment didn't seem to phase Sasha. Livvy wondered how Jen was going to get her cat to cooperate, but she didn't inquire. She continued reading.

Several times, Jen stopped her and scurried across the room, red pencil in hand. "Hold on a minute," she said. "That's dull."

Once, the dialogue sounded too modern for Bible times. "That's too much like new-millennium lingo," Jenna said. "Scratch that line."

Livvy read on. At last, she came to the ending. The stone covering the garden tomb had been rolled away. Jesus was gone—resurrected by God himself!

She could hardly read the finale, it was so exciting. And super wonderful. Looking across the room at Jenna, she said, "I didn't know you could write like this."

"Well, we were pen pals . . . don't you remember my letters?" Jen was laughing now, coming over to sit on the bed.

"Oh sure, they were always fantastic," Livvy agreed. "I didn't mean they weren't. But this . . ." She looked down at the stack of pages in her lap. "This play is going to be really great."

"Too bad Manda has to go to Kansas," Jen said.

Livvy straightened the pages, then handed them back to Jenna. "She must be close to her grandparents."

"I think you're right," Jen said.

Livvy held her breath, worried that Jenna might ask about the situation with Grandma Hudson. When she didn't, Livvy asked, "When can we start practicing?"

"Is it actually ready? What about rewrites?"

She smiled at her friend. "You're starting to sound like our English teacher."

Jenna crossed her eyes. "She'd probably make me edit and proofread it ten more times. At least."

"I have a feeling you've already done that."

Jenna was modest about her play. "Believe it or not, I prayed before I wrote a single word."

"I'm not surprised. It shows." Livvy meant it.

———

At supper, Jenna's mother served a Korean rice dish to her husband and Jenna. She offered an American dish—chicken-fried steak and mashed potatoes—to Livvy.

"Oh, Mrs. Song, you didn't have to make something special just for me."

Jenna's mother, petite and pretty, shook her head. "Not a problem. I always like to make American food for you . . . or anybody who comes for dinner."

Livvy thanked her. "I'll be happy to eat whatever you

make." Mrs. Song's words reminded her of Grandma Hudson's admonition several nights before. But she refused to think about her grandmother just now.

Mrs. Song served her a hearty portion of meat. Of course, Livvy was fine with it. Still, she wished her friend's mother hadn't gone to so much trouble, especially with Jonathan sitting in his high chair across the table. His baby spoon was poised in his chubby hand. Mrs. Song had more important things to do than cook up *two* separate meals!

"Let's give thanks, shall we?" Jenna's father said, bowing his head.

Livvy was glad to have friends like Reverend and Mrs. Song and their daughter, Jenna. The Korean family had been so kind to her and her father when they moved here. They'd invited them for a Saturday evening supper, complete with candlelight, just to welcome them to the community. It was easy to understand why Jenna's father's church was one of the fastest-growing ethnic churches in the area.

Pushing away worrisome thoughts, Livvy picked up her fork. She had come to help Jenna with her fantastic Passion play tonight. Nothing more. It wasn't that she was avoiding Grandma Hudson or whatever was planned at home. No, Livvy wouldn't let those kinds of thoughts spoil her supper at the Songs' home. She was determined not to.

Somehow, though, they inched . . . crept into her mind, especially during dessert. Mrs. Song had baked a cake. Chocolate with creamy butterscotch icing. Her ongoing frustration with Grandma and with the preparations for some sort of celebration seemed to mix together in her head. It was like performing a flying camel to a death drop. Only out of control.

Everything started to spin around her.

Follow the Dream
Chapter Thirteen

"Are you sure you're all right?" Jenna kept asking in the backseat as her father drove Livvy home.

"I'm fine," Livvy assured her.

"Let me walk you up to the door, at least," Jenna persisted.

"I can make it."

"But you said you were dizzy."

Livvy thanked Reverend Song, who sat quietly behind the steering wheel. Then, to Jenna, she said, "I love the play you wrote. It's super."

"Call me later, okay?" Jenna asked, her eyes blinking too fast.

Livvy waved to them as they pulled away from the curb. Then, taking a deep breath, she hurried up the steps to her house.

Inside the house, the living room lights were dim. She headed to the closet to hang up her jacket. She hoped Grandma wouldn't come rushing up to her just now. She felt horribly weak. No, she felt ashamed.

She needed time. . . .

A few minutes later, Dad appeared in the doorway. "I'm glad you remembered," he said.

"Remembered?" She paused a moment. "About coming home for dessert?" She hardly felt well enough to eat anything more.

"Your grandmother has gone to a lot of work," Dad said, his arms crossed.

"Did you ever find out what's going on?"

He smiled then, a full-mouthed grin. She was nearly shocked to see it. How long had it been? "I think you'll be very pleased, honey," he said.

"*I* will?"

He nodded, putting his arm around her shoulders. "I'd forgotten how important this day is to us."

She was confused by the charade. "What's so special about today, Dad?"

They walked the few steps to the dining room. Candlelight cast a golden glow on the wallpaper, the buffet, on everything. A centerpiece basket of yellow and white roses surprised her even more.

"I'll let your grandmother explain," Dad said, pulling out her dining room chair.

He was treating her like a princess.

Seated next to her father, Livvy folded her hands in her lap. What was going on?

Her dad would only smile. Nothing more.

Soon enough, Grandma came in from the kitchen, carrying a beautiful two-layer cake. It was iced with rich, dark chocolate, just as she'd imagined. And there were candles on top.

"This isn't what you think," Grandma said. "We're not having a belated birthday party."

"Must be an *un*-birthday," Dad joked.

Grandma lit the candles, counting each one. Eight in all. "For each of the years since that first spring day," Grandma said, eyes bright.

Livvy wondered what day Grandma meant. But she didn't speak.

"Eight years ago today, you were nearly four years old. Your mother took you by the hand to your first skating lesson," Grandma said. "I happen to know it was the first day of spring." She held up a letter. "It's all right here."

This was so incredible. Livvy could hardly wait to hear more.

"I would like to read your mother's letter, written on that special day," Grandma said, looking squarely across the table.

Nodding, Livvy reached for her father's hand. She held on tight, hoping she wouldn't cry.

"Your mother's letter was written to me," Grandma said, beginning to read.

Dear Beatrice,

Today I did the most exciting thing for my little girl. I have felt for quite some time that our Livvy has an inclination toward athletics. She pretends to spin and jump, as though she's skating on ice . . . hours at a time. I've talked to several skating instructors. Each of them cautioned me: "Three years old is a bit young to be taken too seriously."

But I couldn't ignore what I saw in dear little Livvy. I could be wrong, but I don't think so. I believe our daughter is a natural-born athlete.

Well, I suppose we will find out sooner or later. Because, you see, I signed her up for a Wee Beginners skating group in Riverdale today. It's for preschoolers, and Livvy's the tiniest of all the children. Somehow, I wanted to mark the day—make it special. So I baked a lemon cake with chocolate icing for supper tonight. Livvy and her daddy were delighted. And I took pictures to put in our family scrapbook.

Maybe someday we'll look back on this moment and realize it was the right thing to do. You see, I believe in Livvy's love for skating, even as young as she is. And she took to the ice like a trooper. Her mouth was working hard and her arms flying around to keep her balance. I cried for joy, watching her.

You probably think I'm an overenthusiastic mother, so I'll stop here. Just wanted you and Dad to know.

We love you, Bea. Take care.

Grandma looked up from the letter. "Olivia Kay, do you understand how important this day really is?"

Livvy couldn't speak. She knew if she tried, it would come out all squeaky. And she would probably boo-hoo.

Thank goodness, Dad spoke up. "I guess Livvy and I had long forgotten. Right, kiddo?" He winked at her.

Nodding, Livvy tried to force a smile. She really wasn't sad at all. It was just that her mouth wouldn't cooperate at the moment.

"I think we should hunt down that scrapbook— the one your mother made. Let's have a look at it tonight."

Grandma was nodding. "I should say so."

Livvy excused herself to blow her nose. She closed the bathroom door behind her and leaned against it.

What kind of person am I? she thought.

Going to the sink, she washed her face, patting it dry as she stared at the mirror.

I've resented Grandma so much. . . . Why?

In that moment of reflection, she thought she knew. The truth hit her squarely between the eyes. She was angry at Grandma for trying too hard. And all these months, Livvy had been miserably mistaken. Grandma wasn't trying to take Mom's place at all. Thanks to an amazing letter, things were starting to make some sense. Finally!

———

"Have a piece of cake," Grandma said when Livvy returned to the dining room.

"Thanks, Grandma. What a super surprise."

"A delicious one, too," Dad said, beaming at both his mother and his daughter.

Livvy decided right then that she would share her heart with her grandmother. But it would have to be in private. A heart-to-heart talk was definitely in order. But first, her favorite cake and ice cream awaited. Made by the world's best grandmother!

She could almost hear it now. Jenna, especially, would be thrilled to pieces. But before Livvy spent a single minute on the phone with Jen, she had *two* very important things to do!

Follow the Dream
Chapter Fourteen

Livvy helped her grandmother clean up the kitchen. They scraped the plates and loaded the dishwasher. She wiped the counters, and Grandma wiped off the place mats on the table.

Soon, she and Dad were sitting down with Grandma in the living room. With great interest, they shared the scrapbook on three laps, examining each page. Creatively done, the album featured Livvy's early childhood days.

Liv had to laugh at the various skating outfits. "So cute," she said, pointing.

"Just look how tiny," Grandma said.

Dad, too, seemed surprised at how small the skates were. "I didn't know they made them that little," he commented. "Or . . . did I?"

"You've simply forgotten, that's all," Grandma chided him.

Dad hugged Livvy close. "No more forgetting," he promised. "How about if I go with you to practice tomorrow?"

Livvy held her breath, wondering if Grandma would protest. When no objection came, she nodded. "Maybe you could come twice a week . . . and Grandma twice."

"And what about the other days?" Dad said, a cunning smile on his handsome face.

"On those days, I'll go it alone." She hoped Grandma would keep nodding her head.

"So . . . it's settled, then," Dad said with a clap of his hands.

Livvy realized her father had just now followed through with his promised "talk" to Grandma. He had done what he could to help smooth things out. To pave the way for Livvy's freedom to follow her dream. Of course, he'd accomplished it in a roundabout sort of way. But that was Dad's style, and it was okay.

When he disappeared to return to his studio, Livvy hung around the living room. She stayed curled up on the couch, waiting for Grandma to finish reading a magazine. Full of skating outfits and ideas, the trendy periodical had come in the day's mail.

"I guess you've got your work cut out for you," Liv said hesitantly.

Grandma looked up, her glasses partway down her nose. "What did you say, dear?"

Livvy smiled to herself. "It's all right with me if you want to make my new skating outfit, Grandma."

Her grandmother scratched her head and frowned. "Well, now, I figured you weren't all too interested."

Livvy cringed. Was this conversation headed in the wrong direction? She unfolded her legs and stretched a bit, getting up the courage to speak.

But Grandma beat her to it. "To tell you the truth, Olivia, Mrs. Newton talked me out of it," she admitted.

"She did?" Livvy wondered when Grandma had seen her friend.

"We went shopping together this afternoon . . . for your flowers." Grandma sighed a bit, her hands moving about. "Mrs. Newton advised me not to. She said it was hardly worth the effort sewing an elaborate skating costume."

This didn't sound like Grandma talking. She wondered what else Mrs. Newton had said.

"Oh, before I forget, I have some other letters tucked away for you," Grandma said, getting up.

"What letters?"

"Come, let's go to my room," said Grandma.

Livvy followed her up the stairs. As they went, she

remembered the lovely rose centerpiece. Grandma had gone out of her way to buy flowers and tall white candles for the lovely table.

With each step, she felt even more dismal. Grandma had meant well, just like Dad had said. She was truly kindhearted. Thoughtful, too. To think Livvy'd resisted such loving attention when she needed it most.

The letters Grandma was eager to share turned out to be more writings from Livvy's mother. "They were written to me over the years," Grandma explained. "Especially during the last weeks of your mother's life."

They had been kept—all of them—in a hand-painted oak box. Set beneath the mirror, the treasured box was centered on Grandma's dresser.

Staring at the letters, Livvy felt a shiver. Yet it was comforting to know that Mom had taken time to express herself to her mother-in-law. Bless her heart, Grandma had saved all of them.

"Go on, take them over to the rocking chair," Grandma urged. "Get comfortable."

Livvy caressed the letters in her hands before reading. Then, one by one, she began to read.

Meanwhile, Grandma set about doing other things in the room. It was considerate of her.

Tears began to cloud Livvy's sight, and she stopped reading for a moment.

"Are you all right, Olivia?" asked Grandma.

Livvy sighed. "You and Mom must've been very close."

Grandma nodded from across the room. "She was the daughter I never had. I was mighty glad your father chose such a wonderful young woman to wed."

The words warmed Livvy's heart. She continued her journey, savoring every letter her mother had written.

But it was her mother's final letter that made her sniffle again. She found herself going back and rereading.

My dearest Beatrice,

I am so grateful for the days and weeks you've given to me of your time and energy during my illness. I don't know how I would've coped without your love and care.

This may be my last letter to you, and in it I want to put on paper your promise . . . as I understand it. You are so gracious to agree to help my husband and daughter after my passing. I know you will look after them to the best of your ability.

Whatever you can possibly do, please help my Livvy follow her skating dream. She's going to need your support desperately. There are days, even now, when she is discouraged. Attempt to keep her spirits high—don't let her occasional frustration get the best of you. Livvy's a hard worker, but she's used to seeing me on the sidelines, cheering her on and lending moral support.

You are Livvy's best hope for the Olympics, dear Bea. I know this in my heart of hearts. Not because her father isn't interested. His calling is art, as you know. He needs to focus on his work. My need is to nurture Livvy, our precious Olivia Kay.

So, when the time seems right, will you ease into my place, Bea? I will be ever grateful if you can give my girl a good dose of mothering.

Livvy held the letter close to her heart. *A good dose of mothering . . .* The annoying phrase had come straight from her mother's heart!

She felt like crying. Sobbing, really—to let it all out. All these months, Grandma had been trying to live up to a dying mother's last wish. She was doing what she'd promised by driving Livvy to the ice rink every morning in the wee hours. As for hovering, that was hardly the word for a grandmother who was giving of herself every minute of every day. Giving out good doses of mothering!

Livvy felt like an ungrateful toad. *How could I have been so blind?*

Brushing the tears from her cheeks, she got up, still clutching the letter. "Oh, Grandma, I'm so sorry," she said, crossing the room. She fell into her grandmother's arms.

"There, there . . ." Grandma patted her back.

"I was such a jerk—you have no idea." The bitterness poured out of her like a soda fizzing out of a shaken bottle. "I didn't know what you'd promised Mom. I just didn't know. . . ."

Grandma was silent, still holding her.

"Will you forgive me?" Livvy sobbed. "I'll make it up to you, I promise."

"Oh, honey, there's no need to worry so. Of course you're forgiven. We all are because of Calvary." Grandma found a tissue for her and waited for Livvy to dry her eyes. "Now . . . isn't that what Easter's all about?"

At that moment, Jenna's Passion play became even more of a reality. "You'll never guess what the Girls Only club members are planning," she blurted.

"Must be something about Easter." Grandma Hudson was sharp as a tack.

"That's right."

Grandma's eyes twinkled happily. "Speaking of Easter, your father's going to have a surprise for you in a few days."

"Another one?" She was thinking of her mother's wonderful letters. Especially the one written just before her death. "I don't know if I can handle any more surprises."

Grandma smiled. "This one might be the topping on the cake, so to speak."

Livvy had no idea what to expect. But her curiosity was definitely piqued.

What's up? she wondered.

Follow the Dream
Chapter Fifteen

Three days later, Livvy and Grandma stood precisely where Dad positioned them. "Stand right there," he said, hurrying back to his art table.

Livvy stared at the clock in the shape of an easel, hanging on the studio wall. Numerous large ferns and other greenery softened the corners of the long room. There were framed prints displayed on the wall, mostly drawn or painted by Dad.

Unlike Jenna's attic bedroom, this room had wider and higher windows, letting the light in during the day. Tonight, Dad had drawn the shades, making the place more private.

"I've read and reread all of Mom's letters to Grandma," Livvy said as her Dad scurried about the room.

He stopped moving about and turned to face her. "Letters?"

Grandma was all smiles again. "Oh yes, and you may certainly read them, too."

Livvy was glad to hear it. She would be eager to know what her dad thought of the deathbed wish. He would probably agree with it wholeheartedly—the part that explained why someone other than himself needed to support Livvy's dream. It was a sweet, very dear thing her mother had done.

"I think, perhaps, the time has come," Dad said. "I'd like to read them."

Livvy sighed, relieved. His answer proved that Dad was coming out of his deepest grief. Finally he was emerging, slowly but surely, back into life.

"One more minute . . . and we'll have the unveiling." Rushing around the room, he cleared brushes off his art table. He gathered up small bottles of paint and clustered them together. Then he pushed his chair in and stepped back, surveying the room.

"It's only us—Grandma and me," said Livvy, smiling at Grandma.

"That's right, son. We're not here for a housekeeping inspection. We came for the surprise."

Then Dad proceeded toward the draped easel. Carefully, he lifted the white sheet from the painting.

Livvy gasped in amazement. "Oh, it's super beautiful, Daddy," she whispered. She stared in awe at the face of her mother.

The painting, done in oils, was a portrayal of her youthful mother. Rendered with the aid of an engagement photo, the portrait was breathtakingly real.

Dad displayed the original picture, a newspaper clipping. "This was one of your mother's favorite poses," he explained. "Mine too."

"It's your best work ever," Grandma said. Her voice sounded lumpy with tears.

Both Livvy and Grandma moved toward the painting, standing only a few feet from the easel. Livvy felt her father reach for her hand. Almost without thinking, she reached for Grandma's, too.

"I painted it for you, Livvy," her father was saying.

"It's the most beautiful picture ever," Livvy said softly.

Dad turned and cupped her chin in his free hand. "I pray it will help you remember who first believed in your skating talent." He paused to kiss her forehead. "Never forget who got you started and who was always there for you at the rink. And all those competitions."

Mom's letters . . . and now this painting. How could she possibly forget? It was the coolest present a girl could ever wish for.

"Can we hang it in the living room?" she asked. "We can all enjoy it there . . . every day of our lives."

"That's entirely up to you," Dad said.

"Thank you." She clung to his hand.

They stood quietly in the haven of the studio, gazing in wonder. Livvy saw something of herself in her mother's dear face. The realization made her feel confident, safe somehow.

"Anyone ready for supper?" Grandma asked, breaking the stillness.

"Yes, I'm hungry," Dad said.

"How about you, Olivia Kay?" Grandma asked.

Olivia Kay . . .

The name stuck in her head. It had been a tender expression of love, coming from her mother's pen. She thought of her mother's cherished letters, Grandma's promise and daily sacrifice. Everything that had happened this week.

Livvy glanced at her father's mother. She turned and gazed at her own mother's portrait. Sighing, she knew it was just fine—super, really—for Grandma Hudson to call her Olivia Kay. And as often as she liked. Livvy would never again wince when she said it. Never!

———

"It's hard to believe so many good things can happen in one short week," Livvy told her parrot before bedtime. "I mean, this thing with Grandma's over . . . done . . . finished."

"Grandma . . . Grandma," Coco cawed back.

"I was so messed up about her. I even thought she had her eyes on Coach Sterling!" she confessed. "Jenna was right all along. I should've just relaxed about things."

Coco twittered about the cage, ignoring her.

"I talked to Coach, too," she confessed. "I never understood why he seemed unaware of Grandma at practice. Truth is, he thought she was essential to my success. And you know what? He was exactly right. Now . . . I don't know what I'd do without her. Dad too."

She went to the bookcase, picking up the figurine of the skater. "I was so dense, Coco," she admitted. "So unbelievably stupid."

But for a change, the bird was silent.

"You're a big help," she said sarcastically, replacing the statuette of the skater.

"Help . . . help!" cawed Coco.

"Call 9-1-1," she teased.

He began making his siren sound, and she was immediately sorry she'd ever taught him such a trick.

"Hush, now, you'll have both Dad and Grandma in here."

Thankfully, her parrot calmed down. She said, "Good night, birdie-boy," and covered his cage. Usually that solved most noise problems.

Not tonight. Coco began to warble.

"Better keep it down," she whispered, turning out the light.

"Down, down, down," sang the bird.

"Not down . . . *up*." She went and tapped on the birdcage. "Things are looking up, up, up. And I'm not kidding."

Coco stopped yodeling, just like that!

Climbing into bed, Livvy wondered what part Coco might play in Jenna's play. But then again, maybe birdie-boy best stay home. He was just too unpredictable. Besides, he was a boy. The play was being performed by only girls. Coco was definitely out of the running!

Giggling quietly, she thanked the Lord for her family, including a mom who had always cared and helped her dream big dreams. Never had she doubted that.

"Thanks, Lord, for a dad who's smiling again," she prayed. "And for a grandma whose mothering has made all the difference."

Livvy nestled down under her warm comforter. But her spirits soared up . . . up, high as the best triple flip ever. With divine guidance, she would work hard to follow her dreams. Harder than ever!

Her family and her girl friends would support her from the sidelines. She could count on that. As for Mom . . . well, Livvy had a feeling *she* was cheering her on, too. From the grandstand of heaven.

Girls Only!

Better Than Best

AUTHOR'S NOTE

Once again, I am grateful for the help given me by my young cousin, Alissa Jones of Hutchinson, Kansas, who answered my questions about the thrilling sport of gymnastics. Thanks, Alissa, for being so resourceful!

USA Gymnastics Online also assisted my research. Their official Web site is fascinating for readers eager to know more: *www.usa-gymnastics.org*.

For

Sarah Simmonds,

*who gives her all
to gymnastics.*

Better Than Best
Chapter One

Nothing comes between gymnastics and me, thought Jenna Song. *Nothing!*

Carefully, she taped up her hands for protection before beginning her early-morning training at Alpine Aerial Gymnastics. AAG for short. During the next forty minutes, she planned to warm up her muscles. Stretching exercises were always a great way to get started before *any* sport. Aerobics came next. Last of all, individual routines. Her all-time favorites were floor exercise and the balance beam.

Keeping her focus, Jenna thought through her compulsory elements. She wouldn't allow herself to get off track and think too far ahead, even though the upcoming weekend—a three-day sports camp in Vail—was going to be *very* exciting. All week long, they had been working on individual skills, preparing for the camp.

"Hey, Jen!"

She looked up to see Cassie Peterson, a tall blond sixth grader, bounding across the gym. "Looking good, girl," Jenna said.

"We've gotta nail everything today . . . and I mean *everything*," Cassie said, grinning. She wound her long hair into a quick knot at the back of her head and stuck in a single hair clip.

"Duh!" Jenna gave her teammate a playful pat on the shoulder. "Like I don't know that."

"C'mon, I'm serious."

"And I'm *not?*" Jenna laughed. She and Cassie were both a Level Eight in gymnastics, testing for a Level Nine in a few weeks. They were also on the same All-Around Team.

"Coupled in competition," Coach Kim liked to say about the girls.

Cassie tilted her head, then shook out her arms, rotating her shoulders and neck. "Heard the rumor yet?"

"Which is?" Jenna studied Cassie's face. Something was up.

Cassie leaned closer, whispering, "There's this guy— an elite gymnast—who's going to be a spotter for our All-Around Team. Lara Swenson said she heard it from Coach. And . . . he's supposedly very cute."

"So what?" Jenna couldn't care less. She was team captain and starting to feel *very* annoyed with all this waste-of-time boy talk. "What *I* want to know is, are *you* set for the weekend sports camp?"

Cassie was in her face with more news. "Listen, Jen, this guy's not just *any* male. Lara says he's so gorgeous you'll drop your teeth."

Jenna leaned down and touched her toes. Then again, this time with her hands flat on the floor. "Bottom line: If he's gonna be a spotter, he'd better know what he's doing."

"I'm sure he does, especially if Coach Kim's paying him to do it."

Jenna didn't care to respond to Cassie's comment. "By the way, cute is way overrated. And if I *do* drop my teeth, I'll just have to gum my fruit leather. Won't I?"

Cassie laughed softly. "Spoken like a true team captain. Way to go, girl."

Jenna nodded, feeling better. Finally she'd gotten Cassie's attention off the new boy's physical appearance and on what really counted in their world of competition and mastery of athletic skills. "You said he's a good gymnast, right?" she asked again.

"That's the word around the gym."

"Then he should know how to spot" was all she said.

"Later, Jen." Cassie turned and waved, doing repetitious handsprings across the soft crash pads.

Looking around, Jenna expected to see Coach Kim and his Russian-born wife, Tasya, nearby. Sure enough, the famous twosome were working with Lara Swenson on the balance beam. True professionals, Coach and Tasya were assisting all of them along the path to the Olympics.

Not waiting another second, Jenna blew her whistle, the signal to her seven teammates. Major work had to be done before sports camp this Friday. "Let's get cracking!" she called out, clapping her hands.

Once the girls were gathered on the mats, she began to call out their regular stretching routine. Fifteen long stretches total. She, Cassie, Lara, and the others were a cluster of blue, yellow, and pink warm-up suits. Tall water bottles were lined up, each marked with the individual team member's name.

Soft crash pads were scattered in various sections of the gym. Gymnasts in different levels trained on the uneven parallel bars, the balance beam, and the vault. The large padded carpet in the center of the gym was used for the floor exercise.

Across the expansive gym, Coach Kim and Tasya were busy talking with a tall, slender guy. Their faces were animated, eyes bright as always.

She noticed the young man's confident stance. How

could she miss it? He had that totally self-assured look. His hair was the color of corn, and his eyes . . . Well, she wasn't much for blue eyes, she decided on the spot.

Cassie was right. He was drop-dead gorgeous.

But so what? There were plenty of cute boys in their town of Alpine Lake, situated in the middle of the Colorado Rocky Mountains.

"Stretch and . . . *hold*," Jenna called out the last three long extensions.

She and her teammates would train individually, and as hard as possible. And nothing, not even a cute guy, was going to mess up their concentration!

Better Than Best
Chapter Two

"Mom, I'm home!" Jenna dropped her gym bag near the door.

The three-story brick house was unusually quiet. By now, her adopted baby brother, Jonathan Bryan, would come crawling across the carpet toward her. He would probably be drooling, too, and babbling jumbled-up syllables.

"Anybody home?" she called, heading for the kitchen.

But the counters were washed clean. No dirty dishes in the sink. The place was spotless.

This is too weird, she thought. *Mom's always home.*

Thinking her mother might be busy upstairs with Jonathan, Jenna scurried in the direction of the steps.

"Mom, are you up there?" She asked this in Korean, her first language.

Mom didn't respond. So Jenna hurried to the former guest room, which had been transformed into a nursery for tiny Jon. The room was small but light and airy, decorated in soft shades of yellow and green with white wicker accents. The sweetest nursery ever.

Sighing, she sat on the wicker rocker and leaned back. "Where could they be?" Jenna whispered, feeling drowsy.

Her day had been hectic, working out at the gym before *and* after school. These days, her schedule was exhausting. Up before dawn, early breakfast, rush to the gym, then to school, back to either ballet or the gym. Race like crazy all day long. She knew if she couldn't handle the mental strain, the stress, her own emotions, all of that, she would never attain the success she longed for. At the moment, her goal was to become a member of the Junior National Team.

Getting up, she went to the crib and leaned on the ruffled crib bumpers. She smoothed the folded baby quilt at the bottom. Restless, she reached for the cow-jumped-over-the moon lamp on the bureau and went to sit again in the rocker. She stared at the lamp, very glad to have the support of both her parents. Coach Kim and Tasya were also two of her biggest fans.

And there was the very cool, very exciting Girls Only

club. The other three members were also her closest friends—Livvy Hudson, Heather Bock, and Miranda Garcia. They liked to perform ballets and elaborate dramas for their parents. They also offered enthusiasm and encouragement to Jenna and to one another.

Jenna sometimes wondered how she'd ever managed before the club was created last fall. Livvy was an amazing novice-level figure skater, and Heather was a dazzling, award-winning ice dancer with her brother, Kevin. Manda, their newest member, was a stunning and daring downhill skier. Four girls following a strenuous, yet thrilling, track to the Olympics. They shared athletic dreams and goals, forming a tight-knit friendship.

Jenna's All-Around teammates were cool, too. They worked well individually and as a team. But she was worried about something—*someone.*

Lara Swenson, the youngest of the seven members, had just turned eleven. In the past six weeks, she had grown really fast. Maybe too fast. Right in front of everyone's eyes, she was sprouting up like she might never stop! At the moment, she was just a hair taller than Cassie Peterson, who *had* been the tallest on the team.

Jenna could hardly believe it. Did Lara have an out-of-control pituitary gland or what? Petite Lara was no longer tiny. If she kept up her growth rate, she might end up six feet tall. Jenna worried that Lara wouldn't be able to maintain her exceptional skills as a gymnast. Which would hurt *all* the others on the team.

This week she'd noticed Lara's inability to "stick" her landings perfectly. For the first time, her performances had been less than precise. Lara was struggling for sure.

Jenna really wanted to help. But she had no idea what to do.

———

The phone rang, and Jenna raced down the hall to her parents' bedroom. "Song residence, Jenna speaking," she answered.

"How's life?"

It was Olivia Hudson, Jenna's best friend. "Livvy, hi! Things are going okay . . . I guess you could say."

"Well, by the sound of your voice, I'm not convinced. What's up?"

She cringed. Should she unload on Livvy?

"What *is* it, Jen? Something wrong?"

Putting the phone to her other ear, Jenna said, "I'm worried about my All-Around Team."

"Why, what's up?"

"It's just that, well . . . I think some of us might need some special attention," she said.

"Meaning what?"

Hesitating, Jen wondered what to say. "Well, I think

you know how it is. One of us is having an annoying expansion."

"Speak English," Livvy laughed.

"Meaning one of us has an overactive growth gland."

"Well, *you* don't," Livvy said quickly. "Not yet, anyway."

Her friend's answer took her off guard. "You're right, I'm *not* growing."

"Then who?"

"You remember Lara Swenson?"

Livvy chuckled. "Right. The baby gymnast at AAG."

"Well, try this on for size: Lara's now the *tallest* team member. And it *just* happened."

"You sound . . . sorta jealous," Livvy said. "What's with that?"

Jen bit her lip. "I guess I'm afraid *I* won't grow anymore at all. Maybe I'll stay this small—this short—for the rest of my life."

"Being petite is a good thing for gymnasts, isn't it?" Liv asked.

"So everyone says."

"Then it must be true."

Leave it to Livvy to turn things around, to try to encourage her. Livvy had always been good in the cheering-up department. She'd been Jen's good friend for a long time. They'd started out as pen pals—the snail-mail kind. Then they'd both moved to Alpine Lake with their families before school started last August. Just in time for sixth grade at Alpine Lake Middle School.

"You know what?" Jenna changed the subject. "We've got a new guy helping with the team."

"A guy? You must be kidding." Livvy sounded shocked. "Who is it?"

Jenna had to smile. "His name is Nels Ansgar."

"Sounds Norwegian."

"Might be," replied Jenna.

Livvy was silent for a moment, then continued. "So . . . what's Nels got to do with Lara's growth spurt?"

Jenna sighed. "I guess I'm not making much sense. Nothing really. It's just that Lara's shooting up. Way up. And I'm trapped in pre-puberty."

Livvy was laughing. "Don't go morbid on me."

"I'm not . . . *okay.*" Jenna felt angry and didn't know why.

"Hey, did I say something wrong?" They were silent for a moment, then Livvy asked, "Are you worried? About your height, I mean . . . because of this guy?"

"Sorta." Jenna shrugged, even though Livvy couldn't see her.

"Don't worry. He's just a spotter. It's no big deal."

Maybe not for you, Jen thought.

Just then she heard her mother returning home.

"I better get going," she said, adding a hurried "Bye, Livvy."

"Call me later tonight."

Jenna had tons of homework. "Maybe we'd better talk at school tomorrow instead."

"Okay. I'll meet you at our locker."

"See ya, Liv."

They hung up, and Jenna rushed off to greet her mom and baby brother. "Where were you?" she asked, taking Jonathan from her mother's arms.

"We ran out to buy some more cabbage," her mother explained. "Your father's having his deacon board meeting here on Saturday. He wants me to cook up some kimchi. Lots of it."

"Sounds good."

Jenna's dad was the pastor of the Korean church in Alpine Lake. A small church in a small town. "We can grow . . . and we will," he liked to say when discussing the prospect of attracting new Korean members and their families.

Jostling her baby brother on her hip, Jenna turned toward the kitchen window. She thought of her dad's motto: *"We can grow, and we will."* Would *she* grow? Or would she remain a teeny weeny forever?

Outside, the leaves on their trees were full and green—almost lacy-looking in the fading sunlight. Her mother's red tulips were in full bloom. She stared at the smallest of a clump of aspen trees. The tiny one seemed alone, as it stood out and away from the others.

Stroking her brother's soft head, she cooed to him in Korean. She was actually glad her mom had left the kitchen. "Why am I hung up on my size?" she whispered into baby Jonathan's ear. "What's it matter?"

But she did not breathe a word about Nels, the new spotter. Not in Korean or otherwise.

Better Than Best
Chapter Three

After supper, a light rain began to fall. Soon the April shower turned into a gale of thunder and lightning.

Glancing out her window, Jenna was actually glad for the storm. The weather suited her mood, after all. Rain was the ideal climate for studying for a history test.

American history bored her silly. She would much rather be studying Korean history—her family roots. Often, during class, she had to *make* herself listen to the teacher. She struggled to keep her mind from wandering, especially with gymnastics and ballet and all the thrilling summer events coming up!

She stared at the Olympic rings flag hanging high over her desk. Why was she required to study subjects that didn't interest her? What a waste of her valuable time.

Gymnastics had always been the thing that pumped her up. For as long as she could remember. Since before preschool, she had been testing her balancing ability. On checkered floors, sidewalk cracks . . . anything. Jenna was three years old when her mother signed her up for the Tumble Tots.

She was tapping her pen on the desk top when Mom peered in the open bedroom door. "I don't mean to interrupt, but—"

"Anytime you see this book, feel free," Jenna said, waving the history textbook in the air. "And I'm *not* kidding."

Mom grinned. "Just remember: If it's not worth doing one-hundred-and-ten-percent, it's not worth doing at all." One of Mom's all-time favorite sayings.

"I'm trying, but I can't say it's any fun."

"Fun or not, you must keep up your grades."

Nothing, according to Mom, should ever be done by halves. She believed that God expected—even *required*—our best, as His children. That was her life's philosophy.

"Which leotards and warm-up suits do you want washed for the weekend?" Mom asked.

Jenna shrugged. "Doesn't matter. Just pick out two or three of each."

Mom's smile faded. "I thought you were excited about sports camp, honey."

"I doubt it'll be very cool," she complained.

"But Coach Kim is bringing in a national team coach for the occasion," Mom reminded her. "Won't *that* be exciting?"

She still had gobs of studying to do. "I'd rather not talk about it," Jenna said softly.

Mom touched her shoulder. "I'm here whenever, okay?"

Nodding, Jenna watched her mother head for her closet, pulling several leotards out of the hamper. "Thanks, Mom."

Her mother scurried out of the room, arms loaded down with laundry. "That's what mothers are for, right?"

Jenna couldn't help thinking how similar her mom and Livvy Hudson were. In many ways, they had the same intensely focused, yet happy, approach to life.

She prided herself on having a cheerful attitude. But today she had to pour her thoughts and concentration into the monotonous history questions. Tomorrow she'd be glad she had stuck it out—crammed for the test.

Mom's perspective on life rang in her ears. Doing your best affected every area of learning. Small or tall. Schoolwork was a good training ground for becoming an Olympic athlete.

She spent the rest of the evening preparing for the dreaded test. All the while, Sasha, her prissy kitty, kept her company on the computer desk, purring as if she had not a care in the world.

"Must be nice," Jenna said, leaning her head against the golden-haired cat.

———

"What kept you so long?" Livvy asked the next day. She was primping in the mirror of their shared locker. "I thought you'd never get here."

Jenna glanced at her watch. "I'm not late, am I?"

Livvy turned to look her over. "Not exactly."

"Then what?"

"We have to talk," Livvy whispered.

"About what?"

Livvy jerked her head toward the busy hall of students. "Check it out, over there."

"Should I look now?" Jenna whispered back.

"It's Nels Ansgar, the guy you told me about."

Both girls turned to gawk—discreetly, of course—at a tall boy with golden hair. He was rushing down the hall to a locker on the opposite side.

"Look, he even strides like a gymnast," Livvy remarked.

"You should see him on the uneven bars," replied Jenna. "He makes it look so easy."

"I hear he's thirteen." Livvy commented.

"That would put him in either seventh or eighth grade."

"Probably eighth," Jenna said. "He acts older, don't you think?"

"Maybe he's not enrolled here."

"Then why's he hanging out at school?"

Livvy ignored the question. "He's just so tall and . . . cute."

Everyone thinks tall is best, Jenna thought.

"Why haven't we noticed him around school before?" Livvy asked as they closed the locker.

"Maybe he's new to town."

"Are you sure?" Livvy asked, turning to look at Jenna.

"Not really. Maybe he's a foreign exchange student." She wondered about that. Maybe Nels *wasn't* a permanent fixture here in Alpine Lake. Surely Cassie or Lara would know. Coach Kim and his wife would, too. Jenna wasn't too curious or interested in sticking her neck out to get info. Not for a guy who was as tall as he was cute.

She could just imagine the ongoing distraction a team spotter like Nels might cause.

What *was* Coach thinking?

———

The history test was worse than Jenna anticipated. At one point she closed her eyes, trying to remember the pages she'd read last night. Why had she waited so long to study?

I need to change my game plan about American History class, she thought. *Think of it as a gymnastics meet, where it's best to train way ahead.*

Struggling through five essay questions, she decided she would begin studying tonight for the next test. What a monster of a test. Hardly any multiple-choice questions. Mostly true or false questions—the worst. You either knew it or you didn't.

She took her time, going back to check and double-check her answers. *"Iron the small things,"* Coach Kim always said. Well, she'd have to transfer what she was learning at the gym into her school studies. Especially history.

When she was finished, she sat at her desk, staring at the first page of the test. She didn't get up and turn it in right then. Instead, she prayed silently. She was sorry for putting off the studying part. She prayed she'd get a better-than-passing grade. If not, Mom and Dad would give her the third degree, asking why she'd bombed the test.

She had enough to think about without something like that!

———

Jenna, Cassie, and Lara worked on their aerial cartwheels for over an hour after school, following Natalie Johnston's ballet class. They were really warmed up by the time they arrived at Alpine Aerials Gym.

But Nels had other ideas about warming up. With no effort at all, he'd gathered the girls around him. They watched, nearly transfixed, as he did his pirouettes and saltos with multiple grip changes on the uneven parallel bars. His flight was definitely high. No question, Nels was a superb gymnast.

"What's this, a one-man show?" Jenna whispered to Cassie.

"He's just practicing, that's all," Cassie said flippantly.

"Showing off, don't you mean?"

"What's *your* problem?"

"Sorry I asked." Jenna turned away.

"He's adorable, isn't he?" Lara grabbed Jenna's arm.

"You've lost your focus," she shot back. As far as Jenna was concerned, Nels was hired help—here to help Coach and Tasya spot during sports camp. He would probably head back home to Europe, or wherever, after this weekend. End of story.

Both Cassie and Lara stood gazing at the new boy

like he was an Olympic superstar. They were definitely flipped out.

"I don't believe this," Jenna muttered, walking toward the water fountain. "He's going to be the end of us."

"Who is?"

She turned to see Coach Kim looking up at her from his clipboard.

"Oh, uh . . . nothing," she managed to say to Coach.

"Well, now, other than myself, there's only one *male* in the gym at the moment." His wry smile gave him away.

She could kick herself. Coach had heard her mumbling about Nels Ansgar.

What could she say?

Better Than Best
Chapter Four

Jenna made an attempt to explain herself to Coach Kim. But she was spared the embarrassment when the whistle blew for team warm-ups.

"Time to lead stretching exercises," Coach said. He meant for her to get moving and fill her duty as captain.

Dashing across the maze of mats and equipment, Jenna met up with the girls. But it was Nels who had *her* whistle!

"Excuse me." She put her hands on her hips. "*I'm* the team captain."

Smiling down at her, he said, "Captain Song, is it?"

"Jenna."

"Glad to meet you, Jenna Song. I'm Nels Ansgar."

Grinning, he handed over the silver whistle and stepped back, behind the girls' lineup.

Jenna observed that he was only slightly taller than Lara Swenson. His smiling blue eyes and extraordinary good looks rattled Jenna. She even forgot to wipe off the whistle before putting it to her own lips.

———

Warm-ups went as well as could be expected. As long as Jenna kept her eyes on either Cassie, Lara, or the other girls, she was perfectly fine. But locking eyes with Nels made her flustered.

Did the other girls feel the same way?

During floor routines, Lara stumbled a lot. She was obviously off kilter. Lara had always been well-known for supercharged, brilliant performances. Consistently perfect. She nailed everything—tumbles, acrobatics, and sequences. Every time.

Not today.

Yet Coach was patient with Lara. He and Tasya guided her repeatedly through several sequences and dance movements. "Things will improve over time. . . ." His voice trailed off.

Jenna truly felt sorry for Lara. No longer was her friend a Dominique or Nadia look-alike. She was no longer a pint-size.

And Jenna felt sorry for herself, too. She *still* had a

mini, little-girl body like young Domi and Nadia. She was always first in line of all her teammates when they were arranged as stairsteps at competitions and gymnastic events. But what Jenna wanted most was to be normal. To grow some more. To grow up . . .

What was so wrong with that?

Turning her concentration back to her floor exercise, she fought hard the urge to glance at the girls. All of them were cheering her on.

Coach Kim and Tasya had trained them to encourage one another. "Pump up your teammates," Coach liked to say. "Work as a team. Work hard at caring."

If one member stumbled, they all must feel the pain. The disappointment. Then push past the problem and succeed to perfection. They—all of them—were expected to move, breathe, and live the AAG motto: *Be your best. Be perfect.*

The motto kept her sharp, on her toes at all times.

Nels took his position as spotter.

I don't need him, she thought but wouldn't cause a scene. She would just ignore him. Pretend he wasn't there.

"Hit it, Jenna . . . hit it . . ." the All-Around Team chorused from the sidelines.

The force of their chanting, mixed with Nels' slightly lower voice, inspired her. She was ready to give the routine her best shot.

"Be your best," Cassie hollered.

I'll try for better than best, she thought. She would not miss this moment to excel.

The musical introduction to her floor exercise—"A Whole New World"—spilled out of the speakers. Jenna stared down at the square of carpet, forty feet by forty feet. She would complete each of her skills using every inch of the carpet space. And she would not allow her tiny feet to cross the line.

She saluted the imaginary judges, as she was taught to do. Both arms high over her head, she saluted as if to say, "Look at me! I'm ready to perform perfectly!"

Feeling the burst of confidence, she pointed her toes and began the dance sequence. Next came the tumbling pass. She was so jazzed, she nailed every layout, handspring, and salto. Best of all, she hit her final pose perfectly.

Coach was yelling, "You did it, Jenna! You were wonderful!" He hugged her, twirling her around.

She caught Nels' eye just then. His face was way too serious. Instead of smiling, he was frowning. While the girls clapped and cheered for her, he remained motionless and silent.

Is he jealous? she wondered.

———

It was starting to rain again when her dad parked in front of the gym. "How was practice?" he asked.

"Which one?" She had worked out both before school and after ballet, right after school.

"Both." He waited for her answer before turning into the street.

"Well, this afternoon I really beat the nerves," she was proud to say. "Morning practice wasn't so hot, but that's not *my* problem."

"Oh?"

"Yeah," she muttered. "Did Mom say anything to you?"

A smile spread across his face. "Your mother says lots of things to me." He was such a tease.

"C'mon, Daddy, you know what I mean."

"Well," he said, keeping his attention on the road, "your mother hopes the weekend will be a good experience for you."

"So do I." She wouldn't say more. Mom and Dad were definitely on her side.

He glanced over at her. "You do *want* to go to Vail, don't you?"

She was quiet for a moment. "Sure, I'm planning to go."

"But . . . ?"

She remembered the way Nels had looked at her when her floor exercise was as perfect as they get.

She remembered, too, how he'd blown her whistle for warm-ups. Did he want to take over her position?

"Will you miss me?" she said with confidence.

He reached over and patted her shoulder. "We'll miss you both at home and at church. Your brother will miss your hugs and all the silly baby talk."

Thinking of the baby her parents had adopted back in December, she had to smile. It seemed, nearly over-night, the little tyke had won her heart.

Becoming an extraordinary gymnast meant plenty of sacrifice. But that was part of the training. Three days away from her family might be a little unpleasant. In the end, though, the special emphasis would be worth it.

Now, if only the team would pull together. She hoped and prayed they could, in spite of Nels. She hoped the girls would pay attention to their own skills. Not be so google-eyed over the spotter.

If only Nels hadn't come to Alpine Lake. . . .

Better Than Best
Chapter Five

Jenna was up and packed long before the early-morning departure. Over the past few days, she'd gotten behind in recording her thoughts in her journal.

So she wrote quickly.

Friday (5:30 A.M.), April 7
Dear Diary,

Last night, Livvy and I talked after ballet class. She and the other Girls Only members are going to Vail for the sports camp weekend, too. I'm so jazzed! Of course, we won't be together all that much—only during the ballet segment. But we'll hang out at night in the dorm. We're planning to have a club meeting while we're there. Hope the sponsors don't mind our giggling.

I think Cassie's head over heels about Nels, the new spotter for the All-Around Team. Lara is trying to compete with Cassie for his attention. But he doesn't really seem interested in either of them. Go figure . . .

Gotta run. I hear Dad calling me to bring my luggage downstairs. One little sports bag. Won't he be surprised?

Speaking of surprises, I have a strange feeling about this weekend. But I hope I'm wrong!

Coach Kim and Tasya kept the gymnasts entertained in the van on the ride to Vail. Tasya told amusing and heartwarming tales of national competitions in Russia, and around the world.

"Our tour took us all the way to New York City," Tasya said. "Coach and I fell in love with the Big Apple. And by that time, we were quite disappointed with the Russian government for many reasons."

Jenna and her friends listened intently, eager for more of the story.

"The morning we were scheduled to fly back to Russia, Coach Kim and I spoke to the American officials." She grinned, looking fondly at Coach. "Tell them the rest, dear."

Coach glanced in the rearview mirror. "Can anyone guess what happened?" he bellowed.

Jenna raised her hand. "You stayed in America!"

"Tasya defected from Russia," said Cassie.

The whole van was cheering. "Hooray for Tasya!"

It was a thrilling moment, especially for Jenna. She felt she understood the triumph of being granted asylum because her ancestry was closely tied to another country. She, too, was proud to call herself an American citizen. It was thrilling to hear the national anthem played or sung at gymnastic events.

"On that day, we started all over with nothing," Tasya said softly when the hoopla died down. "Such hard work it was, making a new home in America. But it was worth every struggle."

Just like gymnastics, thought Jenna.

She was thinking of the effort that went into perfecting every single gesture, every movement, every breath. Flashy, impressive moves fell flat if the smallest motions were sloppy or incomplete. Bad habits had to be relearned and replaced with good ones. The overall performance was a make-or-break situation, depending on all of the above.

———

Within minutes of their arrival in Vail, they were registered. Then the intense training began. Physical skills were one thing, the other hurdle was the test for mental toughness. To be a successful gymnast, focusing one hundred percent was most important. Jenna knew that if one tiny detail was overlooked in any of her routines, the whole program was zip.

She was determined to master her skills—to benefit from the three-day sports camp. No matter what.

The first three hours, she did "timers," a trick cut down—abbreviated. She raced along the vault runway and flew into a roundoff handspring. Nels was nearby, but she never once looked at him.

To get the feel of the springboard under her bare feet, she stopped abruptly, not doing the flying skill over the vault. By repeating this many times, she "made friends" with the springboard. This was the goal of the exercise.

"Doing fine?" Lara asked her during the first break.

"Yeah, how about you?"

Lara frowned, patting her own head. "Getting used to extra inches is real tough."

"It'll take time, but you're sticking with it. That's what counts." Jenna sipped some fresh carrot juice.

Lara stared at the juice in Jenna's hand. "How can you stand that stuff?"

Jenna smiled. "Well, if it didn't give me so much energy, I'd probably never drink it."

"You're saying it's an acquired taste?"

Jenna nodded, finishing off the container. "But it's easy on the stomach."

Lara laughed. "You sound like my grandpa. He's always talking about food that 'goes down easy.' "

They giggled at that.

"I'm not *that* old, thank goodness," Jenna said.

"Mom says to enjoy the strength and stamina we have now, as young gymnasts."

"Because it won't last forever?" Jen added.

Lara was nodding her head. "Sounds like your mom and mine are in cahoots."

"Actually," Jenna said, "when we're too old to perform, we can instruct other gymnasts."

"Teaching is the last thing I want to do."

Jenna tossed away her carrot juice container. "For now, all I can think of is Olympic gold. I eat it, drink it, and breathe it."

Lara agreed. "I'm with you. Getting on a national team would be so awesome, wouldn't it?" Suddenly she looked sad. "That is, *if* I can ever get control of my legs again."

Jenna put her arm around her friend. "Keep your chin up. It'll happen. You'll see."

"I'd trade places with you any day," Lara whispered, eyes glistening.

Jenna could hardly believe her ears. They linked arms and hurried back across the gym toward the vaulting horse.

Lara said, "Be thankful you're still so small."

So small . . .

Jenna didn't want to hear that about her size. She wanted to grow taller than this minibody of hers. She wanted to become a normal-sized young woman.

When would it happen?

Better Than Best
Chapter Six

Jenna stared at the vaulting horse—vault for short. It stood four feet high, five feet long, and eleven inches wide. The runway, leading to the vault, was three feet wide and eighty-two feet long. She knew she'd have to be very fast, with a strong burst of energy to build up enough speed.

"You can do it!" Cassie, Lara, and the other girls called from the sidelines.

"Go, Captain Jen," a male voice called.

She saw Nels in the crowd of gymnasts. Some were from the Vail area. Others had driven from as far away as Denver and Grand Junction. Seventy-five young gymnasts, in various levels.

Coach Kim cheered her on, clapping his hands, as

he stood on the sidelines. "You've got what it takes. Think 'the best.' Okay! Push for perfection!"

She faced the horse, focusing deliberately. She thought through her explosive hurdle off the springboard. Her legs must fly high over her head, toes pointed. The next move was a half twist before pushing off the horse with her hands. Her body must create a tall, perfect arc, with an assortment of bends and somersaults.

Last of all, her feet would smack the mat with a deft "stick" landing. Hops and steps backward never cut it with the judges at the competition stage. At all costs, she must avoid any hint of sloppiness in practice.

Be the best, she told herself. *Better than best.*

It was time the All-Around Team saw who was tops. She would show her stuff. She would stretch past her best, to perfection. She was so psyched up, she almost could fly!

———

"You were so amazing," Cassie said as she and Lara gathered around Jenna after the vault.

"Thanks, but believe it or not, I'm not that crazy about the vault," Jenna admitted.

"Could've fooled me," Lara said.

"Me too," said Nels, walking up to them.

Instantly Cassie and Lara clammed up. But Jenna

wasn't going to let Nels' presence spoil her moment of victory. "What's *your* best event?" she asked him.

"Me?" He turned comically, looking behind him.

"Yes, *you.*"

"Uneven bars. What's yours?" His eyes twinkled with interest.

By revealing her best, she would be confessing her weaker skills. She glanced nervously at Cassie and Lara.

Cassie frowned. "What?" she mouthed silently.

My girlfriends know the truth, she thought. Both Cassie and Lara—Coach too—knew her preferred events.

"C'mon, Captain. Cough it up." Nels' smile made her soften. Maybe telling him wasn't such a big deal, after all.

But no, something kept her back. Both the floor exercise and the balance beam were her all-time best. Her greatest passions in gymnastics. But she wanted to keep this to herself for now. She shrugged him off. "I . . . uh, later," she managed to say.

Nels looked puzzled but didn't push the question. "Whatever," he said, following the girls into the cafeteria.

They kept pace, the three of them, side by side.

"Guess who's tagging along?" Cassie whispered.

"And guess who likes *you?*" Lara teased.

Jenna smirked. "Guess who's *toast?*"

Cassie and Lara gave her confused looks, but they said no more.

Jenna had already guessed that Nels had singled her out. That he liked her. But cute or not, he was obnoxiously competitive. Not that an ambitious spirit wasn't *totally* essential for an athlete. But Nels Ansgar was a pain about it. He acted like a medalhead or something.

Jenna decided to try to throw him off, just a bit. So she waited till Cassie and Lara were out of earshot. "You asked about my favorite event?" she taunted him.

He'd already sat down at a long table. "Sure, what is it?"

"Can you guess?"

"The beam?"

She grimaced. "It's okay, I guess."

"Floor exercise?"

She shook her head, but her heart pounded. "Floor exercise stinks."

"You're kidding, right?"

"Nope."

His eyes squinted. She had him. He could *not* figure her out. "I saw you training yesterday at the gym. Your floor routine was outstanding." He didn't crack a smile. His eyes held hers. He was testing her, she was fairly certain.

"I just give it all I've got, no matter the skill."

It was his turn to shrug her off. "Every good gymnast is *supposed* to do that."

"So what do *you* like best?" she asked.

Cassie and Lara were waving her over. Looked like they'd found a table near the juice stand.

"Well, gotta go. See ya around," she said.

"Hey, I thought—"

"Later," she interrupted.

"So long, Captain Song." There was a knowing ring in his voice. It was as if he were taunting her.

She didn't like it one bit. She resented his scoffing her name. He'd made fun of her title, too. She wished he'd stayed in his own country, far away from Colorado.

Why had Coach Kim and Tasya bothered to bring him all the way to America just for a few days of sports camp? It made no sense.

Marching toward Cassie and Lara, she was secretly glad she had tricked Nels. For all she cared, he could mistakenly think she disliked the floor exercise.

Lie or not, it served him right!

Better Than Best
Chapter Seven

All four Girls Only club members relaxed in the third-floor dorm above the sports center overlooking the Vail mountains. Posters of various celebrity-status sports heroes decorated the walls across the long, narrow room. There were showers and bathrooms at the opposite end of each wing, complete with hair dryers. A first!

"We survived our first day of camp," Jenna said, lying back on her bunk.

"It was hard work but lots of fun," said Livvy. She towel-dried her auburn hair as she sat on Jenna's bunk. "I'm glad ballet sessions are happening all weekend."

Jenna nodded, filing her fingernails. "If the ballet segment wasn't being offered, the Girls Only club wouldn't be meeting here tonight."

"Supercool," replied Livvy. "I'm glad we have *one* sport in common."

"Me too," Manda spoke up. She was curled up on her bunk, leaning back on two pillows. "Otherwise, I know you three wouldn't be hanging out with *me* on the ski slopes, right?"

"Hey, you can't say that," Heather insisted. Her blond hair billowed down over her shoulders. "Some of us are big risk takers. Right, Livvy?"

Livvy laughed. "Well, I'd rather not gamble with my life on ski runs like that. You're the fearless one of us, Manda."

Heather's face drooped a bit. "Really? Well, let me tell you about fearless." She began to describe in detail several new stunts she and her ice-dancing brother and partner were learning. "One wrong move, or one half inch off, and my head's crashing into the ice! Now, if that's not daring, I don't know what is."

Jenna spoke up. "You're right. Both you and Manda are the thrill seekers."

Livvy said no more. Obviously, she wasn't going to fight for a slot on the most-daring list. Not tonight.

Jenna knew what truly motivated Livvy. It was all about excelling in her sport and had nothing to do with thrills and chills. Liv had already gone through a frightening experience. Nearly one year ago, her mother had lost her battle with cancer. Jenna was positively sure her best friend was more cautious than the other club members because of her deep loss.

———

The official start of the Girls Only meeting began with prayer. Jenna usually prayed, but instead, she asked Livvy Hudson, the vice-president.

"Dear heavenly Father," Livvy began, "thanks for giving us the chance to come here. Help us stay focused on the things we need to learn and perfect. For your honor and glory, we pray these things. Amen."

After the prayer, Manda stared at Jenna. "What's wrong—why didn't *you* pray?" she asked, sitting cross-legged at the foot of her mattress.

"Nothing's wrong," Jenna replied quickly.

"Right," mocked Heather Bock. "You can't fool us."

Manda twisted her dark locks. "My guess? Something happened today. Something got you off on the wrong foot."

"Hopefully not one of the coaches," Heather said smugly.

All three girls were staring a hole in her. Jenna knew she'd have to level with them sooner or later. "Time for the reading of the minutes," she said, ignoring them. "Will the secretary please bring us up-to-date on last month's meeting?"

Heather's eyes widened. "I didn't bring along the minutes notebook," she confessed. "I didn't know we were having a formal club meeting."

Jenna looked at Livvy and shrugged. Manda and Heather exchanged glances and frowned.

"Maybe you could *recite* the minutes from memory," Jenna suggested.

Manda grinned. "Yeah, and we'll help fill in any holes if you forget something."

"Me, forget?" Heather joked.

"Well, there's no forgetting the Passion Play we performed last month," Livvy pointed out. "Remember that?"

Only three of the girls had been involved in the creative presentation called *Resurrection*. Manda had gone to Kansas for Easter, so she couldn't be in the play.

"Remember those quick changes we had to make, because each of us played two different parts?" said Heather.

"I thought it was supercool," Livvy said softly. "We should make it an annual event."

"Right, and next year Manda gets a lead part, okay?" Jenna said, tossing a pillow at their Hispanic friend.

"Oh, I can't wait," Manda said sarcastically. "But what I want to know right now is, what's bugging *you,* Jen?"

Scratching her head, Jenna pretended not to hear.

"C'mon, don't do that," Heather protested.

"Do what?" Jenna said, frowning.

"You know" was all Heather said.

Unexpectedly, Cassie and Lara flounced into the room. They were sharing the space in two more bunks. "Are we interrupting anything?" Lara asked.

"Not really," Jenna was quick to say.

"Oh, it's your club thing, right?" Lara said, standing taller than ever.

"Actually, I think we're finished," said Jenna. "Aren't we, girls?"

Manda was shaking her head. "Not till you answer my question, *President* Jenna. What's bugging you?"

Jenna felt the heat rise into her cheeks. "I say the meeting's adjourned."

"Okay, have it your way." Manda got up and draped her arm around Heather. She whispered something, and both girls glanced Jenna's way.

"Hey . . . no secrets," Livvy said, obviously sticking up for Jenna.

But Jenna didn't care if Manda and Heather talked behind her back. Besides, she had every right to keep her opinions to herself. No way was she going to say why she was ticked off. Mainly because she was so upset with herself.

Better Than Best
Chapter Eight

Jenna tossed and turned, trying to get comfortable in bed. The narrow bunk, probably a twin-size, seemed smaller than that. At least it wasn't lumpy like the mattresses at other sports camps she'd attended. Something to be thankful for!

When she finally *did* fall asleep, she dreamed she was riding bikes with Lara Swenson. The wind was in their hair as they flew over the bluffs on the outskirts of Alpine Lake.

Midway down the hill, she realized her feet didn't reach the pedals. Surprised, she saw that the bike was a minibike with training wheels!

This is crazy. I know I'm bigger than this! She panicked.

She awakened with a start and sat straight up in the bunk. The dorm was dark and still. The other girls were sound asleep. Lara Swenson was snoring. Livvy, in the next bunk, was half in, half out of bed, with one leg flung over the side.

Slowly, Jenna leaned back onto the mattress, wondering about the weird dream. Was she so worried about her size that her subconscious had kicked in with the ridiculous dream?

She decided she would try to brush it off. She would wake up in the morning and probably forget the bike dream ever happened.

———

Forgetting the dream is exactly what Jenna *tried* to do, except that during breakfast, she could think of nothing else. The dream about riding a beginner's bike plagued her thoughts.

Is that really how I feel about my body? she wondered. Am I too small for who I want to be?

"Hey, wake up, daydreamer."

Jen looked up to see Livvy sitting across the table from her. She had a fruit plate of fresh strawberries, bananas, apple slices, and a bran muffin. "You look wiped out, and the day's just starting," said Livvy. "You okay?"

"Sure," Jenna replied. "Did *you* sleep all right?"

"Sure," Liv said flatly.

The girls' gazes met and held.

"So . . . how's it feel?" Livvy said.

"What're you talking about?"

"Saying 'sure' when you don't mean it."

There was no getting around Livvy Hudson. She knew and understood Jenna through and through.

Sighing, Jenna took a long drink of her orange juice. Then she said, "I did a lousy thing."

Livvy kept her focus on Jenna, never flinching. She'd pulled her hair back into a tight ponytail, snapping on a Scrunchie. The intense look in Livvy's green eyes got Jen's attention.

"I'm a pastor's daughter. I should know better," Jenna said softly.

"Doesn't make you perfect, does it?"

"But still . . ." Jenna sighed. She really didn't want to tell Livvy what was on her mind. But knowing Livvy the way she did, she hardly had a choice.

"I think deep down you want to tell me, Jenna. C'mon, you know you can trust me."

Sure she could. Jenna knew that. But . . .

"Is this about your hang-up . . . you know, over your size?"

"Maybe."

Livvy leaned closer, nearly in her face. "Or is this about Nels, the new spotter for your team?"

Jenna thought about the peculiar dream. She remembered the way she'd deceived Nels on purpose.

She thought about tiny Lara Swenson passing up Cassie Peterson in height, all in a few short weeks.

"I'm a rotten person, that's all," she said at last.

Livvy was shaking her head. "You're *what?*"

"You heard me. I'm rotten—I lied."

"Who to?"

"Nels Ansgar."

Livvy's eyes were blinking nearly out of control. "Well, since you've confessed, maybe you could explain."

"There's nothing more to say. I just did a dumb thing."

"So . . . apologize to him, why don't you?"

She was silent. What would Nels think if she said she was sorry? He might want to know the truth.

"Jenna?" Livvy reached to touch her hand. "What's wrong?"

"I wish I knew," she blurted out, tears welling up.

"Maybe you should talk to someone," Livvy said, glancing around.

Feeling worse than ever, Jenna nodded her head. "Sure, I know who I can talk to. Besides you, Liv."

"Who?"

Jenna whispered, "My mom. She'll know what to do."

Livvy withdrew her hand. She looked hurt.

"Don't misunderstand, Liv. I just need to ask Mom something."

"Okay," Livvy said, "but if you get things figured out, will you let me know?"

Jenna smiled. What a great friend she had in Livvy. "I'll think about it," she teased.

"You *better!*" Livvy gathered up the trash from both trays and waved to her. "We've got ballet class in ten minutes."

"I'll catch up with you." She drank the rest of her juice and picked at her whole-grain toast. The bike dream loomed in her mind. Just then Lara floated past Jenna's table.

From where Jenna sat, Lara seemed to have grown another two inches or more overnight. This was too much!

She groaned and hurried out the door without speaking to Lara or anyone else. There was a public telephone in the lobby of the sports center. If she hurried, she could call home and have a quick chat before the first session of the day.

Mom won't think I'm silly, she thought. *She'll be glad I called.*

———

Dad answered on the first ring. "Your mother's busy with Jonathan," he said. "Shall I call her to the phone?"

"No, Daddy, just tell her I was checking in."

"Having a great time?" he asked.

She told him about the national team coach. "Ever hear of Sandy Williamson?"

"Male or female?" Dad asked.

"Sandy's a man, and he's one terrific coach."

"I'm sure if Coach Kim chose him for this camp, you're in excellent hands." Dad had lots of confidence in Coach Kim and Tasya. He had interviewed them extensively before enrolling Jenna.

"Okay, well, I've got to hurry off to ballet now. Tell Mom I called."

"Sure will."

"Love you both."

"We love *you*, kiddo."

Kiddo.

The word rang in her head like a bell. She couldn't seem to shake free of it.

First Lara, then the dream. Now this!

Better Than Best
Chapter Nine

Saturday afternoon, April 8

Dear Diary,

I almost didn't bring my journal to sports camp, but now I'm glad I did. To start off the day, Livvy gave me an earful about what I ought to do. She knows me as well as if she were my sister, I think.

I told Livvy the truth, that I lied to Nels. But something's keeping me from wanting to apologize. And I backed out and couldn't ask Dad to get Mom on the phone.

What's my problem?

Why am I so focused on what I'm not (tall) more than WHO I am (a first-rate gymnast)? Why can't I stop playing games with myself?

All my Girls Only friends know something's bugging

me. Cassie and Lara, too. If I could just get my head screwed on, I could work this out.

Oh, I almost forgot. Nels ate lunch at my table at noon. I'm trying not to let him distract me. It's hard because he's always hanging around.

Ballet is very cool. Natalie Johnston's here, working with a group of us. Some of the gymnasts haven't had as much ballet background as I do. I'm glad Mom and Dad got me started early. Ballet makes me a better gymnast.

I'm supposed to be resting, but I feel so jittery. Now I better hide this or my girl friends will know too much about me.

I might read this diary years from now and think that what I'm going to write next is weird. But I don't care—I really miss my cat, Sasha. She's such a prissy creature, but I relate to her very precise movements. The way she walks across the windowsill is so poised and graceful. I think she has the same perfection hang-ups I do.

Thirty minutes till floor-exercise training! I wonder if Nels will start to see through my lie. . . .

———

The pressure was on.

Coach Williamson, the national team coach, gave specific comments after watching each of the teams warm up and perform. Jenna craved excellence and wanted to learn all she could from both coaches. Tasya, who was always nearby, especially at the uneven bars or the balance beam, made helpful corrections or whispered, "Perfection is within your reach . . . *today.*"

Extra striving would go a long way toward testing to a higher level a few weeks from now. Jenna knew that well. Eventually, she hoped to win gold medals. Olympic gold. Being able to follow through and really deliver during the most intense pressure made one athlete stand out from another.

She wanted today to make a difference. She was determined to do whatever it took to get noticed by the national team coach.

All across the gym, there were younger girls—boys' teams, too—working out. Colorful images of leotards soared here and there. The atmosphere was charged with emotional electricity.

Cassie was in a strange mood, though, and Jenna wondered why she seemed overly confident. A good trait to have, true. But this was very different from Cassie's usual attitude. "I adore this leotard," she said, pulling on the tight-fitting white sleeve. "I always do super well when I'm wearing it."

"Sounds superstitious," said Jenna.

"Maybe to you, but it's not really. I just like the feel of it—the way it fits me. I have my red-and-white one that's exactly like this," she said, still stroking her arm.

"Did you bring the other one along for tomorrow?"

Cassie grinned. "You bet I did."

Jenna watched Cassie work through some of the difficult skills in her floor exercise. Then it was her turn. She was glad because waiting around sometimes made her body stiff, like it was freezing up.

Be sure to wow the coaches, Jenna told herself. Knock their socks off!

She prepared to take her stance on the diagonal point of the carpet. While she paced, Coach Kim and Tasya called out encouragement. "Point your toes! Reach! Focus on perfection! Okay! You can do it!"

"Looking good, Jen!" Cassie called from the sidelines.

Jenna wished Cassie, and Lara, too, wouldn't call out to her once she got this close to her performance. It was one thing for Coach and Tasya to pump her up, but somehow she resented the same from her teammates.

Except for her sudden feeling of resentment toward Cassie, Jenna felt totally confident. She was going to impress all of them. Again!

She was absolutely certain she could perform every single trick. After months of training, the skills would come easily. Like breathing.

Coach Kim picked up on her mood, cheering her on even more. "Be your best, Jenna! Show your stuff!

Okay!" All the while, he clapped his big hands, grinning and nodding.

Better than best, she thought. *Show off really big today. Go, girl!*

As soon as the music began—a medley of songs from *Miss Saigon*—she was really into her routine. She and Coach Kim had listened to dozens of musical renditions of Broadway show tunes. Everything from *Music Man* to *Phantom of the Opera*. But during the first hearing of the assortment of songs, Jenna knew she'd found what she was looking for.

Her routine began with a sequence of dances, choreographed flawlessly to the music. The program was only eighty seconds long. During that time, every shade and emotion in the music was translated into leg and arm movements. Even her neck and head were involved. Every muscle strained to respond, as she had drilled repeatedly hundreds and hundreds of times. Second nature by now. No problem.

The dance shifted seamlessly into a tumbling pass. Jenna loved to fly from one end of the carpet to the other, using saltos and front full twists, roundoffs and front walkovers. Spinning and turning was everything. She was glad there were four more required acrobatic passes in her program.

Unexpectedly, on the second tumbling pass, one foot stepped off the mat. She lost her height and distance on the third pass. Sloppy—the most despised word in a gymnast's vocabulary!

From then on, her scope and distance were way off. With things falling apart, it was no wonder her landing was less than perfect. She fumbled and nearly forgot to salute at the end.

Disappointed, she wanted to crawl under the carpet. Coach Kim and Tasya were right there, consoling her, encouraging her to try harder. "You'll do better next time."

Out of the corner of her eye, she saw Nels. He hadn't been her spotter this program. She hadn't needed one. Not for safety purposes, at least.

Looking away, she hid her emotions. She couldn't bear for him to see her frustration. Angry at her performance, yes, but upset about more than that.

Nels probably *believed* her lie for sure now.

She was convinced of one thing. Her lousy performance was her own fault. She'd set herself up for it.

Better Than Best
Chapter Ten

Cassie was next. She, too, was scheduled for the floor exercise. Flaxen hair pulled back in her trademark knot, Cassie stood tall like a model. Long, slender legs, tiny waist, and square shoulders. The perfect stance.

Jenna gritted her teeth, standing on the sidelines. She ought to be rooting for her teammate, but she couldn't make herself cheer or call out upbeat remarks. Instead, she stood a few feet from the padded carpet, close to the spot where she'd stepped off, ruining her floor exercise. Where a whole string of problems, one after another, had begun.

Oh, how she had wanted to impress the coaches! Desperately, she had. But she'd *not* succeeded in getting positive attention for her skills, especially from her teammates. Worst of all, she had been sloppy.

She felt miserable—angry at herself. Sure, she'd flubbed big time. But worse than that, she'd twisted things around to Nels Ansgar. And he'd *liked* her!

Cassie, erect and poised, saluted Coach Kim and Coach Williamson for practice. She began working through her program beautifully. The strains of violin music filled the gymnasium as Cassie ironed *all* the small things and nailed everything else.

I have a choice each day about how I will react to what happens to me, Jenna thought as she watched. But she was still ticked off about her routine, how she'd completely bombed.

She struggled emotionally over Cassie's solid performance. Everything was going so well for her teammate. Jenna was actually discouraged that Cassie was doing so well. Not the best thing for the team mentality. For the team captain!

They'd strived so hard on their individual work, competing against one another for weeks before camp. Now it was hard to be a close-knit team.

Think sisters, Coach would often say.

For Jenna, team sisterhood was vanishing fast. Uppermost in her mind, as she watched Cassie perform, was being the best gymnast at camp. Nothing else—and no one else—mattered.

———

Lara Swenson—the growth gland—was up next, after Cassie. Jenna noticed the overeager look in Lara's eyes. Until a few weeks ago, Lara had been the infant of the team. Smaller than all the others, she had a pleasant personality and winning smile. Lara had passed them up in height, but she was trying her best to put forth a team effort.

She's going to do well, too. Just like Cassie, Jenna thought, clenching her fists.

Angry tears blurred her eyes. She could scarcely see through the haze as Lara finished out her floor routine, ending it with a perfect "stick" landing.

Everyone was cheering and calling, "Lara . . . Lara. You did it! You're the best."

No, I'm the best! Jenna pondered the words so hard, she nearly blurted them out loud.

Better Than Best
Chapter Eleven

During a snack break, Cassie caught up with Jenna. "I've never seen you perform so—"

"Badly?" Jenna interrupted.

"Uh, well, I guess you could say that." Cassie reached for a large bottle of apple juice. "So . . . what was wrong on the floor?" she asked.

"I'm having a lousy day. Isn't that what Coach always tells us?" She wanted to run away and nibble on her healthy snacks somewhere alone. But she stayed, letting Cassie pummel her with questions.

"Was your timing off? Did you anticipate what went wrong?"

"Look, do we really have to talk about this?"

Cassie pushed her bangs back and let them fall

forward again. "You're mad at me, aren't you?" There was fury in her voice. "I didn't *do* anything, Jen."

"Whatever." Jenna got up and went to the water fountain. When she returned to the table, Lara and two other girls from the All-Around Team had sat down.

"What *happened* during your floor exercise?" Lara asked immediately.

"Everyone has an 'off' afternoon once in a while, right?" she shot back.

Lara and Cassie exchanged puzzled looks. The other girls did the same to each other. "That's not like you," Lara said softly. "You're always so . . . well, confident. You never excuse yourself for a bad performance."

"Nothing's changed," she muttered back.

"That's not what Nels thinks," Cassie retorted.

"Keep him out of this." She felt the anger clench her throat muscles.

Cassie's eyes were wide with astonishment. "He can't stop talking about the floor exercise you performed back at AAG. He said you were the best young woman gymnast he'd seen."

Young woman?

"That was then," she replied.

"Was your concentration off?" Cassie pushed.

"Look, I need some space, okay?" Jenna said.

Lara and Cassie exchanged scornful looks. Lara

spoke up. "Something's very weird here. If you ask me, I think there's too much competition going on."

"It's called jealousy," Cassie added.

"Nobody asked you," Jenna shot back.

"Jealousy makes people do wild and crazy things," Cassie jeered. Loudly, she bit into her celery stick. "I'm with Lara on this. You're envious of your own team members, Jenna. That makes no sense."

Jenna felt she was losing it. She wouldn't sit here for another second. "Who asked either of you?"

Getting up, she marched straight for the exit without looking back. *They can't talk that way to their team captain!* she decided.

But Lara was calling after her. "What's happening, Jenna? Where are you going?"

Where *was* she going athletically . . . emotionally?

She didn't want to think about it. She didn't care anymore. Being the best was her only focus. It was more important than certain team members' petty feelings. More important than a guy spotter getting wrong information about her.

She *had* to be the best. At sports camp weekends. At Junior Nationals—when and if she made it. At anything connected with her gymnastics dreams and goals.

Rushing back to the dorm, she threw herself across her bunk, sobbing. What *had* made her mess up today?

No answers came.

She could only cry, not caring if she missed her next session. Ballet with Natalie Johnston could wait.

Livvy burst into the room. "What's wrong?" she asked. "Are you sick . . . hurt, what?"

"I'm freaking out."

Livvy waited for her to blow her nose and wash up. "I think it's time we had a long talk."

Jenna muttered, "Me too."

"But there's no time," Livvy said, glancing at the wall clock. "Rythmic ballet starts in three minutes." She smiled, brushing her hair into a ponytail. "And maybe that's a *good* thing."

Jenna sighed. "What do you mean?"

"Read my lips . . . *ballet.*"

Jenna stared at the mirror. She saw a petite, bleary-eyed gymnast. "I think I know what you're trying to say."

"Fierce competition can do you in. You need a change of scenery."

"You said it," Jenna agreed. "So let's have some fun!"

Livvy laughed, and Jenna followed her out of the dorm. The sun was twinkling over the tops of the tallest Ponderosa pine trees she'd ever seen. She tried not to think about their size.

"I don't mean to bring up a sore point," Livvy said as they walked together.

"Then don't."

Livvy scrunched up her face. "Well, I think I'd better."

"What?"

"I heard Nels is coming to ballet class."

Jenna could hardly think about him without getting upset. "What for? We don't need spotters at ballet."

"He's not going as a spotter."

Jenna was confused. "Then *what?*"

Livvy draped her arm over Jenna's shoulder. "He's coming as a student."

Jenna shook her head. "Oh," she groaned, "this is just great."

What's his problem? she wondered.

Better Than Best
Chapter Twelve

Jenna, Livvy, Heather, and Manda hung out together during most of ballet. "We could have a quick Girls Only meeting," Manda said, laughing. She wore a hot pink leotard with white stars across the bodice.

"I doubt Natalie would appreciate that," Heather said, warming up at the barre.

Natalie Johnston, their ballet and dance instructor, also coached beginner through intermediate ice skating. Her home-based studio was on Main Street in Alpine Lake, two houses down from the remodeled Victorian where Livvy, her dad, and her grandmother lived. Natalie was young and petite, with a single honey-blond French braid down the back of her head.

Jenna couldn't keep her eyes off Manda's seriously pink leotard. It reminded her of one she'd worn when she was five years old. Eons ago, it seemed. Her mother had allowed her to choose a leotard for a gymnastics event. She'd picked out the hot pink one.

Thinking back, she remembered that Mom had been the one to instill a competitive spirit in her. *"Never give up till you're the best,"* Mom had always said. She expected her daughter to give her all to the sport. Everyone who observed young Jenna in action instantly recognized her remarkable talent. So why had she messed up today, of all days?

The ballet students lined up, each putting one leg on the barre next to the wall of mirrors.

Pointing her toes, Jenna stretched, leaning her head and upper body forward. She firmly touched her forehead to her kneecap. In the mirror she caught her reflection. Not smiling as she usually would be during stretching exercises.

"Grin and bear it," Natalie liked to say.

Forcing a half smile, Jenna continued the exercise. On either side of her, Livvy and Heather gracefully extended their flexible bodies forward. Jenna caught occasional glimpses of her closest friends in the mirror. For the time being, she remained silent, concentrating, focusing. Stretching . . .

Livvy seemed deep in thought. Heather, the more bubbly of the two girls, hummed a tune from *West Side Story.*

In the far corner of the wide room, the pianist began to play classical music by Haydn. Natalie distributed "the ribbon" to each student.

Jenna was glad about *one* thing. She loved to create the spiral look, a beautiful, twirly motion in midair. The ribbon was approximately fifteen feet in length, made of satin fabric and attached to a lightweight stick. She held the stick, swiveling the ribbon in rapid figure eights. Other motions were snakes and spirals.

Natalie reminded them that the ribbon must be "in motion at all times."

Or points can be lost at competition, Jenna remembered.

Standing at the core of their large circle, Natalie demonstrated the rotating motion for all fifteen ballet dancers. Some of them were new to this form of rhythmic ballet, with elements from both ballet and artistic gymnastics.

Jenna watched Natalie leap across the floor, twirling the long ribbon beside her.

Swoosh! With a flick of her wrist the long ribbon glimmered like a graceful wand as their instructor walked them through the simple routine.

"This exercise is not a time to show off individual skills. It is excellent practice for working together . . . as a unit," Natalie said. "Teamwork is important for both ballet and gymnastic performances."

Excellent practice . . .

Jenna was reluctant to accept the idea of teamwork at the moment. Yet it would be essential to the ballet activity they would be doing. If they were to do it well.

She took her stance, holding the stick of the ribbon securely in her right hand. Her left hand balanced her gracefully.

Jenna regarded her Girls Only friends. Livvy, Heather, and Manda seemed to be enjoying themselves. She also observed her All-Around teammates, who stood together in a row around the circumference of the circle. Cassie's jaw was tense and determined, while Lara appeared to be more relaxed.

Raising her stick, Jenna waited for the music to begin.

Natalie called out, "One . . . two . . . three . . . and four!"

And they began.

Jenna attempted to match, stay in sync with, the person to both her right and left. She kept her eyes on her own ribbon, but followed Natalie's instructions and worked at paying attention to the other ballet dancers and their movements.

But in the back of her mind, she couldn't wait to call home. When could she catch a quick phone conversation—this time with her mom? She decided she'd try again right before supper.

Near the end of the ribbon exercise, she saw Nels. He and several other boys were across the circle from her, at about the nine-o'clock position. When he caught her eye, she was startled. Was that a smile?

On second thought, she didn't want to look at him again. Not now. She didn't want to gawk, secretly or not, and end up colliding with the dancers on either side of her.

She was positive he was *not* smiling at his own success with the rhythmic gymnastic exercise. He had been grinning at her. Why?

Her thoughts flew back to their first encounter. He had been polite. Nice, really. Complimentary, too. And he'd held her whistle between his lips.

What was she thinking? She groaned audibly. Her life was gymnastics. So why was she sneaking looks at Nels?

She continued with the routine until the music slowed to a gentle *ritardando.* The grand finale came as each dancer slowly lifted the ribbon high into the air, making a fast spiral.

"That was lovely for a first practice," Natalie said. "Now, let's try it again. This time, think *stage performance.*"

Jenna smiled to herself. Natalie liked to refer to show time. Of course, they wouldn't have the benefit of an audience, but Natalie had a way of getting them psyched to acquire the *feel* of a live presentation.

That's when she noticed Nels again. He *was* smiling at her. What did it mean? Did he truly like her as Lara had said?

They waited again for the musical cue from the pianist. Working through the routine, they paid closer attention to unity and the harmony of their movements than before.

When the activity was finished, Natalie seemed very pleased. "We'll do this again tomorrow. Same time, same place."

"A Sunday filled up with ballet and gymnastics will be real different," she told Livvy on the way back to the dorm.

"For me, too," said Liv. "I'm always at church on Sundays. So are you."

"I wonder how things are going at home," she let slip.

Livvy stopped walking and frowned. "Are you worried about your family?"

"No, nothing like that." Jenna wouldn't admit to being a bit homesick, even though that was nothing new for her. She often felt the sinking, half-sad feeling in the pit of her stomach when leaving home for sports events.

"Did you ever get through to your mom?" Livvy said out of the blue.

"Well, no . . ."

"Maybe you should try again."

"I might." Jenna was glad for the prodding, because she'd planned to anyway. She just didn't know how Livvy or the other girls might react if they knew she'd called home. Twice. On top of everything else, she didn't want to be pegged "Mama's girl."

Even though, deep down, she probably still was.

Better Than Best
Chapter Thirteen

Jenna dialed the operator and got through to her mom right away. "Hi," she said, glad to hear the cheerful voice.

"Honey, how is the camp?"

"Oh, you know, we're busy all the time."

"That's what your father pays for."

They exchanged small talk—what the weather was like in Alpine Lake. Unimportant stuff.

"Are you missing out on an activity by calling?"

"No, I'm ready for supper."

"Are you eating well?"

She pondered that. "Well, there's plenty of healthy food here, if that's what you mean. You'd be proud of me, Mom. I'm mostly doing the vegetarian thing. No pop or candy."

They talked about her baby brother and what he was doing. "He's getting into everything," Mom said.

"I hope he doesn't grow up too much while I'm gone." She could hardly wait to see her baby brother again. Her parents, too.

"I miss you, Mom," she said softly.

"And we miss you, too."

She wanted to bring up the lie she'd told. Get it out in the open. But each time she tried, Mom got her off track, talking about something else.

Finally she blurted, "I want you and Dad to pray about something."

"What is it?"

"Something's bugging me. No, not really something . . . *I'm* bugging me."

Mom's voice took on the soft and familiar quality, and she switched to Korean. "Your dad and I pray for you every morning."

She felt at ease enough to tell on herself. How she'd purposely led someone astray. "I lied, but the worst part is that I *still* don't want to set the record straight."

"Ask God to help you. Remember, you belong to Him."

She felt better. Comforted by her mother's words.

"How is everything else going?" Mom was more pointed now.

"Okay." Jenna looked around. There were gymnasts

filing past her, moving toward the cafeteria. "I'd better get going."

"You're in Vail to learn and train," Mom reminded her.

"You don't have to worry. I'd rather train than eat."

"Don't compete against others," Mom said out of nowhere, like she knew the problem. "Compete against yourself."

Why hadn't Jenna remembered this? "That's probably the best advice I've heard all weekend," she admitted.

"Well, have a good time."

"I will, Mom. See you tomorrow."

They said good-bye and hung up.

Jenna was glad she'd made the phone call. Now, if only she could put into practice everything her mother had said. Starting with letting God help her.

You belong to Him. . . .

Talking to Mom had made a difference.

She knew she had to get past the competitive thing with Nels. Stop letting it consume her with, yes, jealousy. If she did that, then she could offer him a sincere apology. Tell him the truth about her gymnastics strengths. Possibly make friends with him.

She almost laughed. *Friends with Nels Ansgar?*

The idea seemed ridiculous at best. Impossible was more like it.

Better Than Best
Chapter Fourteen

"How'd it go with your phone call?" Livvy asked at supper before the others gathered at the table.

Jenna couldn't just announce how cool she thought her mom was. Especially with Livvy missing *her* mother these days. "I got some good advice," she replied.

Livvy's eyebrows rose high above her pretty green eyes. "Like what?"

"Wouldn't you like to know," Jenna teased. "Seriously, I'll tell you about it sometime."

Livvy would only press so far. She wasn't pushy that way. "Did you lay everything on the line for your mom?"

"Let's just say we talked about *important* things."

"Okay . . . okay, I know when to quit," Livvy said. Jenna was relieved.

———

When Nels and two other guys came and sat at the girls' table, Jenna kept quiet. Tall and beautiful, Cassie and Lara could do the talking. They were the ones most interested in Nels anyway.

Things were awkward. She desperately wished she could get past her resentful feelings toward Nels. And she wished she didn't feel so out of it, compared to the other girls.

Looking up and down the table, she realized once again that she was definitely the smallest and shortest girl gymnast there.

"Hey!" Natalie Johnston called, coming over to stand behind them.

"Want to sit with us?" Heather asked, sliding over, causing a pileup on one side of her.

"Sure, why not." Natalie squeezed in between Heather and Manda. "What's everybody eating?" she asked.

"Food," Manda piped up.

"But no meat for me," Livvy said, showing off her plate of pasta and cooked veggies.

"Everyone having a good time?" Natalie asked, leaning past Heather to look down the table.

"Great!" Nels said, glancing at Jenna.

Several others responded in gleeful cheers. But Lara

was the only girl who spoke up. "This is one of the best camps I've been to."

"Really?" Natalie looked surprised. "What makes this camp so special for you?"

Lara's eyes moved rapidly back and forth. "Well, I guess it just has this *feel* about it." Then she grinned at Nels and the other boys.

"What sort of feeling?" Natalie was like that. She wouldn't let you *not* finish what you started.

Lara frowned, then looked around the table. "We're like one big family, I guess."

"Is it a happy family?" Natalie asked.

Lara nodded. "Sure, why not?"

Jenna, on the other hand, was thinking the opposite. The togetherness thing, the feeling of sisterhood, for her was long gone. She was actually surprised to hear Lara express that *she* felt like a family up here in the woods.

"What's everybody else think?" Natalie persisted.

Cassie looked at Jenna. "I can't speak for anyone else, but *I'm* having a good time."

"And learning a lot," Livvy spoke up.

Manda nodded her agreement. "Fun, but hard work. It's good for us."

Natalie was looking at Jenna now. "What do you think, Jen?"

She really hated being put on the spot. "It's a cool place."

Lara frowned. "Natalie didn't ask about the place."

Spiteful feelings sprang up in her. "I *heard* what Natalie said."

The table got very quiet.

"Excuse me." Jenna stood up with her tray. She was sure everyone must be staring at her as she walked away. But she couldn't help it. The former pip-squeak who'd outgrown all the girls on the team wasn't going to corner her.

"Work hard at caring . . ."

Coach Kim's words stuck in her head. Jenna wished she could ignore them, and she tried. But she couldn't free her thoughts of the truth.

Better Than Best
Chapter Fifteen

Saturday evening, April 8

Dear Diary,

What a long day! I don't remember when I've felt so tired. Thank goodness Livvy's so understanding. I'm grateful for her friendship and the other Girls Only club members, too. I just wish everyone would stop asking me what's wrong—all the time!

Sure, I admit I did another dumb thing at supper tonight. But why do I have to get the third degree?

For instance, Lara asked why I hated her so much.

"Hate you?" I said. "Don't you think that's a little strong?"

She said she was pretty sure I disliked her. A lot. When I tried to change the subject, she tuned me out.

She's convinced I don't like her because she's taller than me. I wasn't stupid enough to say this, but even if she was the same size as before, I'd be disgusted about her catty ways.

So . . . I'm not the most popular team captain around. Guess Mom nailed it when she said to ask God for help. How long will I wait?

Tomorrow, I'm going on a hike before dawn. I'll leave and head for the bluffs before anyone else is up. I have to be alone!

"What are you writing?" Cassie asked just as Jenna closed her diary.

"Just stuff."

"Like what?"

She wasn't going to reveal that she'd brought along her diary. That she was unloading her wrath onto the pages of an innocent-looking journal book.

Cassie sat on Jenna's bunk, staring at Jenna's diary. "Is that what I think it is?"

Jenna remembered how Cassie had called out at her when Jenna took her gymnastic stance. Prior to a routine—seconds before!

Even though Cassie probably meant well with her cheer of encouragement, it *always* rattled Jenna's nerves. "You know, I've been wanting to talk to you about something," she began.

Cassie wrinkled up her face. "Oh, please spare me this."

"No, I'm serious." She pushed her diary under her pillow. "You probably don't know it, but there's something you do that really bugs me."

Cassie pulled the clip out of her long hair. The blond locks came billowing down. She ran her fingers through the thick strands. "I'm thinking I couldn't care less, but for some strange reason, I'm still listening."

Before she got cold feet, Jenna said, "Do you have to cheer for me a split second before I perform a routine?"

There, she'd said it. What would Cassie's response be?

Cassie stood up abruptly. "You know, I'm really sick of you, Jenna Song. Why do you have to pick on everyone?"

With that, she marched out of the room.

"So much for caring," Jenna muttered.

Pulling her journal out from under the pillow, she added a P.S. to the day's entry.

I did my best to level with Cassie. Big mistake. She's carrying a chip on her shoulder. Or maybe she thinks I am.

Anyway, if I could just sleep without dreaming another freaky dream, I might feel better tomorrow.

Meanwhile, there's something I'm going to do.

Premeditated mischief. Boy, will Cassie be surprised . . .
and mad!

She couldn't stop thinking about the way Cassie had
lashed out at her. Because the dorm room was free of
girls, she knew now was her chance. In one fell swoop,
she could get even with Cassie Peterson.

Darting past several bunks, she located Cassie's suitcase. There, neatly folded in the back, Jenna found the
sleek red-and-white leotard. Cassie's precious leotard.

"I always do super well when I'm wearing this," Cassie had
told her smugly.

"Let's see just how well you do tomorrow," Jenna
whispered, removing the one-piece garment.

Hurrying back to her bunk, she stuffed the leotard
in her own bag. She wouldn't keep it for long. It would
easily reappear tomorrow afternoon before they headed
back to Alpine Lake. She would hide it just long enough
to teach Cassie a lesson in respect. Let her act all huffy
when Jenna wanted to share out of a sincere heart.
Sure, let Cassie be that way.

But even as Jenna put away her diary, she felt an
unbearable heaviness. *Really* heavy.

Better Than Best
Chapter Sixteen

She had set her watch to play a soft tune instead of the beeping alarm. That way she could slip out of bed and watch the sunrise high on the bluffs. Without anyone knowing or stopping her.

Not a single dream had harassed her last night. At least, if there was, she didn't remember it. Just as well. She had enough on her mind.

Silently, she dressed as Lara snored lightly in the bunk nearby. She glanced at Cassie and wondered how she might freak out about the missing leotard, but, oh well, too late now. The deed was done, and Cassie would just have to endure a less-than-perfect day at the gym.

Sneaking out of the dorm was easy. She was glad for the non-squeaky doors. There were no rules about taking a walk alone. But before dawn? Well, she didn't know. But she wasn't worried. She'd stayed in this neck of the woods several times before. It wasn't hard to remember a place like this. And she had her trusty flashlight.

The air was fresh and clean as she stepped out into the predawn. Glad she'd brought her scuffed-up tennies, she sat on the porch and slipped them on, tying them quickly.

She'd seen the trailhead east of the main building, out behind the cafeteria. Stopping to get a drink at the lone water fountain, she shivered with excitement.

A brisk walk in the morning was a good thing. She'd learned this practice from her father, also an early riser. Not out of necessity, as was Jenna's schedule, but because Dad preferred getting up before the sun rose over the horizon.

"I do some of my best praying before sunrise," he'd told her on many occasions.

Maybe because half the earth is still asleep, God has more time to listen, Jenna used to think when she was younger.

As a preteen, she knew better. God was always available. Anytime, night or day. She just hadn't talked with Him much lately. Not at the Girls Only meeting. Not during her quiet time, either. In fact, instead of reading her devotional, she'd preferred to write in her diary.

Pushing ahead, up the path, she could see the

slightest hint of pink in the sky. If she hurried, she could make it to the pinnacle of the hill to watch the world say "hello" to the light.

A tree branch brushed against her face. It frightened her, but only a little. Though her pulse sped up, she kept moving forward. She wasn't really scared. Not in the least.

God is with me, she thought.

Replaying her conversation with Mom yesterday was a good thing to do right about now. What was it her mother had said? Oh yes.

"Remember, Jenna, you belong to God."

True. She knew that, with every ounce of her. She was a child of God. But her actions hadn't measured up. She had been jealous, angry, and spiteful. And more. She was sure she had displeased her heavenly Father.

———

Reaching the highest point of the trail, she sat on a boulder, her flashlight pointed at the ground. She looked out across the sky, to the horizon. In the distance, puffs of pinkish clouds foretold the sun's rising.

"Won't be long now," she said aloud.

Behind her, she heard rustling in the bushes.

Turning to look, she expected to see someone coming up the trail. But no one was there.

"Hello?" she called timidly at first. Then, "Who's there?"

Suddenly the small frame of a woman emerged on the crest of the path. She wasn't sure, but she thought the person might be Natalie Johnston.

"Is that you, Jenna?" called Natalie softly.

"Sure is." She moved over on the boulder, and Natalie sat down.

"Wow, what an invigorating walk up here."

"Nice, huh?"

They were quiet for a moment, then Natalie spoke again. "I saw you sneak out of the dorm. Anything wrong?"

There it was again. Someone asking her the same old question.

"I just need some time alone."

"So should I leave?" Natalie asked.

"Oh, that's all right. It's not you I'm running from."

Natalie didn't question her, and Jenna was glad. The rays of the sun began to streak upward across the deep blue of the sky. They sat in silent awe.

"God sure knows how to put on a light show," Natalie said.

Jen was surprised to hear her ballet coach talk about God that way. "My dad's probably watching the sunrise from his study right now. He's a minister and likes to read his Bible early in the morning."

"Well, it *is* Sunday morning, after all," Natalie said. "An ideal time to think—get some things squared away."

Jenna didn't respond. She wondered if Cassie and Lara had been talking to Natalie.

"Competition can be brutal. It causes hard feelings between friends, especially teammates."

Jenna sucked in some air and held it in. So Cassie and Lara *had* blabbed their complaints. "Then . . . you must know what's going on with certain people?" she asked hesitantly.

"I see what I see."

Natalie had admitted, in so many words, that she knew about the ongoing conflict. Jenna was actually relieved.

"What's the biggest hassle between you and the other girls?" Natalie came right out and asked.

Jenna thought about her answer. It might sound strange to say she resented Cassie and Lara for growing a few inches. "It's complicated," she said in a near whisper.

"Try me, Jen."

Taking another deep breath, Jenna considered. She wanted to tell someone the truth. Someone like Natalie, who was also *very* small in stature. "I'm afraid of something." She paused, thinking. "I really don't want to be stuck being this size my whole life."

Natalie nodded. "I understand where you're coming from. Because, you see, I'm the same size now as I was at fifteen."

Jenna worried. "You mean you didn't grow after that?"

"Not a millimeter. And I was always small to begin with." She glanced at Jenna and smiled a sympathetic smile.

Such bad news, Jenna thought. "So I'm basically the size I'm going to be? Is that what you're saying?"

Natalie shook her head. "Not necessarily."

"How will I know?"

"You won't, Jen. But one way to determine your height is to look at your own parents."

Jenna sighed. "Well, that's a problem. They're very small."

Natalie chuckled. "I know your parents, Jen, and I never think of them as short people."

"You don't?" She was shocked to hear this. "Why not?"

"Some people stand out as tall in my thinking," Natalie explained. "You don't even notice their size because they're so consistently bighearted. Know what I mean?"

Her parents *were* very generous people. Exactly as

Natalie said. "Then there's a good chance I'll be about the size of my mom or dad?"

"Most likely, unless you have a very tall aunt or uncle somewhere in the family."

"All of us are fairly short."

Natalie stood up just as the sun peeked over the horizon.

Jenna joined her quickly. "I've been so jealous of Lara. Cassie too."

"Because they're taller than you?"

"Sounds lousy, I know."

Natalie went on to tell her, in great detail, how she'd had to overcome her envy toward certain tall friends. "I wanted to switch places with all of them somehow."

"That's how I feel now," she confessed. "But I don't want height to get in the way of teamwork."

"Or friendship?" Natalie said, turning to face her.

She pushed her hands into her pockets. "Friends are forever."

"Push for perfection, but don't push your friends away to get there."

"I've stepped on some toes trying to get to the top."

"You're not alone in that," Natalie said.

They shared even more openly, waiting for the full-blown sunrise. When it came, Jenna said, "Thank you for finding me up here."

Her ballet teacher and friend smiled. "I'm very glad I did."

They headed down the trail together. Jenna quickened her pace as the trailhead appeared.

"Are you late for something?" Natalie asked.

"I hope not." She was worried, wishing she hadn't taken Cassie's leotard. Jenna dashed across the lawn. Was it too late?

Better Than Best
Chapter Seventeen

The dorm was in chaos when Jenna walked in. Mattresses were upturned, suitcases were in disarray, girls were fussing.

"There's the culprit!" shouted Cassie, pointing at her.

Jenna cringed. *I'm too late,* she thought.

"You stole Cassie's leotard, didn't you?" screeched Lara.

Livvy looked on in stunned disbelief.

Before Jenna could say a word, Cassie rushed over, carrying the red-and-white leotard. She dangled it in Jenna's face. "How could you do this?"

"You . . . found it?" Jenna said, knowing.

Lara's hands were on her hips. "In your suitcase. What's with *that?*"

Cassie didn't wait for an answer. "Wait'll Coach Kim hears about this," she hissed.

Coach Kim!

This was crazy. Things were way out of control.

She could plead with Cassie not to tell Coach and Tasya. But that wouldn't help the real problem. No, the more she protested, the worse things might get.

There was only way to handle this mess. "I hid your leotard because I wanted revenge," Jenna admitted. "I wanted you to have a bad day at the gym, Cassie."

The girls gasped, staring at her.

"But I was wrong," Jenna continued. "I'm sorry."

Cassie's eyes nearly bugged out. "That's it? You're *sorry?*"

"You won't believe this, but I was on my way to return it," she said.

"That's hard to believe," Lara snipped.

Livvy stepped forward. "Stay out of it, Lara. Listen to your team captain."

Lara rolled her eyes, mumbling as she sat on a bunk. "Some rotten captain we have."

"This is between Jenna and me," Cassie said, scowling at Livvy.

Heather stood on her bunk, like she was about to conduct a meeting. "Let Jenna talk!" she shouted.

Cassie blinked and sat next to Lara. Livvy, Heather, and

Manda sat down, too. All in a row, like their togetherness was meant to be moral support for Jenna.

Looking around, Jenna felt so ashamed. "I've let all
of you down," she said, measuring her words.

"You go, girl," Heather whispered.

"Shh!" said Cassie.

Jenna sighed and sat on the bunk across from Cassie
and Lara. She looked right at them. "More than anything,
I wanted to be the best gymnast on the team. But in
the process, I forgot to be the best *person*."

The dorm was quiet. No one blinked an eye.

"It's not easy admitting this, but I'm telling you
straight—I shouldn't have taken your leotard, Cassie.
And I shouldn't have let jealousy get to me, Lara."

Lara's face broke into a smile. "You were jealous
of me?"

"You're growing and I'm not." This was tough
stuff.

The atmosphere was charged. Not the way it was at
a gymnastic meet. This was way different.

Cassie's eyes glistened. Some of the other girls were
sniffling. Livvy, Heather, and Manda linked arms.

Brushing her tears away, Cassie stood up. "I was
wrong, too, Jen," she said.

Lara's eyes widened. "You?"

Cassie looked only at Jenna. "You called it right.
You accused me of yelling at a critical time—before

you perform. I wanted to distract you, get your focus messed up." She put her head down. "I was jealous of you, too."

"Whoa, heavy stuff," Lara said, a glint in her eye.

"Telling it like it is makes you feel light inside," Jenna spoke up. "Nothing heavy about that."

Lara's mouth dropped open. Was she going to spout off something snippy?

Jenna hoped not.

"You're better than best, Jen. I'm not kidding." Lara surprised her, and by the looks on their faces, Lara had surprised everyone else.

"What's that supposed to mean?" Cassie said, turning and sitting on the bunk with Jenna.

"The whole team's been selfish. Anyone can see that," Lara insisted. "But Jenna's the only one who had the nerve to apologize. She isn't team captain for nothing."

Jenna was amazed at the turnaround.

"I say we team up and start caring about each other again," Lara continued.

"The way we used to," Cassie said, leaning her head on Jenna's shoulder.

"I'm in." Jenna raised her hand.

"Me too," said Lara.

"Me three," said Cassie.

Livvy, Heather, and Manda were grinning, sticking their thumbs up.

The girls spent the next fifteen minutes cleaning up the dorm room. Mattresses were replaced on the bunks, suitcases were put in order. Towels and sheets were tossed into the large hamper provided. Most of the girls packed their suitcases for the return trip home. Jenna helped Cassie straighten up her bunk and Lara's, too.

"I thought this day was going to be shot to pieces," Cassie said. "It's mind-boggling. I never thought we'd be working together like this."

Lara was quiet, but she nodded her head.

" 'Think sisters,' remember?" Jenna said.

"Boy, won't Coach be surprised!" Cassie said.

"He'll definitely see a difference in us today," Lara spoke up.

"You bet he will!" Jenna was pumped up with confidence. But there was something else she had to do. "Does anybody know anything about Nels?" she asked, knowing full well she was asking for it.

"Nels who?" Lara joked.

Jenna smiled. "Very funny. Is he a foreign exchange student or what?"

"Beats me," Cassie said. "He seems so European somehow."

"Why don't you ask him, if you're curious?" Lara said.

"Good idea," Jenna said.

The All-Around Team, as well as Livvy, Heather, and Manda, headed off to the cafeteria together. They ate breakfast and attended the early-bird ballet session.

But there was something Jenna had to do alone. Something very important. Something involving Nels Ansgar.

Dear Lord, help me pull this off!

Better Than Best
Chapter Eighteen

Ballet with Natalie Johnston was extra special today. Several times Jenna caught her eye. Then there was her occasional knowing smile.

Jenna was glad she'd gone to the bluffs. Especially because Natalie had shown up. She wasn't positively sure why her ballet coach had gone hiking in the first place. Jenna hadn't asked her that question. Yet she felt Natalie had come looking for her.

The sunrise experience had been a turning point. That, and the nightmare of a showdown at the dorm. Thank goodness she hadn't lost her cool and lashed out at Cassie. Her first instinct was to do just that. In the end, making peace and telling the truth was the better way.

"Better than best," Lara had said of her.

Well, she wasn't going to let that give her a big head. There was only one reason why she had been able to pull it off. And in front of all the girls. Only one. God had helped her. Just like Mom had said.

She could hardly wait to get it all down in her journal. Tonight, for sure.

———

After ballet class, Nels followed her out the door. He fell into step with her. "Mind if I walk with you?"

She smiled. Typically, she might've said, "You're walking, aren't you?" But she wanted to bridge the gap of friendship, if that was possible. She wouldn't know till she tried. "Sure, let's walk," she said, not looking at him. "I was hoping we could talk."

"So was I."

His comment puzzled her. "Really?"

"Why is that surprising?" he asked.

"I thought—"

"You thought I was angry with you," he interrupted.

She nodded. "You have every right to be." They followed the narrow roadway, taking the long way to the gymnasium. "I lied to you, Nels."

"I know," he said softly.

They stopped walking and stood under a tree.

"You do?"

His smile warmed her heart. "I'm not blind, am I?" He leaned on the tree trunk. "I saw your floor exercise at my uncle's gym. You were a perfect ten."

"Thanks." This was a switch, coming from Nels.

"You're very good, Jenna."

"Wait a minute." Her breath caught in her throat. "Did you say your uncle?"

Nels ran his hand through his hair. "Coach Kim is my uncle because his brother-in-law—my father—adopted me."

This was too much information all at once. A total surprise to her. "Wow," she said. "I had no idea."

"Nobody at the gym knows, except Coach Kim and Tasya, of course."

She hardly knew what to say. "My baby brother's adopted. Adoption is very cool."

Nels grinned at her. "Someday he'll be proud to call you his sister."

"That's nice of you to say."

"I mean it, Jenna."

They walked across the wide lawn in front of the gymnasium. The sun, having risen only a few hours before, shone brilliantly. Not a single cloud in the sky. The day was exceptionally warm for April in the mountains.

"I'm sorry I deceived you," she got up the courage

to say. At last. "I don't know why I didn't just tell you my best skills."

"Probably my fault for being such an odious bore."

She laughed. "The last thing you are is boring." Then she caught herself. "I mean—"

"What *do* you mean, Captain Song?"

She turned to face him. "Will you please stop calling me that?"

"Only if you'll agree to call me your friend."

This was exactly what she'd hoped for. Prayed for. But she'd never dreamed a conversation with Nels Ansgar would turn out like this.

"Call you friend? Sure, why not?"

He held the door for her as they entered the gym.

"Before I forget, my father wants to speak with you."

His father?

She was completely baffled. "What?"

"My father, Sandy Williamson, is the national team coach."

Gasping, she clutched her throat. "Coach Williamson is your dad?"

He nodded, grinning as they climbed the stairs. "Has been for ten years now."

She made the mental calculation. Nels must've been adopted around age three. Maybe that was the reason for his different last name. She rejected the urge to know. She would not ask nosy questions. "This is so unbelievable!"

"Well, you can believe it, Jenna, because my father is very impressed with you."

"With me?"

"I should let *him* tell you," Nels said, waving to her.

They headed in opposite directions. Nels to the men's locker room, and Jenna to the women's. She scarcely knew what to think. So many surprises in one morning. And such an early morning at that.

She kept the news to herself. It wouldn't be the coolest thing to blurt out this info to her teammates. Not after everything they'd just been through. And survived!

No, she wouldn't breathe a word. Not to Cassie or Lara. Not even to Livvy and the rest of the Girls Only club members. She had to hold this close to her heart for now.

Changing into her warm-up suit, she thought of her chat with Nels. He was the adopted son of the well-known national team coach. And both of them were related to Coach Kim and Tasya. Wow!

She hadn't thought to ask Nels if he was planning to stay in Alpine Lake after camp. Or if he had enrolled in school for the rest of the semester. Surely not, because school would be over in less than two months.

So many questions, yet she didn't want to pry. Maybe Nels would tell her on his own. Now that they were friends, maybe he would.

She had to make herself walk and not fly across the gym floor. Coach Williamson wanted to speak with her. His *son* had said so.

Better Than Best
Chapter Nineteen

Jenna took the lead in helping unify the team during warm-ups. Instead of taking a tough approach as captain, she decided to think of herself as an extension of the group.

Coach must've noticed. "Nice job today, Jenna," he said, wearing his AAG shirt. "By the way, Coach Williamson wants to chat with you after this next session."

She couldn't help but grin.

"Tasya and I will sit in on the meeting with you."

The meeting?

She could hardly wait. What was this all about?

Tasya demonstrated a point by hanging from the uneven parallel bars. "Tuck up very tightly to make the turn," she said, following through with a visual presentation.

Jenna watched carefully, memorizing every move Tasya made. She was eager to try the skill but waited her turn. While she did, she stood with Cassie and Lara. "How're we doing?" she aked softly.

"We're pulling together," Cassie said, wearing her red-and-white leotard.

"Yeah, we really are," Lara added.

"It's a good feeling, isn't it?" Jenna said, reaching around and hugging her teammates.

"Actually, I'm glad you stole my leotard," Cassie said.

"*Hid,* don't you mean?" said Jenna.

"Well . . . you know." Cassie grinned. "We cleared the air."

"Big time!" Lara said, laughing.

"We sure did," Jenna said. As strong a competitor as she was, she was beginning to feel like part of the team again. She would never stop comparing herself with the others. With Tasya, Kim, and the outstanding Olympic gymnasts—Nadia and Mary Lou Retton. Even with someone like Nels, who had such agility, as well as explosive movements. She wanted to observe and learn from *everyone.*

———

"Coach Williamson is very interested in you," Coach Kim said as she walked with him across the gym.

"I can't believe this. I'm still so young."

Coach grinned, patting her on the back. "Just wait till you hear what he has to say."

She stood in a little circle with the two coaches and Tasya, her eyes dancing. Jenna had a hard time standing still, she was so excited.

Coach Williamson had some big ideas. He wanted to help her with consistency in performance, building on her physical abilities, as well. "Jenna, I believe you have amazing potential. I can see you going very far in this sport," he told her. "You'll have to continue to work hard."

Coach Kim nodded. "Jenna never quits," he said, grinning at her. "She has nerves of steel."

"And she's the perfect size for a first-class gymnast," Tasya said.

Jenna's spirits soared. Yes, being small was very cool!

Coach Williamson continued. "On recommendation from your coach, I'd like to refer you to the University of Arizona. They're offering a terrific short-term program for gymnasts of your stature."

The way he talked, she felt tall! It was happening. Her dreams were coming true.

"I think you're much too talented not to stretch yourself, Jenna."

"And I agree," Coach Kim said as Tasya winked at her.

"Thank you very much," Jenna replied softly. But inside she was shouting for joy.

———

Sunday, April 9

This has to be one of the best days of my life, and it all started with a heart-to-heart talk on a hiking trail in Vail. And a view of the sunrise with my ballet coach.

Mom and Dad are so excited for me. Arizona, here I come! I'll be on my way the minute school's out in June.

Nels and I are going to be good friends, I think. He and I are much too focused on our sport for any romantic stuff. Besides, we're both too young for anything but friendship. He'll be doing some one-on-one training with his uncle and aunt—Coach Kim and Tasya. I'll see him at school, too, because he's finishing up seventh grade in Alpine Lake. It's a very small world!

My short-term goal is to shoot for the Junior Olympics. Livvy, Heather, and Manda are thrilled. So are Cassie, Lara, and the other All-Around Team members.

No more stepping on toes to get where I want to be. Life's too short to shut out friends. I'm glad I finally got my head on straight. Thank heaven—and that's the truth!

Girls Only!

Photo Perfect

AUTHOR'S NOTE

I wish to thank my daughter Julie for her help with the modeling-agency scene in this book. Thanks so much, honey!

Also, my great appreciation to the U.S. Figure Skating Association and the International Skating Union (*http://www.usfsa.org* and *http://www.isu.org* for additional information about ice dancing and free skating).

To
Janell Hall,
a faithful fan
(and homeschooler!)
in Fortson, Georgia.

Photo Perfect
Chapter One

It all started at Dottie Forster's Boutique, situated across from the skating rink in Alpine Lake's shopping mall. Heather Bock sat waiting for her mother, who was getting another one of her funky, too-curly perms. Eager to pass the time, Heather reached for a teen magazine and began paging through until she came to the fashion and trends section. Her gaze zeroed in on an article titled, "Pin Thin: The Stick Clique."

She peered closely at the young and glamorous models featured on the two-page spread. "Wow, that *is* skinny," she whispered.

"What's up?" asked Mom from the beautician's chair.

"Oh, it's just these pencil-thin jeans," she replied,

absorbed in the new spring styles. "I think it's time *I* get some new clothes."

"Well, save your pennies," Dottie Forster piped up from her salon cabinet, where hair-color concoctions and clean combs and brushes were stored. "That's what *my* mother always used to say."

Yeah... back during the Great Depression, thought Heather, dismissing the beautician's offhanded remark.

But the mental picture of tall and super-lean girls smiling back from the pages of the fashion magazine stayed with Heather the rest of the day. Even as she dusted and vacuumed her bedroom, and later worked at her computer, doing research for a homeschool project, thoughts of the ultra-thin models lingered in her mind.

Writing the final paragraphs of her paper, Heather stopped for a moment and stared up at her poster of world-renowned British ice dancers, Olympic stars Torvill and Dean. She daydreamed about her own athletic goals, well within reach. With every ounce of zip and vigor, she longed to be a skating sensation, right along with her older brother and ice-dancing partner, Kevin, who was just as blond and nearly as focused. No, he was as *equally* caught up in the sport as she.

Sometimes, though, she convinced herself that between the two of them, *she* was the skater most eager for Olympic gold. The sound of boisterous applause thrilled her, as well as the unmistakable echo of the loudspeaker broadcasting her name—with Kevin's, of course.

Finished with her assignment—the history of the Olympics—she stood and stretched at her desk. Then, turning toward her calendar, she flipped it to the month of July, counting the weeks and months until the next big skate contest. She circled the second Saturday and wrote in big letters: *Summer Ice Spectacular.*

Only four more months. If she and Kevin could land a first-place medal for that event, they'd have a good shot at the Junior Olympics. She hugged herself, ready to take on the world of ice dancing.

———

Joanne, Heather's six-year-old adopted sister, came in without knocking. The chubby brunette sat down hard on Heather's bed, her feet dangling. "Can you help me?"

"With what?" Heather went and sprawled out on the bed, waiting to hear what Joanne had to say. "What's spinning around in your little head tonight?"

"Nothin's spinning," came the quick reply. "And my head's not little!"

"Oh, really?"

"Yep, and besides, I've been thinking that it's time I start getting in shape."

"For what?"

Her sister's eyes were playful. "You know, in case I decide to go out for something like . . ." She stopped for a second, then continued. "Something like ice hockey or maybe even Alpine skiing, like your friend Miranda."

Heather didn't dare laugh. Even though Joanne's eyes twinkled with mischief, Heather wasn't sure just how serious her sis was. "Have you been thinking about this for a long time?"

Joanne's head bobbed up and down. "Oh yes. I want to build up my muscle tone, start doing more sit-ups every day. Like Mommy does with her workout DVD."

"That's nice."

"No, really . . . I *want* to be a healthy vessel for God."

Heather let a tiny laugh slip past her lips. This was too much. "Don't you mean a *willing* vessel?"

"Sure . . . that, too." Joanne jumped off the bed and bounced toward the door, her long hair hanging loose around her shoulders. "So . . . will you help me?"

She had no idea where this conversation was headed. "What do you want me to do?"

"Help me get rid of my flabby muscles." Joanne pointed to her upper arms.

"You've got to be kidding." Heather eyed her sister. Slightly plump around the middle, but lots of six-year-olds had little or no waistline. Nothing to worry about. "You're fine, Joanne. Kids your age are supposed to be chubby. Besides, when you grow a bit taller in a few years, you'll slim right down."

"But I don't want to wait." Abruptly, Joanne turned and left the room.

What's that about? wondered Heather, reaching for her teen devotional Bible.

Morning training sessions came very early in the Bock household. Both she and Kevin had a long day tomorrow, and Coach McDonald expected them to be prompt. After practice, they'd have to hurry home to shower, change clothes, and hit the books around the dining-room table, with Mom as their teacher. At the present time, one of their homeschool study units was personal hygiene and nutrition. Mom's idea, as usual. She was a stickler for eating healthy foods and, in general, taking good care of "God's property," as she liked to refer to her children's bodies.

Opening the pages to the devotional for the day, Heather was caught off guard. Surprised, really. The Scripture reading was 1 Timothy 4:8. "For physical training is of some value, but godliness has value for all things, holding promise for both the present life and the life to come."

She thought of Joanne's comments about wanting to get in shape. Had her sister been reading Heather's devotional book? Joanne was a good reader, advanced beyond her years, one of the benefits of being schooled at home—you didn't get stuck in a single grade level for a full year.

Hmm. She wondered about her suspicions. Not that Joanne was ever known to nose around in her big sister's bedroom. Mom was totally opposed to it. And the younger children—Joanne and Tommy, both—knew enough not to cross any of the clearly defined boundaries set up in the house. Joanne must have come up with the notion to work out entirely on her own.

Heather hurried to her dresser and picked up her brush, beginning her nightly ritual of brushing her shoulder-length hair twenty-five times on each side. As she did, she thought of the skinny-minny models she'd seen in the magazine at Dottie Forster's Boutique. Did they exercise vigorously to look that skeletal, or did they go without eating? And what would cause a girl to want to starve herself that way?

Photo Perfect
Chapter Two

Heather flew through her day, dragging out of bed before dawn, dressing for practice. She breathed a prayer before rushing out the door with Mom and Kevin. "Help us meet our skating goals for today, dear Lord," she whispered.

"You're rehearsing your lifts today," Mom reminded them on the drive to the skating rink.

"I'm ready," Kevin said, grinning and proudly showing off his arm muscles. "I'm in great shape."

Mom nodded. "You're strong because you lift weights. Keep up the good work."

Kevin groaned. Lifting arm and leg weights wasn't his favorite thing to do, but it was essential to build and strengthen the upper torso, as well as a skater's legs.

"Thank goodness I'm still shorter than Kevin," added Heather.

"If you pass me up, maybe *you* can start doing the lifts, with me over your head," Kevin said, laughing.

"No, thanks," she replied.

When it came to lifts, there was no set rule that the guy had to be the one to lift the girl. Actually, a short girl lifting a taller partner would shock the judges. And no skater wanted to risk offending or upsetting a judge.

Heather was ready for anything today. Totally pumped and eager to work.

————

Mom pulled into the mall parking lot, pausing to look at each of them before opening the door. "I'm so proud of you both," she said. "You work so hard."

"Coach McDonald insists on it. We have no choice." Kevin grinned at Heather, his blue eyes shining.

"Okay, so let's get going." Heather opened the car door and raced her brother to the mall entrance.

Coach greeted them with a grin and a wave and sported a bright red tie. He always wore a pressed white dress shirt and a bright tie when coaching. His trademark.

To warm up—to avoid tearing muscles—both Heather and Kevin did their off-ice training, working on calf, thigh, and hip muscles, as well as spine, shoulders, and neck. Flexibility was important, the foundation of all aspects of skating. Stretching and bending three or four times a day, for several minutes at a time, was crucial to good skating—something Coach McDonald had instilled in them. So was ballet class, which Heather took from dance instructor Natalie Johnston, along with three other Girls Only Club members.

Physical conditioning, the regular scheduled routine of exercise and repetitions, was their *protocol.* Heather and her brother trained this way without fail each day, except for one full rest day per week. In addition to that, one other training day was less of a workout day.

After the off-ice warm-ups, they laced up their skates and did some hard stroking on the ice, including high-speed skating. The stroking helped develop their upper-body strength. Holding arms at a level between the chest and waist, they skated separately for a full two and a half minutes, the time required for the short program.

"Judges like to watch for drooping arms," Coach McDonald reminded them, "especially toward the final seconds of a program."

Heather knew this to be true. Coach pounded away at certain things during each session. Practicing four days a week—every other weekend was spent training in Colorado Springs, at the Olympic Training Center—

helped strengthen their late jumps and lessen the chance of fatigue happening in the upper body.

"Let's work on your lifts," Coach said, skating close to them. He followed them around the rink, spotting them, especially on the armpit lifts. Though they were the easiest group of overhead lifts, Coach liked to play it safe.

Today, Heather was going to practice something for the first time. She would spring off the ice, into the armpit lift. Once Kevin's arms were completely extended and she was fully off the ice, he would lower her back to the ice, very gently, turning around while supporting her in midair.

Coach insisted on spotting her, even though she had done the less-advanced move with her hands resting on Kevin's shoulders. "You're absolutely ready for this," Coach said, guiding them through as he skated backward, facing them. "Think through each step, every move and turn."

They skated another half length down the ice. On cue, Heather sprang up and off the ice. Up . . . up she flew, resisting the urge to touch her brother's shoulders. Yes! She could do this without assurance of a prop. No crutches needed.

Easy.

Then it happened. While she was being lifted, scary as it already was, Kevin caught an edge and fell backward. Head forward, Heather saw the ice rushing to meet her. She reached out her hands to catch her fall, and when she did, her knee hit the ice. She cried out as searing pain shot through her knee.

Instantly, Coach was there. Kevin got up and brushed himself off, seemingly not hurt, only stunned by the sudden fall.

Heather sat on the ice, holding her knee, trying to rub the pain away. She'd trusted her brother. Yet, in spite of their long history, knowing each other's rhythm—in spite of that—she felt he'd let her down. Literally.

"I can't believe you dropped me, Kevin."

"It was an accident, and you know it."

She was crying now. "You . . . *hurt* me!"

Kevin muttered, "Well, if you weren't so heavy . . ."

"What did you say?" she shot back.

"Uh . . . forget it."

But she'd heard him. "You think I'm fat?" she spouted. "Is that it?"

Coach intervened. "Nobody's fat here. Things like this happen, even to the most experienced skaters." He inspected Heather's bruised knee. "I guess we'll have to call it a day. Have your doctor take a look, and stay off the leg for a couple of days."

"We won't be trying *that* lift anytime soon," Kevin said as Coach helped Heather off the rink.

"We'll see how she's doing next Monday," Coach said.

Mom was worried, as usual, assisting Heather with her skates, getting her safely to the car. "Don't worry, honey," Mom said. "You'll be as good as new."

Yeah, right, thought Heather, still upset.

What bothered her even more were Kevin's words on the ice: *"If you weren't so heavy."* "Maybe it's my partner who's got the problem," she whispered in the backseat.

Mom held her cell phone, waiting for the doctor's office. "What's that, dear?"

"Oh, nothing," Heather replied.

But it *was* something. She felt absolutely rotten. Being accused falsely like that was . . . well, she *knew* she wasn't too heavy for her brother to lift. Not when they had the right momentum. Not when she helped him by bounding off the ice, getting herself up in the air. Besides, he had done the move hundreds of times before. She refused to accept Kevin's heartless comment. There was no truth in it. None.

Stopping by the doctor's office took less than thirty minutes. "One of the benefits of living in a small town," Mom pointed out on the drive home.

Heather nursed her knee on the living-room sofa, keeping it iced and elevated. *Two days out of training is disaster,* she thought. Especially with the July skate event coming up in the near future. Kevin, of course, could carry on without her, keeping in shape and toned. Knowing him, he would, too. When it came to skating, nothing kept her brother down. Not even minor injuries.

Meanwhile, she read and wrote her homeschool assignments while lying down, following both the doctor's and Coach's orders. At midmorning break, Joanne and Tommy came to check on her. Typically, she would have been pleased with their thoughtful attention. But today, after what happened at the rink, she felt annoyed by their kindness and concern. "I'm fine," she snapped. "Don't baby me."

"Doesn't look like you're fine," Joanne said.

"Nope." Tommy stuck out his lower lip. "Your knee's real messed up."

She shooed them out of the living room. "Doesn't Mom need you in the kitchen?"

Tommy shook his head. "She wants us here, with you."

Thrilling. What she preferred was to be alone, sulking about the dreadful morning—Kevin's fall, his dropping her. The accident had spoiled everything.

Photo Perfect
Chapter Three

The members of the Girls Only Club met that afternoon. Jenna Song, team captain and award-winning gymnast, was their club president. Livvy Hudson, skater extraordinaire, was vice president. And Miranda Garcia, known as Manda, a first-class Alpine skier, was their newest member.

All three girls showed up at Heather's house after school. In the past, they'd met at Jenna's because her enormous bedroom was set up with a barre and a wall of mirrors on one side. The girls liked to do stretches, centerwork, and pointe technique together.

When the others had heard of Heather's bruised knee, though, they quickly changed the location.

Heather's mom was all for it. "We'll have fun serving

frozen yogurt with fresh strawberries," she said, making a place for the girls at the kitchen table.

Joanne and Tommy pushed an extra chair up close to Heather, so she could prop up her leg. Then they scooted off, leaving the foursome snug in the large country kitchen. Mom closed the door behind her as she left.

"Wow," whispered Livvy, "this is really great of your mom."

"No kidding," Jenna said. "Be sure to thank her for us."

Miranda nodded. "Maybe we ought to rotate our club meeting locations."

Heather wondered what everyone thought of that. But nothing more was said, and no one moved to put it to a vote. The truth was, Jenna's remodeled attic bedroom was the ideal place for their meetings.

Livvy launched the touchy subject first. "How'd Kevin drop you?"

Momentarily, Heather relived the startling instant. "He caught an edge and went down backward. No fun."

"And you came crashing onto the ice?" Livvy asked, the one club member who could relate most.

"Let's put it this way: If I hadn't caught myself, my head might be in traction right now . . . or worse."

"Worse?" Jenna asked, her beautiful Korean eyes squinting nearly shut.

"Well, you know. . . ."

"No, *tell* us," Jenna prodded, and Miranda leaned on her elbows, scooting forward.

"Ever hear of a concussion?" she asked. "Not a good thing for a skater."

"Or *anyone,*" said Manda, pulling on her dark hair. "Believe me, I know what I'm talking about."

"You had a concussion?" asked Heather.

Manda nodded. "Yes, and it's unbearable. Your head throbs, and you're totally out of it." She sighed. "The worst thing is everyone babies you because your skull and your brain collided."

"Thank goodness Heather doesn't have *that.*" Jenna reached over and patted Heather's arm.

"Yeah," said Livvy softly.

Heather did not reveal the first thing out of Kevin's mouth after they'd fallen. She would say nothing about it—she could just hear her girl friends laugh. They were always telling her how thin she was, and she didn't want them thinking less of Kevin because of his comment about her weight.

Jenna called the meeting to order, then Heather read the minutes from last week's meeting. "Any corrections or additions?" she asked.

"Sounds fine to me," Manda said, sitting across the table.

"Me too," said Livvy.

"What new business do we have to discuss?" Jenna asked.

"I propose a craft project," Livvy said, her face growing a bit pink as soon as she spoke up.

"You mean like *making* something . . . with our *hands?*" Manda asked. She looked horrified.

"Sure." Livvy nodded. "To raise money for our club."

Jenna jumped on the idea. "We could use some extra cash, you know, for costumes and things . . . when we put on ballet presentations for our families."

"I like the idea," Heather said. "But what'll we make?"

"My mom's a little over the edge about birdhouses," Manda said. "Maybe we could get some old wood somewhere and make some, then paint them real cute."

"Yeah, that's a possibility," Livvy agreed. But Heather could tell she wasn't overly wild about the idea. No one else seemed to be, either. "What about collecting recipes . . . healthy ones, for the athletically inclined?" suggested Livvy.

"Hey, great idea," Heather said.

Manda, too, was swayed by either their enthusiasm or the fact that she truly enjoyed creating healthy foods and drinks.

"So should we vote on doing a cookbook?" Jenna asked, with a flick of her dark brown hair.

The girls agreed. The vote was unanimous.

Jenna asked Livvy to coordinate the recipes, since the project had been her idea. "How much for our club cookbook?" asked Heather.

"Is five bucks too much?" asked Manda.

"I could run them off on my dad's computer printer," Livvy volunteered, "so it shouldn't cost us too much for production."

"Five dollars seems just right to me," Jenna said.

They voted. Five bucks it was. They also discussed sectioning off the book by recipes for specific times: After Training, Before Training, and High-Energy Snacks.

"This is a cool idea," Jenna said.

"Sure is," Heather said, wishing she'd thought of it.

Livvy smiled, quiet as usual. But Heather could see that her auburn-haired friend was very pleased.

"When do we start?" asked Manda.

"Tonight," Heather said. "That'll give me something to do while I'm waiting for my bum knee to mend."

The meeting was adjourned. Heather's mom emerged

from the living room when they called to her. Serving up frozen vanilla yogurt with juicy red strawberries, Mom hummed as she worked.

"Thanks for letting us have our meeting here," Heather told her.

Mom glanced up, smiling. "Any time."

Manda whispered, "Let's tell your mom about our cookbook idea."

"Yeah, see what she says," Jenna said.

Heather filled her mother in on the fund-raising idea. "We'll take our finished product around to neighbors, family, and friends. So . . . what do you think?"

Mom was all for it. "I have a bunch of recipes to donate, if you'd like."

"Thanks!" Livvy said, bursting with delight.

The girls giggled at Livvy's enthusiasm. "Looks like *all* of us are on board with this," Jenna said.

Heather could see that it was true.

———

After the girls left, Heather helped her mom clean up the kitchen as best as she could with her hurt knee. "You have some terrific friends," Mom said as they wiped the table clean.

Heather thought how glad she was to have solid

Christian girl friends. "And we're all on track for the Olympics. Isn't that the coolest thing?"

Mom nodded. "First, we've got to get your knee back to normal."

"Don't I know it." Heather sat down again, rubbing her kneecap. "I still can't believe Kevin and I fell like that."

Mom said no more, but busied herself with preparing supper. Heather hobbled upstairs to her room. She had intended to begin gathering a few recipes for the Girls Only cookbook, but weariness overtook her. She fell onto her bed, thinking she'd rest for a few minutes.

Soon, she was dreaming, flying in the air while Kevin sped on the ice. Heather felt so free, so limber . . . so high above the rink. But then Kevin dropped her flat on the ice, awakening her.

When she opened her eyes, she saw Joanne standing over her. "Uh . . . what's going on?" she asked, sitting up.

"Supper's ready, sleepyhead," came the little-girl reply.

"So soon?"

"Mom says you've been out for almost an hour."

An hour?

"Better come to the table," Joanne said, "so the food won't get cold."

She massaged her knee, feeling slightly dizzy as she moved toward the edge of the bed. "I'll be right down."

"Don't fall on the stairs," Joanne warned.

"Don't worry." Then she remembered something. "Oh, Joanne . . . have you been, uh, in my room?"

"Nope."

"Reading my devotional book, maybe?"

"Nope."

"You're sure?"

"I don't tell lies," Joanne insisted, wide-eyed.

"I didn't say you did," she replied, even though her sister had already dashed out of the room.

At supper, Dad prayed exceptionally long, blessing the food and asking the Lord "to bring strength and healing to my daughter's knee." There was some talk about the club recipe book, and Dad promised to purchase several copies. "I'll take them to the office and sell them there when they're finished."

"Really? You'd do that for the club?" Heather said, surprised her father was so interested.

Dad chuckled. "We have two secretaries who could use some trimming down. So sure. It'll help the cause."

Mom nodded. "Might just help someone feel healthier, too."

Kevin glared at Heather just then. His intense glower made her wonder. What was he trying to say? Surely not that he thought *she* needed to go on a diet!

Photo Perfect
Chapter Four

After supper, Heather got busy at the computer, going online to check through various sites featuring recipes. She decided the High-Energy Snacks section of the Girls Only cookbook might be her biggest interest.

Maybe if Kevin had eaten something like that, I wouldn't have fallen. . . .

But she knew better. Anyone can fall on the ice. Energy or no energy. She'd have to forgive him, sooner or later.

Meanwhile, she printed off three different copyright-free on-line recipes: Bars of Iron with raisins, dark molasses, oats, and ginger; Powdered Milk Energy Bars; and Oat Bars with sesame seeds, dried apricots, and chopped almonds. Power food for sure. Livvy would be pleased.

———

By Monday, Heather's knee was much improved. Enough for her to skate freely around the rink. Coach McDonald was obviously pleased, but he didn't push for any lifts or jumps. And Kevin kept his mouth shut about further insults. *He better,* she thought.

After practice, when they'd arrived home, Heather noticed a mailer lying on the coffee table in the living room. "What's this?" she asked Kevin as he hung up his jacket.

"Looks like overnight mail." He came close and looked over her shoulder.

Mom had gone to the kitchen, so Heather called to her, asking if they could open the envelope. "Go ahead," Mom said. "It's probably the new pictures."

Heather felt her pulse quicken. Recently, Mom and Dad had hired a professional photographer from Denver. He'd met them several weeks ago, taking numerous rolls of film "to get a few good ones," the photographer had said.

"How do you think they turned out?" she asked her brother.

"Open it and see," Kevin said.

Tearing the envelope open, she discovered the proofs of her and Kevin. Dressed in ivory with dazzling Austrian sequins, they posed happily, taking bows. The shots had been taken at the finale of their two-minute original dance in Colorado Springs, at the World Arena. Every other weekend, they practiced there when they could get ice time.

One after another, Heather studied the pictures. "What do you think of them?" she asked Kevin.

"Cool," was all he said.

"But do you *like* them?"

"Yep. Don't you?"

She wasn't sure. Not exactly. In fact, the more she looked at them, scrutinizing every inch of each photo, the more she second-guessed the poses—the way the photographer had captured their "look."

"We don't look enough alike," she said softly.

Kevin squinted at the proofs. "I don't get it," he replied. "What's wrong?"

Their coach had trained them to move, breathe, and nearly think alike. On the ice, at least. When they skated in competition, or any event, for that matter, they always wore matching costumes, just like other ice-dancing partners. But these glitzy white costumes in the photos didn't offer the mirror image Heather had imagined. No, the long pants and double-breasted coat made Kevin look taller . . . *thinner.* Her outfit had been fashioned out of the same fabric, but the skirt, she decided as she inspected the picture, was too short. Showed too much of her leg.

She heard Kevin mutter something about being hungry. He headed off to the kitchen, probably to grab a quick snack before school started. Meanwhile, she took the pictures over to the bay window and sat in the overstuffed chair. Holding them up to the window, she stared at the poses. Slowly, she sifted through the pictures.

I hate these, she thought. But it wasn't the pictures she despised. It was the reflection of herself in the camera that bugged her.

"Am I getting fat?" she asked Manda that afternoon on the phone.

Manda laughed. "You can't be serious."

"Come on, Manda," she insisted. If she wasn't serious, she wouldn't be asking her friend's opinion. "I'm not joking here. I want your honest opinion."

"Are you deaf? I *gave* you my honest opinion, girl. No way are you fat."

"Not even a little?"

Manda sighed into the phone. "Well, if you are, then it's invisible . . . or in your head."

"So, I'm a fathead?"

That got a laugh.

Heather continued. "Maybe you should take a look at these new pics that just arrived at my house."

"Of you?"

"Yeah, they're of Kevin and me." She propped the phone against her chin and shoulder as she slid the photos back into the large envelope. "Except my brother looks so tall and slender."

Like I used to, she thought.

"You're stick thin, Heather, and I'm not kidding."

She wished she could believe her friend. "Guess you'll just have to see the pics," she said. "Then decide."

"Bring them to ballet in an hour. Jenna, Livvy, and I will give you our honest opinion . . . that is, if we see the least hint of flab."

They said good-bye, and Heather hung up the phone.

———

At Natalie Johnston's ballet class, Heather worked extra hard during centerwork. And later, during pointe technique, she felt downright gloomy. Jenna and Livvy must've picked up on her mood, and during the break, when they stood around with small cartons of carrot juice and apple juice, Heather bought nothing to either drink or snack.

"Are you feeling all right?" asked Jenna.

"Uh-huh," she said.

"Want me to get you something?" Livvy offered.

"I'm fine, thanks."

"So what's with you today?" Jenna asked, grabbing a handful of carrot sticks.

"Nothing, why?"

"You just seem so . . . uh, I don't know." Jenna crunched her carrots loudly.

"Out of it?" she said. "Not myself?"

Jenna eyed her without saying more.

Livvy came over and stood beside her. "Is training getting to you?"

She wondered if she should tell them what was bothering her. But no, like Manda, they'd probably just laugh. Wouldn't understand that she'd begun to feel as fat as the pictures looked. As heavy as Kevin had said she was the day of their fall.

"Maybe you're tired," suggested Jenna. "Is that it?"

"I got some photos back from Denver," she began.

"Oh yeah, those," Jenna said. "Manda said you were bringing them to show us."

She wondered if Manda had also gone to the trouble of revealing what was troubling Heather. "Where's Manda, anyway?"

They turned to see their friend talking with Natalie near the piano. "Looks like she's tied up right now," said Livvy.

Heather cringed. She hoped Manda hadn't told Jenna

and Livvy what she'd shared on the phone. For now, wanting to whittle down her figure was just *her* business.

It turned out the girls didn't stick around after ballet, as they often did. So Heather carried the envelope of photos home with her without ever showing them to her friends.

Just as well, she decided.

———

She didn't let on to her mother that she thought several of the photos made her look a little chunky. *Might just be the camera angle,* she thought. *Photos always make people look bigger.*

Mom seemed almost too excited about the portfolio photos. She talked of nothing else at supper. Even took the pictures out and held them up as she stood at the foot of the table, opposite Dad. "Have you ever seen such great photos of *any* ice dancers?" she gushed to all of them. "Let alone *our* own children?"

Dad, too, seemed impressed, asking to see the pictures more closely. Mom and Dad, their heads together, made a big to-do about the shots. "We'll definitely use this photographer again, won't we, dear?" Dad said, his face bright with satisfaction.

Mom rested her hand on Dad's shoulder and beamed.

"We couldn't be more proud of you both," she told Heather and Kevin.

Joanne and Tommy seemed interested, but only for a short time. After a while, they were more interested in knowing when and where dessert was than poring over photos of their older siblings.

"I'm gonna be as strong as Kevin when I grow up," Tommy said, squirming.

Joanne nodded her head, eyes twinkling. "And *I'm* going to look as slim as Kevin when I finish working out."

Nobody seemed to notice the remarks from the younger children. But Heather did, and she felt horrible. Crushed. Wasn't it obvious who Joanne and Tommy thought looked better? After all, Tommy had said Kevin was strong. And just now, Joanne minced no words about wanting to trim down, lose her baby fat—"look as slim as Kevin."

So . . . it was true what Kevin had said on the ice last Friday. She *was* too heavy.

Well, not for long. Starting this minute, she was going to make some changes. Some *big* changes!

Photo Perfect
Chapter Five

"Skinny is beautiful . . . skinny is beautiful," Heather chanted over and over.

She had been studying, doing her math homework in her room, when she got up to stretch. Going over to the window, she pulled back the curtains trimmed in pink rickrack and looked out.

It was mid-March, and the ground was beginning to peek through melting snow. No one could tell how much more snowfall they'd get this season. Snow was known to come in blizzard size this time of year in Alpine Lake, nestled high in the Rocky Mountains. But the fact that there were more than just a few brave blades of grass showing through the layer of white meant spring wasn't too far off.

With spring coming fast, the summer skate competition

was on their heels. That's how Heather had been pro-grammed to think. Skaters—any athletes involved in competitive sports—knew there was no time like the present to get it together. Never any time to waste.

Turning away from the window, she moved toward the tall, oval mirror and stared. She scanned every inch of herself. Then, glancing up at the poster of world-famous ice dancers Jayne Torvill and Christopher Dean, she looked at their overall body types.

They're stick thin. Just like the models in the magazine at Dottie Forster's Boutique, she thought.

Going back to her desk, she wondered how long before she might begin to notice a difference in her own weight. Then a brain wave hit. She hurried out of the room, heading to the bathroom. There she weighed herself—one hundred and five pounds. She hadn't lost a speck of fat since refusing dessert last evening! She'd also made a point of not eating or drinking during their break at ballet.

Mom had frowned, but only slightly, when Heather asked for cold cereal this morning instead of eggs. She'd only picked at her toast, not buttering it at all. And turned up her nose at warm cocoa.

Must take several days, she thought, determining to cut back on her food intake.

She'd do it, little by little, so no one would notice or protest. Maybe then Kevin would say nicer things about her, his long-time skating partner. And maybe Joanne would say she wanted to be as slim and pretty as her big *sister* when she grew up.

She knew Mom would be her biggest hurdle. Her mother was hooked into healthy foods, wanted her kids to feel good—"the picture of health," Mom often said.

Well, Heather had gone Mom's route for nearly twelve years. It was time to do things *her* way.

———

When she finished her math assignment, she stayed at her desk. For a while, she doodled on a blank sheet of paper, daydreaming as she did. Then she began to write her name in cursive, over and over: *Heather Elayne Bock* . . .

Thinking back to the photos—the ones she hadn't shown to her Girls Only Club members—Heather imagined what it would be like to ice-dance with someone other than Kevin. Brother-sister pairs were supposed to be ideal. At least, until a skater reached the late teens. But even then, Coach McDonald had always said a brother-sister team was the way to go. The best hope for Junior Olympics.

Her biggest hang-up was having to look so much like Kevin. She was her own person, wasn't she? Yet they dressed nearly exactly alike on the ice, moving in perfect symmetry, smiling on cue, flowing to the music, performing difficult stunts.

Like puppets on a string, she thought. *Look-alike puppets.*

It had been Mom's idea to get them started in ice dancing. They worked so well together, maybe because they were less than two years apart in age. And they both shared a love for skating, as well as being part of a close-knit homeschooling family.

Their hair color was identical. They even had the same shade of blue eyes. Twins in every way except age. That is, if you could call yourself a twin with your *older* brother. Kevin was thirteen, going on fourteen, and as skinny as a handrail. She, on the other hand, was a girl, not even a teen. A "heavy" girl, at that.

Lifting up her sweater cautiously, Heather looked at herself in the mirror, trying to see her ribs. Someday soon, she'd be able to count them. That was her goal— to get down to nothing. Just like the magazine models. She'd show her skating partner. Little sister, too.

As for Mom, Heather felt pent-up anger toward her. She didn't quite know why. Unless it had something to do with being pushed too hard and fast into a mold. The brother-sister thing? Maybe that was the trigger.

Whatever it was, Heather was unhappy. Dissatisfied with how she looked.

———

"What're you doing?" Joanne asked, standing at the door, looking in.

Startled, Heather pushed down her sweater quickly. "Don't you ever knock?"

Joanne smirked and opened the door wider, coming into the room. "I saw you peeking under your sweater," she said in an accusing tone. "That's really weird, you know."

"Mind your own business."

"What were you looking at?" came the next awkward question.

"Listen, Joanne, I'm really tired, and it's late. Don't you have to brush your teeth or something?"

"Only when you tell me what you were doing in the mirror." Her sister marched over to the dresser and leaned on the front, her hands on her hips.

"Who said you could even come in here?"

"*You* didn't stop me." Joanne's eyes were serious.

"Well, I'm asking you to leave. Now."

Her sister's eyes were blinking fast. "Don't be so mean, Heather. That's not what Jesus wants you to be."

"I'm *not* being anything to you. Now, get out of my room!" With that, she scooted Joanne along toward the door.

"I'm telling Mommy."

"Please do."

Joanne turned and stuck out her tongue. "Don't make me!"

"Well, if *you* don't tell Mom, then I will."

That silenced Joanne. She pulled another face and ran off down the hall to her own room.

Relieved, Heather turned her attention back to the mirror. This time, she kept her sweater down. Instead, she leaned over and rolled up her jeans. She looked long and hard at her ankles. "Could use some slimming," she whispered.

Though she was preoccupied with her figure, Heather thought through the steps and moves to the American Waltz as she showered. Letting the water beat on her back, she performed the dance in her head. She and Kevin planned to skate for the Novice level silver dance test next November. Their first shot at Novice. They would present the dance in July at the summer event, too. It was a good chance to practice and compete with a "live" audience.

The meter was in three-four time: *one,* two, three— with the accent on the first beat, a typical waltz beat. The tempo was sixty-six measures of three beats. One-hundred-ninety-eight beats per minute. Smooth and flowing, the waltz had stylish direction changes, graceful and uniform in pace. Knees bent, corresponding with the heavy beat in each measure, they would skate in perfect unison.

Ice dancing was much different from pairs skating. In pairs, there were side-by-side jumps, spins, and other moves. But ice dancing was all about footwork— mostly fancy steps performed in precise time with dance rhythms such as the polka, tango, waltz, and fox-trot. The steps of each dance were drawn on a diagram of the ice rink. The International Skating Union and U.S. Figure Skating Association preserved music libraries with suitable music for each of the compulsory dances. Techniques such as conformity to the style and mood of the music, placement of steps, movements of both partners, good form and style, edge technique, dancing to the beat, and character of the music were essential elements for a top mark by a judge.

As much as Heather wanted to test to the next level, which would set them up for the Junior level international competition, possibly as soon as next year, she struggled with the *twin image* thing. How far did they have to take it? Would she ever be her own person?

On the other hand, she knew better than to question her future. Ice dancing with Kevin was the surest way to Olympic fame and success. She'd gone through tough times, struggling with the notion of becoming a free skater, going it alone. In the end, though, she knew where she belonged—as Kevin's skating partner. They were fantastic skaters together. Coach McDonald told them so, and often. They were headed for gold.

Someday.

Photo Perfect
Chapter Six

At breakfast, Heather sat down to a full plate of food. Mom had been up very early, making her delicious whole-grain bread and homemade granola cereal. There was fresh fruit, too—cantaloupe, bananas, and straw-berries.

Heather looked down at the plate, just staring at it. Mom had gone out of her way to prepare a good "skater's breakfast," as she liked to call it. Small dishes of yogurt were set off to the left of both hers and Kevin's plates.

I'm not hungry, Heather told herself.

Knowing full well that Mom would expect her to eat heartily, she slowly ate two spoonfuls of granola softened with skim milk. She figured if she took her time, ate at a snail's pace, she could prolong the meal until it was too late to finish.

"You're not eating, Heather." Mom had noticed.

She shrugged. "Don't feel like it."

Mom glanced at the wall clock. "Well, you can't sit there and just look at your food. Not when you're expected to train at the rink this morning. You'll need the nourishment."

"I'm not hungry."

Kevin looked up. "Since when?"

"Since now." With that, she got up from the table and trounced out of the kitchen. She could hear the not-so-discreet comments whispered in her absence. This was just the beginning, and Mom did *not* understand.

———

She was actually a little surprised that she got through the day till lunch without feeling too weak or light-headed. No symptoms she might've experienced by now, due to her new eat-less approach to life, seemed to be evident. Best of all, she'd felt lighter while on the ice, after scarcely any breakfast. A great feeling.

After their homeschool sessions, she decided to head over to Natalie's ballet studio, a short walk away. Every other Wednesday, Natalie offered "free workout" sessions for super-dedicated students. Heather wanted to work on limbering up her knee a little while.

In the locker room, she dressed in her warm-up tights, then sneaked a peek at herself in the full-length mirror.

Still too fat, she thought, noticing the slightest pad of flesh around her knees.

Livvy Hudson soon caught up with her at the practice barre. "You look tired," she said. "Feeling okay?"

Heather nodded. Now wasn't the time to get into the "going skeletal" thing with Livvy. Her friend would never understand. Besides, Livvy was an only child. How could she begin to relate to a younger sister's flippant remark? Or an older brother's crude comment? All good motivations to drop some pounds.

Livvy was pushing harder, doing longer stretches than Heather had the energy for. "Are you sure you're all right?" Livvy asked.

"Why shouldn't I be?" This was annoying, coming from Alpine Lake's award-winning free skater.

Livvy eyed her curiously. "I don't know. It's just that—"

"What?"

"You look pale, that's all."

Heather smirked and increased her efforts, still cautious of her knee. She refused to accept the fact that she *did* feel a bit weak. After more stretches and moves, she drank lots of water. *Water never made anyone fat,* Heather thought. The water seemed to take the edge off her hunger pangs.

During break, she purposely denied herself her usual snack intake, pitching half the turkey and Swiss cheese sandwich her mother had packed—*"just in case you're hungry,"* Mom had said.

Jenna caught her trashing part of the food. "Whoa, girl, isn't that the whole-grain, super-good stuff your mom bakes?"

"Yeah, so?"

Jenna's eyes were intent on her, squinting nearly shut as they walked to the small room just off the studio area. Natalie's students hung out there before continuing workout sessions.

Manda was waiting, obviously glad to see them. Jen chatted with Manda for a moment, then fell into a plump chair, turning to Heather. "Hey, that's great stuff." She meant the sandwich. "Next time you don't want your mom's good snacks, just hand them over. Okay?"

Manda got a kick out of Jen's comment. "Sounds like she's very serious," Manda said, munching on a celery stick.

Jenna smiled. "I wish *my* mother had time to bake bread."

Livvy joined them about the time Heather was finished. "Are you leaving so soon?"

"Yep," Heather said. "Gotta run."

"Where to?" asked Jenna.

"Yeah, what's the rush?" asked Manda.

The room was filling up with other ballet students. "I need some fresh air," she said, waving at the girls. She purposely kept moving, otherwise one of them might call her back. Might try to get to the bottom of what was going on in her head. She had to avoid more conversation at all costs.

———

Heather headed straight to the mall ice rink, taking time to warm up again before ever going out on the ice. Her knee still required special attention after the fall last Friday. So she spent extra time—more than usual—stretching her quad muscles. They were the muscles that began just below the outside of her hips, ending just below her knee.

She stood erect and tilted her hips backward just a bit. Then, lifting her right knee so her right thigh was parallel to the floor, she grabbed her ankle with her right hand. She went through the exercise process, repeating the *quadriceps* stretch several times on both sides. Careful not to bounce or stretch at all in short surges—because bouncing can tear muscles—she used constant pressure during the fifteen-second segments. Then she rested, only to repeat the stretch.

On the ice now, she stroked forward on the inside edge of her right skate, several times around the rink. Other skaters were practicing, too. Some of them were Natalie Johnston's beginning skaters. Natalie was not only the best ballet teacher around, she also taught a few skating classes in Alpine Lake.

Since bruising her knee, Heather knew she needed time on the ice, limbering up again. She wanted to get back her confidence. Kevin's words—*"If you weren't so heavy"*—still rang loudly in her ears.

"Hey, looking good!" one of Natalie's students called to her.

She waved to the boy across the ice. It was Micky Waller, Natalie's best male free skater. How long had it been since a cute boy had said something like that to her? On the ice, no less?

So . . . her idea to cool it with eating was paying off. In fact, Micky was actually still smiling at her from across the rink. Really grinning now as he turned and skated toward her.

Nice run of blade, she thought as he powerfully stroked, looking like a top-level skater—well balanced and flowing well over the ice. She wondered how long Micky had been training with Natalie.

"Haven't seen you for a while," he said, falling into rhythm with her.

"I'm here nearly every day," she said. "How about you?"

"Me too."

She wondered what Kevin would think when he showed up. Mom and Dad weren't exactly thrilled about her hanging out with boys. Her parents were pretty strict about the boy-girl thing. She figured she wouldn't be dating till she was twenty-five or older. At least, that's how Dad joked about it.

Micky was close to Kevin's age, she was pretty sure. And she wasn't so much interested in him as a friend as she was curious. He'd singled her out from all the other girls on the ice just now.

Skinny is beautiful, she thought, determined to lose even more of her excess weight in the coming days and weeks.

Obviously, Micky had noticed. How long before Kevin and Joanne did, too?

At the rate she was going, she could drop to a size zero in the blink of an eye. And she would. Nothing could stop her now.

Photo Perfect
Chapter Seven

She should've known.

Heather got into it with Mom the second she pushed back from the table after only a few bites of sirloin steak, rich gravy, and baked potatoes.

"Honey, what's wrong?" Mom's frown lines grew deeper by the second.

"I'm full." She hoped her excuse would fly. If not, she had no idea what she'd say or do next.

Dad looked puzzled from his end of the table. Now *he* was getting in on the question thing. "Heather, are you ill?"

"Just full, Daddy."

"It's not like you," Mom insisted.

Joanne stared across the table, her little eyes peering at Heather. She was only slightly taller than the table.

Usually, they had her sit on the telephone book or other stacked books. Tonight, though, Joanne looked like a midget. "If Heather worked out enough, she'd be hungrier," came her little voice.

Tommy began nodding his head, joining in the campaign.

"What do *you* know about working out?" Heather shot back.

"Mommy!" whined Joanne.

"That's quite enough, young lady," Mom directed her rebuke to Heather.

"What did *I* say?" Heather was fed up. She wanted to leave the table, but she tried not to lose it in front of Dad. Her father liked a peaceful atmosphere at mealtime.

Mom's expression turned from a frown to a pretend scowl. She stood there, scrutinizing Heather. "Who *are* you, really, and what did you do with my daughter?" Mom quipped.

Tommy looked completely confused, then started to laugh.

"Yeah, what did you do with my big sister, Heather, who used to like to eat?" Joanne asked, giggling a little till Dad intervened.

"Let's get back to the business of supper," Dad said firmly, yet softly. "Your mother made a terrific meal." He looked over at Mom, winking at her. "Thanks, dear."

Mom merely nodded, still looking a bit frazzled.

"Save room for some delicious no-fat frozen yogurt for dessert," was all she said.

Yogurt, either low-fat or no-fat, did not sound very appealing to Heather. She wished she could excuse herself and get a head start on Mom's hefty history assignment before the prayer service tonight at church. But she thought better of it, staying put. The last thing she wanted to do, judging from her parents' serious expressions, was cause another ruckus.

———

Heather was more than miserable during the Bible study and prayer meeting. Kevin took Joanne and Tommy off to the children's classes. Her older brother had been assisting the junior boys' group recently.

Their youth pastor was out of town, so the teens and preteens were stuck in the main service with the adults. Several other kids were sitting with their parents, slumped down in the pew like it was some horribly hideous thing.

She was smarter than that. Besides, Dad had shown his disapproval after supper. He'd made it obvious to her by hanging around the kitchen while she and Mom and Joanne cleaned things up. It was like he didn't trust her or something. Maybe he thought she was going to continue the scuffle with Mom in the privacy of the kitchen.

Well, she had no intention of keeping the conflict going. Mom was behaving like a good mother, encouraging Heather to eat and enjoy her great cooking. How could that be Mom's fault?

So here they were, all lined up in the church pew. Dad, Mom, and her. Of all the nights for youth group to be canceled. She'd have to grin and bear it, because she wouldn't risk catching Dad's eye during the Bible study or prayer. She knew better. She also knew how to conduct herself in church, whether Wednesday night or Sunday morning. She'd been raised in this church, attending nearly every time the doors were open.

Yet this evening, she felt she was only partially present. Sure, she was sitting there, hearing the minister expound on one of the epistles, the apostle's letter to a church in Corinth. But her heart and brain were elsewhere. She could hardly wait to drop by Dottie Forster's Boutique tomorrow. Maybe she'd ask Dottie if she needed the teen magazine, the one with the skinny models. If not, maybe Dottie would let her borrow it. She really hoped so. She wanted to compare her ankles and other parts of her body with the very thin girls in the fashion section.

" 'Godliness has value for all things . . . ' " Their pastor's words, a direct quote from the Bible, took her off guard. She'd read precisely the same thing in her own devotional book a few days ago. What was going on?

After church, there was a message on their voice mail. She could hear Livvy's voice, but it sounded strange . . . far away. "Is something wrong?" she asked Mom.

"Not that I know of." Mom came over and listened to Livvy's message. "I see what you mean, though. Does sound a bit garbled."

For a second, Heather wondered if Livvy was sick. But when she called her, Heather discovered a bubbly friend waiting by the phone. "You'll never guess what," Livvy said.

"What's going on? You sound breathless."

Livvy laughed softly. "This is really amazing."

"What is?"

"Micky Waller—remember him?—wants to give you a call."

Heather sucked in her breath. "What?"

"Yeah, I ran into him at the mall rink late this afternoon," Livvy said. "He asked me for your number."

She groaned inwardly. "Uh, you didn't just give it to him, I hope."

"That's why I'm calling *you,* silly," Livvy replied. "So . . . what should I do?"

She had to think about that. "Better not . . . at least for now."

"How come?"

Glancing toward the living room, she spied Dad sitting in his easy chair, reading a magazine. "I just better not," she said more softly.

"I don't get it. Micky just wants to talk to you."

"I know, but it's a mistake. Bad timing."

"Know what *I* think?" Livvy wasn't giving up.

Heather fell silent, not too eager to hear what was on her friend's mind. But she listened.

"Heather, you still there?"

"Go ahead. I'm listening . . ."

"I think Micky's really cute," Livvy said. "You'd be crazy not to let him call you."

Heather sighed. "Maybe what he really wants is *your* phone number."

"I don't know. To tell you the truth, my dad's dragging his feet about me starting to talk to boys on the phone. And Grandma Hudson would probably hit the roof."

"Yeah."

"Maybe it's for the best," Livvy volunteered. "Liking boys can get very distracting."

"Right. We both have too much work to do . . . to reach our skating goals. There's really no time for boys." She'd said what she really believed.

Just maybe Dad was—right now—overhearing her end of the conversation. What she'd said about boys might earn her some points. After all, she needed to do what she could to make up for behaving badly at supper.

———————

After she hung up, she tried to slip upstairs to her room without being noticed. But Dad called to her just as she reached the hallway. "Heather, do you have a minute?"

"Sure, Daddy." She bounded into the living room, sitting across from him on the sofa.

He put his magazine away, sliding it under the coffee table. "I'm glad we have this chance to chat," he began. "Your mother and I are concerned. You ate very little today—far less than usual. Is something upsetting you?"

She wouldn't unload on him, spill out the remarks that had gotten her thinking about her weight in the first place. Dad wouldn't be interested in either Joanne's or Kevin's comments, either. "I'm fine," she said.

He leaned back in his chair. "You can say you're fine, but I think there may be something behind all this."

"Like what?"

Dad was smiling. "I was hoping you could tell *me*."

Just then, Mom came into the room. She was carrying the stack of professional photo proofs. Sitting down, she suddenly looked very tired as she shuffled through them. "I hope your not eating doesn't have anything to do with these wonderful pictures of you and Kevin," Mom said softly.

What could Heather say?

She noticed the dark circles under her dad's normally bright blue eyes. Tonight, his hair was a bit disheveled. Maybe from raking his long fingers through it while Heather was talking nonsense on the phone with Livvy. Yep, that's probably what was bothering him.

"I don't want either of you to worry," she said, getting up. "I'm feeling just great."

"But you're pale," Mom said, reaching out her hand.

"I feel fine." She didn't really feel all that terrific, but there was no turning back now. She was on track to reach her goal—do or die.

Photo Perfect
Chapter Eight

Dottie Forster's eyes actually lit up when Heather strolled nonchalantly into the beauty salon after homeschool hours. "What can I do for you, cutie?" asked the middle-aged beautician.

"Just thought I'd check in." Heather eyed the magazine rack, hoping Dottie wouldn't notice. "Everything cool here?"

"Always." Dottie turned the gray-haired woman who was getting a color. The client faced away from the mirror. "Need a trim?" asked Dottie.

"Sometime, just not today."

"Okay. Call me whenever."

Heather sat down, picking up the first magazine she saw. "Mind if I sit here?"

"No problem, and help yourself to some magazines,"

Dottie said. "I get so many piled up here . . . lots of them are out-of-date, too. Take them, if you like."

Mom had always said that Dottie had been around the block more than once. Was this evidence of her perception? Could Dottie tell by the look in Heather's eyes that she was on the lookout for that one special teen magazine?

Wow, and I thought Mom was bad. . . .

She sat there reading one monotonous magazine after another. At last, she finally found the courage to pick up the one she *really* wanted. She looked at the date. Too bad, it was the March issue, the current month. Dottie wouldn't be ready to let this one go. But Heather asked anyway.

"Hmm, let's see," Dottie said, coming over. She thumbed through the magazine, never hesitating on the article that had caught Heather's attention. "Sure, take it. I have plenty of teen mags floating around here."

Heather was overjoyed. "Are you sure?"

Dottie waved her hands. "I'm sure . . . I'm sure. Hey, enjoy."

All the way home, she stared at the lanky models— six pages worth. The girls were all very tall. Lots taller than she was. But then, she knew she still had several years left to grow. Being tall was a major plus in the fashion circles. But being not only petite but short gave a skater somewhat of an advantage. "You're closer to the ice," Livvy's grandmother liked to say.

Kevin had often told Heather that, too. "The closer you are to the ice, the softer the fall."

Her response was to laugh it off. Now she wasn't sure. Height gave a girl the lean lines Heather longed for. Both Dad and Mom were fairly tall. And Kevin was starting to shoot up, too. So there was hope for her.

Nearing her house, she rolled up the magazine and stuffed it into her backpack. No need to share this with Mom. She'd freak for sure, figure that Heather had gotten the notion not to eat merely from these skinny models. Well, maybe that had started the ball rolling, but there was much more to it. More than Heather cared to discuss with her mother. Or anyone.

———

Finishing off her homework, Heather rushed to the basement. Her parents had set up a workout area there for her and Kevin especially. Dad used it often, though. Mom too. And sometimes she saw Joanne there trying to lift the smallest weights.

"Physical training is of some value," the Bible verse stated.

She decided to set the treadmill for forty-five minutes this time, upping the amount of time by fifteen minutes.

305

Each day, she planned to increase her time. No longer was she satisfied with her performance. She felt compelled to push harder, go farther, work longer.

I can get as thin as those models, she thought. *I can!*

She visualized herself as one of the girls in the magazine. Sporting the sleek, thin jeans and tight boots. Yeah, she could fit into a size nothing real soon.

When Mom called, Heather scarcely heard. Joanne came running downstairs to alert her. "Mom's been calling. Didn't you hear?"

"Huh?"

"Mom wants you to make the salad. Hurry!" The younger girl turned and left the room.

Heather had spaced out on the time completely. Gone past her set time on the treadmill. She was actually beginning to love this workout regimen. Besides that, Coach McDonald would be pleased when he realized how terrific her stamina was.

Tomorrow she would check herself on the ice. Surely, the additional exercising would benefit her skating. Not to mention getting her slimmed way down.

She went to make the vegetable salad for Mom. Then, when she was finished, she climbed the steps to the second floor. She was surprised to see Joanne coming out of *her* private domain—Heather's bedroom. Actually, it seemed that she'd caught her little sister in the act of something. Just what, she didn't know. "What're you doing in my room?" she demanded.

"Oh, nothing." Joanne shrugged her shoulders innocently enough.

"Right . . . nothing. You keep saying that." Heather took the last three steps with a single bound. She towered over her little sister. "I know you were in my room."

"I just borrowed something, that's all."

"Borrowed what?"

Joanne shrugged again, tilting her mischievous little head to the side.

"C'mon," Heather urged.

But Joanne shook her head silently.

"So you're not going to tell me? Is that it?" She was mad. "I won't play twenty questions with you. You'd better tell me now or . . ."

How far should she take this? If Mom was witness to this exchange, they'd both be in trouble. They'd been taught to respect not only each other's privacy, but to treat each other with esteem. "Where's Mom?" she asked, curious.

Joanne shook her head. "I don't know."

"I think you do," she shot back. "And you know you're not supposed to snoop in my room or anyone else's. So . . . Mom must be downstairs somewhere."

Tommy emerged from his own bedroom, a Lego creation in his hand. "Mommy's in the family room."

Heather straightened. "Do you really have to eavesdrop?"

"What's *that* mean?" Poor Tommy. He was stuck in the middle.

She glared at both of them. "Look, you two . . ." She stopped from almost lashing out at her brother and sister. It was a good thing she'd bit her tongue, because Mom's footsteps were on the stairs just now.

Heather turned to see her mother's arms loaded down with folded laundry. "I could use some help, kids," Mom said. Usually, she didn't have to say much about helping. They all liked to pitch in and pull their weight with chores.

Joanne and Tommy stood at the landing, waiting with arms outstretched.

Perfect little brother and sister, she thought, staring at the twosome. But she knew the truth. They weren't even close to perfect.

Sooner or later, Mom would find it out.

———

When the laundry was put away, Heather closed the door to her room. Looking around, she tried to figure out what Joanne had borrowed. She went to her dresser. No drawers were hanging out. Nothing seemed to be missing. At least, not that she noticed. Her bed wasn't even rumpled. So what did Joanne need so badly that she was willing to risk getting caught?

Going to her mirror, Heather stared at her reflection. *Cool outfit,* she thought, looking at the gold and black jogging suit. Mom had purchased it during the after-Christmas sales a couple of months back. She especially liked the color gold, which seemed to point out the blond highlights in her hair.

Turning her back to the mirror, she glimpsed the back of her. She thought she *might* be a teeny bit thinner. But she couldn't be sure. Not without undressing. Tonight, after her shower, she would check to see how she *really* looked.

Just then, a knock came at her door. She hurried to see who was there.

It was Mom, standing in the hallway. "Heather, I'd like to talk with you when you have a minute."

The tone of Mom's voice spelled trouble. What had Joanne told her? Or was Tommy the culprit this time?

"Am I in trouble?" she said before thinking. She'd practically told on herself.

"Sounds like you have a guilty conscience." Mom smiled, reaching out to squeeze her arm. "Meet me in my bedroom in a few minutes. Okay, honey?"

Now she *knew* this was serious. "Sure, Mom."

She slipped her jogger top over her head, wearing

only the short-sleeved black T-shirt underneath. One more quick look in the mirror gave her the nerve to think about what little she could get by with eating at supper. She'd smelled the meaty aroma of roasted chicken. One of Mom's most delicious recipes. Delicious or not, Heather had a plan that did not include eating much of the specialty dish at all. Sure, her stomach had been rumbling all day long. She'd fought hard against the ongoing hunger pangs. Pretty soon they'd go away. They *had* to.

Mom was waiting for her in the master suite, standing by the window. "What's up?" Heather asked, hoping for an off-the-cuff reply. But Mom motioned for her to close the door. Another danger sign.

They stood at the foot of her parents' bed for a moment. Then Mom suggested they sit down. So Heather chose to perch on the bed, while her mother sat in a chair across the room. "I wish I didn't have to talk to you about this," Mom began. "I think by now you should know better."

Here it comes . . .

"I happened to overhear your conversation with Joanne earlier." Mom paused, probably searching for the right words. "Your sister looks up to you, Heather. She's learning from you each day. Tommy too."

Heather wished Mom would bring Kevin into this

lecture. Why wasn't her older brother included? Was *he* the ideal role model?

She refused to mention Kevin. She kept quiet—something she should've done when she first caught Joanne scurrying out of her room. Just what did Mom know about any of that?

"We've studied very thoroughly godly character traits," Mom continued.

True. Heather—the whole family, for that matter—had studied and learned thoroughly the Bible-based attributes. She could recite them, each one corresponding to a fruit of the Spirit. But then, so could Joanne and Tommy.

Why was Mom picking on her?

"I'd like you to go easy on your sister . . . about whatever she was borrowing," Mom said straight out.

"But Joanne's constantly messing around in my room."

"Be gentle and patient with her when you bring it up again. All right?" Mom's eyes reflected her own kind spirit.

Yet Heather could not contain her anger about the situation. "I'm sick and tired of Joanne waltzing in and out of my room at will. She's doing something in there. I know she is!"

"I'll talk to Joanne," Mom said quickly. "In the meantime, can you please watch your attitude a bit?"

Watch my attitude? She felt the anger rising. But she wouldn't sass her mother. The ultimate no-no.

She ought to be sorry for her tone of voice with Joanne. She ought to act as an example to her younger sister. But she didn't feel a bit sorry. Not at the moment.

Maybe not at all.

Photo Perfect
Chapter Nine

Any other evening, Heather might've asked to be excused and hurried off to bed. Homework was completed and double-checked, just the way Mom liked it. But Dad was probably waiting in the living room eager to get family devotions going. There was no getting out of that. And she didn't really want to dodge out of it. Just needed some space.

Her head ached and her stomach growled. She knew she should've eaten more of Mom's tasty and tender chicken. She'd hardly eaten a speck of food.

My own fault, she thought, sitting next to her little brother.

Quietly, she turned to the Bible. Dad had asked specifically for Galatians 5:14. She should've recognized the verse before she ever turned to it. Dad had helped both her and Kevin memorize the passage years ago. Even before little Joanne and Tommy had come into their lives through adoption.

The living room was quiet. Dad and Mom sat together on the sofa. Joanne was perched at Dad's feet. Heather and Tommy were snug on the loveseat.

Dad started with a general, family-type prayer. Then he asked her to begin reading.

" 'The entire law is summed up in a single command: Love your neighbor as yourself,' " she read, feeling her face growing warm. But the room remained still.

Heather fully expected Dad to comment on the verse, the way he usually did. But not tonight. Instead, Dad asked Kevin to read another Scripture, which just so happened to be about getting along with others in the family of God.

So was this a specific lesson for the whole family? Or was Dad focusing in on her?

No use getting huffy about it. Better to listen and learn—and repent, as Dad always suggested—than to get herself in a stew over something minor. She and Joanne didn't need to be at each other's throats.

Still, the idea of Joanne getting by with snooping bugged her. She was starting to feel she had no control over much of anything anymore.

While Dad talked about the importance of getting along in a cheerful manner, Heather let her mind wander. She thought about the things she *could* control in her life. Things like her food intake. Things like how many hours a day she exercised. And nope, she wasn't ready to give up trying to lose weight. No matter what anybody said.

By the time Dad was finished talking and reading from his Bible, she was eager to get to bed. Morning couldn't come early enough for her this night. She could hardly wait to hit the ice. Besides that, tomorrow afternoon was the next Girls Only Club meeting. She had several fantastic recipes to add to Livvy's cookbook.

To think she was collecting recipes when she'd given up eating. What a hoot!

———

Before turning out the light, Heather curled up on her bed. She skimmed through the teen magazine once again, enjoying the pictures immensely. She wondered how thin she'd look this time next week. Would anyone notice? What would Coach say? How about Kevin?

Kevin . . .

At least, maybe he wouldn't drop her on their lifts. Soon, she'd be lots lighter. That alone was good enough reason to shed some pounds.

Scooting off the bed, she went and stood in front of the large floor mirror in the corner of the room. Yes, she could see the slightest changes—or she thought so. Wearing only her baby-doll pajamas, she thought her legs . . . and maybe her ankles, too, seemed a little slimmer. Yes, they *were* thinner. She was sure of it.

Good, she thought. *I'm on the right track.*

But when she finally did slip into bed, she had a hard time relaxing. Falling asleep had never been a problem before. The gnawing in her stomach and the dizzy feeling in her head kept her tossing and turning.

Around eleven, she got up and tiptoed downstairs. One little bite of a graham cracker and a swallow of milk wouldn't hurt anything. She had to do something. So she crept out of her room and down the stairs.

She was surprised to find Mom downstairs, too. Sitting in the dark, her mother was praying in the living room. Heather wouldn't have known she was there, except she heard someone whispering her name as she came down the steps.

"Lord, please help my Heather . . . whatever is bothering her," Mom prayed softly.

Heather swallowed hard. She didn't know what to think. Mom, up this late? How would she feel when five o'clock in the morning rolled around?

It wasn't hard for Heather to know how *she* would feel, dragging out of bed. Ten hours of sleep a night was essential for active athletes during the growing years. Physical exertion demanded recovery time. She'd pushed her body extra hard today, working out on the treadmill far longer than ever. She knew from past experience she could only stretch her limits so far.

She would pay dearly if she didn't get proper rest. And Coach McDonald would see right through the balance and concentration problems that were sure to crop up. Even after only one night of poor sleep.

Hurrying to the kitchen, she ate three crackers, then poured a tiny bit of milk. She limited herself to just one third of a cup. Tomorrow, she'd do better about not snacking. She promised herself.

Photo Perfect
Chapter Ten

At breakfast, Heather purposely suppressed the urge to eat. She also made excuses about why she was late coming to the table. "I couldn't find the warm-up suit I wanted," she said, feeling terribly tired and irritable.

Mom's eyebrows rose briefly, but she said nothing. Dad was nowhere around, as he'd gotten an even earlier start on his day. He wasn't there to either witness her explanation or intervene.

Kevin, though, stared at her curiously. "What's with the zero appetite?" he asked.

Before Heather could say a word, their mother quickly changed the subject. So nothing more was said, and Heather was relieved. She was too exhausted to put up much of a fight. Especially with Kevin.

After sitting only a few minutes at the table, she

pushed back her half-full glass of orange juice. She'd taken only a few bites of her fresh pear, then bravely she asked to be excused.

Thankfully, Mom seemed cool enough about it. *Good,* thought Heather. She could put her plan into action more easily with some breathing room.

"Someone should call the phone company about our voice mail," Kevin reminded Mom.

"Yeah, it's messed up," Heather spoke up, remembering Livvy's hazy message.

"I'll look into it," Mom assured them. She also told them about getting together with two other homeschooling families. "We plan to meet here after lunch."

Kevin seemed interested. "We're starting another new history unit, right?"

Mom nodded. "It's time we delve more deeply into the American Constitution."

"Cool," Heather said.

At least it wasn't another one of Mom's nutrition units. The history study with other families of kids was great news. Joanne and Tommy would be studying on different levels, and Heather and Kevin would pair up with some of the older kids. Mom was good about having all four of them work on similar themes, but she also had a knack for bringing the subject matter down to each of their comprehension levels, even including Joanne with mazes, puzzles, and age-appropriate material.

———

Somehow, Heather made it through her morning ice session. But she was really beginning to drag as she sat on the bench to remove her skates. Kevin waited around for her, leaning on the barrier. He was obviously impatient, too, by the way he shuffled about. But he didn't bring up anything troublesome, and she was glad.

The walk home seemed longer than usual. Heather's legs felt more like rubber than flesh and bone and muscle. Mom hadn't accompanied them to the early-morning session. Often, she let them walk to and from. Today, though, Heather wished her mother had driven them.

"What's wrong with you?" Kevin asked.

"Nothing."

"Anyone can see you're worn out," he persisted.

She sighed. Her brother didn't need to know that she'd been up prowling around the kitchen for something to eat so late in the night. "I'm fine," she insisted.

"Say what you like. I can see you're exhausted."

"Why don't you just . . . leave me alone?"

"Oh yeah, sure . . . that's a great suggestion." He paused as they walked in silence. Then—"So is it really none of my business that my skating partner is falling off balance and skating way under her ability today?"

He had her. She scuffed her feet against the sidewalk, saying nothing.

"Look, Heather, if you have to go on some stupid crash course, or whatever it is you're doing to your body, I think you'd better bounce it off me first. Okay?"

"Says who?"

"Coach, for one . . . and Mom and Dad, too, since they're paying big bucks for our training. In case you forgot. They're behind us all the way, helping us push ourselves ahead to our goal." He stopped and turned to look at her. "It *is* still your goal, right?"

"To get to Junior Olympics, sure." There was no question in her mind.

"Then, how about if you start eating?"

They began walking again. This time, she forged ahead, leaving her brother behind.

"Aw, don't do this," Kevin called to her.

"Don't do *what*—walk faster than you?" She didn't even stop to glance over her shoulder. She was losing it faster than her own stride.

"Your head's jumbled," he said flatly.

That got her attention. She turned and waited for him. "Since when is it fair for you to call all the shots for us?"

"It's fair only when I see my sister doing harm to herself." He sighed loudly. "I wish I knew what was bugging you."

"Whatever." She turned away.

"No, Heather, I mean it." Kevin reached and grabbed

her arm. "You're not heavy, if that's what you think." His eyes were kind. He *was* concerned.

"We're not having this conversation." And that was the end of it.

Weary before the day had scarcely begun, she mustered up enough energy to run ahead of him. At her side, her skates flip-flopped nearly out of control as she attempted to steady them.

Photo Perfect
Chapter Eleven

"I don't feel well," she admitted to her mother during a short break in the history unit that afternoon.

Mom had been talking with two other students, slightly older than Heather. Two boys from their church were also homeschooled. Kevin was hanging around with them, deciding what essays to write. "A discussion on the balance of power would be great," one of the other boys suggested.

Kevin seemed to like the idea. Heather could tell by his wide, bright eyes. She, on the other hand, could scarcely stand up. She'd pushed herself this far through, but now felt so tired she just wanted to put her head down on the table and give in to sleep.

Mom looked at her over her glasses. "Are you ill or just tired?"

She wanted to say "both," but that wasn't true. Fact was, she was dog tired. Her own fault. "I'm really wiped out," she said.

"Well, why don't you sit on the couch to do some reading?" Mom suggested.

What she really wanted was to go to her room and lie down there in the quiet. Why hadn't she gone to bed earlier last night? But she knew the answer. The truth was, she'd denied herself food and paid the price—much to the anger of her skating partner and older brother. How was she going to get down to nothing with Kevin hounding her?

She carried her books to the living room, as Mom recommended. Getting settled into the cushions, she knew right off this was a mistake. The sofa was far too comfortable, and the movement of her eyes on the page only served to make her sleepier. Almost before she knew it, she was sound asleep.

But in her dreams, she was light as a feather. She was also hungry, the empty feeling in her stomach exaggerated. As the dream progressed, she realized that she was beginning to get hooked on the hunger pangs. The feeling was actually enticing, something she liked. Somehow, though, she could sense that her family and friends, and even the Girls Only Club members, were afraid for her. But that, of course, was only in her dream.

When she awakened, the other kids had left. Mom, Joanne, and Tommy were doing an art project at the dining-room table. "Where's Kevin?" she asked.

"Lifting weights," said Mom. "Want to join him?"

"Too tired." She headed toward the stairs.

"School's not finished for the day," Mom said suddenly.

Returning, Heather asked, "What's next?"

It was clear that Mom was displeased. "Well, if you're too tired to do your schoolwork, then you must certainly be too tired to attend ballet class . . . and later, your Girls Only Club."

Mom was smart that way. She had her coming and going. Without saying more, Heather waited for her next assignment—a writing project—from her teacher-mother. She shouldn't have been too surprised at her own usually tenacious spirit. It was obvious she'd inherited persistence from Guess Who.

———

Heather yanked on the locker-room door at Natalie's Ballet School. Rushing inside, she was eager to get ballet class over for the day. Livvy and the other girls were already dressed and chattering at one of the mirrors, looking at something posted on the wall.

She couldn't care less. Not the way she felt at the moment. She wandered over to her own small locker,

worked the combination lock, and pulled it open. Inside
the locker door, smiling Russian ice dancers taunted her.
Yet she knew better than to feel upset about the poster.
After all, she'd searched high and low for the fantastic picture of ice dancers Pasha Grishuk and Evgeny
Platov. She knew the grueling schedule and dietary
provisions these superior skaters certainly must have
adhered to, to get what they wanted. To reach their
goals and dreams.

She found herself staring at them, wishing she could
speak their language. Wishing she could get a grip on
her life as a great skater . . .

Just then, Jenna and Manda came dashing over to
her. "Have you heard?" Jenna said.

Still almost in a daze, she turned slowly. "Heard
what?"

"Newman's department store is hosting a modeling
agency," Jenna said.

Manda's eyes were absolutely twinkling. "They're
interviewing prospective models next Wednesday."

Livvy wandered over to join them. "Yeah, but it's
too bad."

"What do you mean?" asked Heather.

"None of us has any extra time," Livvy said
glumly.

Jenna nodded, too, as if reality were sinking in.
"True."

"Wait a minute," Heather said. "How'd you hear about this?"

Manda pointed to the poster near the mirror, across the locker room. "Check it out for yourself."

"I will!" And she charged off, feeling an unexpected surge of energy.

She scanned the ad with her eyes. It was *very* interesting. She read every word carefully. There were going to be agency directors flying in from New York City next week. They would look at portfolios—*no problem,* she thought—as well as narrow down the number of contestants. Whoever made the final cut was offered a modeling contract.

"Is it runway modeling, commercial, or catalogs?" she asked the others.

"Probably any of that, if you're good enough," Jenna said. "But it clearly says they train you, teach you everything you need to know. Even set up appointments for your work."

"But only if you have the look they want," Manda added.

The look . . .

She wondered what that might be. If they meant the hollowed-out look, like the young models in her teen magazine at home, she thought she could pull *that* off by Wednesday. Less than a week away, she could maybe do it if she went without eating between now and then. Yes, that's what she'd do.

"I think I'll show up and see what it's all about," she said.

Livvy wrinkled up her nose. "You're kidding, right?"

She whirled around, bending and limbering up. "This is just what I've been waiting for."

Jenna and Manda exchanged glances. "How come you've never said anything to us about modeling before?" Jenna asked.

"Maybe you weren't listening."

"But we hang at Girls Only together, and never once have you said anything." Jenna was unwavering.

"Guess I don't say everything I'm thinking." Heather shrugged it off.

Livvy frowned. "What about your summer ice event, Heather? How will you place there if you're attending modeling classes or whatever?"

"Not *classes*." She spun around. "Didn't you read the ad? They find you *work*."

Manda joined her in bending and warming up. "I'd rather keep focused on one thing at a time. Life gets less complicated that way."

"Yeah, one thing at a time," Jenna echoed.

Livvy suggested they go to the barre and get ready

for class. "Modeling's not for me, I can tell you that right now."

Heather was surprised—that comment coming from beautiful Livvy. "How will you know if you don't try out?"

Livvy shook her head. "I don't have the look they want, I'm sure of it."

Jenna grinned. "But maybe Heather does."

Heather wondered what Jenna meant by that. "Which means?"

"It's just that you're so tiny . . . the way they like models to be," Jenna replied.

Heather knew she probably wasn't even close to being tall enough. Models that made it big were usually close to six feet tall. Never much shorter. There was no chance she'd grow that much in a few days.

"Personally, I think it's silly," Manda said.

Think what you want, Heather decided.

"The four of us have athletic goals, in case you forgot," Jenna joined in the chorus.

"Who said anything about giving up goals?" she asked.

Jenna shot her a weird look. "Well, what will Kevin say?"

She should've known that was coming. Her girl friends always cared too much about what Kevin thought about everything. "My brother has nothing to say about it."

"But he's the other half of your skating partnership," Livvy said softly. "Doesn't that count for something?"

Of course it counted. She knew it did. But Heather was feeling just stubborn enough to stand firm in her quest. "Everyone, just back off."

"Fine," said Manda, pouting.

"It's time for ballet, besides," said Jenna, turning to go.

Livvy gave Heather a puzzled look but kept quiet.

When Natalie called for centerwork, Heather was glad. What did Manda, Jenna, and Livvy know about anything, anyway?

Photo Perfect
Chapter Twelve

At home, Heather stayed in the shower much longer than usual, trying to rinse away the memory of her girl friends' stinging remarks. So what if they weren't interested in showing up for the modeling try-outs. Who cared what *they* thought?

Lathering up for the second time, she remembered how outspoken Livvy had been. Livvy Hudson, typically sweet and considerate, had been downright direct. What had come over her? Was it that she was really interested but knew she couldn't honestly take on one more event in her week? Was that it? Or was there more to it?

Livvy and her father barely made ends meet sometimes. That was partly the reason for Livvy's grandmother coming to live with them. *"Out of necessity,"* Livvy had said early in the year.

Of course, Heather wouldn't be rude and bring up such a thing. But she suspected that to be the reason behind Livvy's disinterest. What else?

Manda and Jenna had been equally hostile. Well, maybe hostile was stating it a little strongly. But they *were* defensive. Drying her hair, Heather wondered why.

In her room, she chose a soft blue warm-up suit to wear to Jenna's house. Girls Only Club meetings were some of the best times of each week. It was fun to wear something comfortable. Sometimes, they worked together to come up with new ballet routines.

Today she was eager to see how many healthy recipes had been gathered since last Friday. Livvy's idea of a cookbook was really a terrific one. They could sell lots of copies at church and around the neighborhood. Another good place to market them was the homeschooling network in town. Mom knew all sorts of folks devoted to home teaching. Families who might appreciate a cool cookbook like theirs.

When she headed to the basement, Heather found Kevin playing with Tommy. "Where's Mom?" she asked.

"She ran an errand," Kevin said, looking up. "Where are you headed?"

"If it's Friday, it must be Girls Only," she taunted him.

"Oh yeah." There was a mischievous twinkle in his

eye. "You're making a cookbook to raise money . . . for what?"

She wouldn't go there. It was a setup. She could see it on her brother's face. "Never mind."

He shook his head. "You know, it's kinda hard to overlook something so completely ridiculous," he muttered. "You've quit eating, but you're putting together a cookbook. How does that make any sense?"

"Oh, what do *you* know?" she said under her breath.

He stood tall just then, grabbing Tommy and swinging him around the room. Tommy let out a few screams of delight. "Faster . . . swing me faster," their younger brother hollered.

"Stop it!" Heather shouted. "Just stop it."

Kevin slowed Tommy down and stopped. He frowned. "Relax, Heather. Nobody's out of control here."

No one except me, she thought.

———

Heather was the first to arrive at the Songs' home. Jenna Song was lying on her bed, talking to her furry feline, Sasha, high in her attic bedroom. The room was the largest bedroom Heather had seen in her life. When Jenna and her family moved to Alpine Lake last fall, they'd knocked out a wall in order to make the upstairs room a combination bedroom and ballet practice area. The only thing the room lacked was a hardwood floor for full-blown dances.

"Hey! You're early," Jenna said, spying her in the doorway. "Come in and relax."

Heather inched into the room, going to the corner near the window. "It's nice and quiet up here."

"Isn't it, though?" Jenna tickled her cat's nose.

Heather was silent, staring down at the rooftops of the other houses.

"Something on your mind?" asked Jenna.

"Oh, I don't know."

Jenna chuckled. "Well, if you don't . . . I sure don't."

Heather thought about that. Should she tell her friend about her nagging desire to be skin and bones? What would Jenna think?

"C'mon, Heather, talk to me." Jenna came over and sat on the floor across from her.

"You won't laugh?"

"Never."

She'd have to test the waters first. See if Jenna was the kind of friend she thought she was. "Bet you've never wanted to starve yourself skinny . . . have you?"

Jenna frowned, pulling on one side of her short hair. "Hey, I've heard all about eating disorders, if that's what you're talking about."

"I didn't say anything about disorders." Now she was stalled. Maybe talking to Jen wasn't such a good idea, after all.

"So what are you saying?" Jenna twisted first one side of her dark hair, then the other. Her deep brown eyes were very serious, like she was struggling to understand.

Heather pushed ahead, unsure of herself. "My brother thinks I'm fat."

Jenna laughed softly. "I doubt that."

"No, I'm serious. Kevin said I was too heavy one day during our practice."

Jenna sat with her knees under her chin. "Surely he was joking."

"I don't think so." She sighed. This was harder than she thought. "I want to be thin, Jen. Thinner than you are . . . thinner than I am now."

Frowning, Jenna looked at her. Really looked. "Hey, girl, you're starting to scare me. Am I hearing you right?"

Heather nodded. "I've never been more serious."

"So . . . what's it you're doing? Cutting out eating, is that it?"

"And I'm working out a lot."

"Working out? Like how much?" Jenna's eyes glistened.

"Several extra hours a day."

Jenna scrunched up her mouth. "Does your coach know?"

"Nobody knows but you." At last, she'd told someone. What would Jenna's reaction be?

"Wanna know what I think?" Jenna said softly, reaching out her hand.

"Sure."

"From everything I've heard and read—and, believe me, stuff like this gets around—you do *not* want to get caught up in the anorexic thing. I've seen girls my age get so high from the endorphins released during the starvation process, they actually get hooked on them. It's addictive." She scooted over next to Heather. "Please, don't even think of losing weight that way. It's dangerous."

She was frustrated at Jenna's reaction. "I don't get it. You think it's wrong not to eat?"

"Wrong and stupid, you pick. I've heard of some girls who'd rather cut off their arm than eat. They get sucked into the craving for the starvation high. Ten percent of them end up dead."

"Really? Dead?"

"Hey, if you don't eat, you die. Simple as that."

Heather hadn't thought of it quite that way. "You're sure about this?"

"My gymnastic coach could tell you a thing or two. That is, if you don't believe me."

She didn't know what to think. Jenna seemed so convincing. Sure of herself. And Jen ought to know this stuff, coming from the athletic world she, too, lived and breathed daily.

"Don't say anything to Livvy and Manda, okay?" she said, beginning to tremble.

"Well, I won't promise forever. I'm a better friend than that. If you need to control something in a major way, I would never suggest the food-less route."

They were silent for a moment. Then Heather whispered, "I'm sorry, Jen. I want to be skinny. I really do."

"And right now you're shaking. So how's that going to help you enjoy the club meeting in a few minutes?" Jenna's face was solemn. "When's the last time you ate?"

She wouldn't tell. That was her business. Her secret. Getting up, she went to the barre. "Sorry, Jen. Guess I made a mistake."

Jenna followed her over, staring at her in the mirror. "You're wrong about that. You did the right thing telling me. Because I refuse to let you get sucked into this dead end you're headed for."

Heather was nearly too weak to protest. But her silence was her best defense. So she said no more.

Photo Perfect
Chapter Thirteen

Both Livvy and Manda arrived late to Girls Only. Heather really wished they'd shown up on time. Maybe then she wouldn't have blabbed her soul to Jenna. Now, someone else in the world knew what was going on in her head. And she wasn't so sure her gymnast friend would keep quiet about it.

"What recipes did you bring?" Livvy asked as the meeting had come to order.

Heather had carefully printed out the recipes she thought fit best under the High-Energy Snacks heading. She showed the Bars of Iron recipe first.

"Read off some of the ingredients," Jenna said.

She wasn't so sure she wanted to think about food, let alone read about it. But she did, for the sake of the club. "There are raisins and molasses in it."

Manda wrinkled up her nose at the molasses.

"Oats and ginger, too," Heather said. Just the sound of the word *raisins* made her mouth water. She was so hungry.

But no, she wouldn't think about it. Not now. Not with Jenna, Livvy, and Manda sitting here, staring at her with bright eyes and full stomaches. Nope, she'd stick it out as long as possible. At least until the modeling agency came to their little town.

———

They were in the middle of voting on a title for their cookbook when Jenna's mother knocked on the door. "Jenna, dear, can you watch your baby brother for me?"

Jenna glanced over her shoulder at the rest of the girls. "You don't mind, do you?" she asked the rest of the club members.

"No problem," Manda spoke up.

"We'll help you entertain him," Heather offered.

Livvy nodded her head, agreeing that they'd all pitch in and baby-sit. "It'll be fun."

Jenna left the room and returned with little Jonathan in her arms. The baby's olive skin tone matched Jenna's, and his eyes widened as he looked around at all of them. Then his face lit up with a big smile when he spotted

Heather. "Aw, he's adorable," she said, getting up and going over to Jenna. "May I hold him?"

Jenna gave her the strangest look. "Are you strong enough?" Jen whispered.

She knew what Jen was getting at. "Well, maybe I . . ."

Jenna moved past her and went to sit on the floor with her baby brother. "He's crawling everywhere now," she said, setting him down in the middle of the floor.

Just then, the cat jumped down off the bed, and tiny Jonathan pointed at Sasha. "Oh," he said, crawling toward the furry creature.

"Watch this," Jenna said.

The girls were spellbound, watching Jonathan's every move. His cute little hands sprang out, and he began crawling toward the golden-haired cat. But Sasha only allowed the baby to get within inches of her. Then she skittered under the bed skirt to a safe hiding place.

Baby Jonathan just blinked his dark eyes, making sweet, high-pitched sounds.

"Does he talk?" Manda asked.

Jenna nodded. "He says 'Mama,' 'bye-bye,' 'hi,' and 'Da-da.' "

"What's he call you?" asked Livvy.

Jenna smiled. "My brother only points at me and grunts."

"That's interesting," Heather said, observing the small child. She wondered what would happen if a baby didn't eat. How long before he or she would starve? Like the children on TV, in Third-World countries where every day babies die by the thousands.

Jenna's voice brought her out of her reverie. "Let's do our best to compile the recipes today. Then when we're ready, I'll make the cover. Unless someone else wants to."

"Go for it," Manda said.

"Yeah, you'll come up with a nice design," Livvy said.

"Use your computer program, maybe," suggested Heather. But her thoughts were on getting home, lying down. She felt so terribly weak.

———

Heather was glad Mom was out doing some shopping when she arrived home. Quickly, she slipped off to her bedroom, eager for a nap. But her rest was short-lived. Joanne knocked on her bedroom door, waking Heather.

"What do you want?" she asked.

Joanne poked her head inside. "Are you awake?"

"Not really."

"Kevin said to tell you that someone left a phone message for you, he thinks." Joanne's lips curled into a smile.

"What do you mean, 'he thinks'?"

Joanne stared back at her. "Just what I said."

She sat up in bed, groaning. "Will you just please tell me what you mean?"

"It's hard to hear who's on the voice mail," came the reply.

"So . . . it's still not fixed?"

"Better go listen," Joanne said. "Maybe you'll recognize the voice."

Why should I care?

Joanne stood there, like she was waiting for Heather to get up and go to the phone. "Well, are you going?"

"Not now . . . I'm tired."

"And crabby," Joanne whispered.

But Heather had heard her sister. "Please close the door."

"You want me to leave?"

"Please." *The sooner the better,* she thought.

Taking her time, Joanne shut the door behind her. And Heather leaned back on her bed, closing her eyes. But now it was impossible to fall asleep again. She was too curious. Who had left the message? One of her friends from church, probably. Or maybe one of her Girls Only friends.

But she'd just been with Jenna, Livvy, and Manda. So . . . what would *they* want? The more she thought about it, the more she wondered, secretly, if Micky Waller had called.

"Micky wants to talk to you," Livvy had said on the phone the other day.

That got her up. She slipped down the hall to her parents' room and checked the voice mail. Joanne was right. It was almost impossible to hear who was talking. Almost.

Thank goodness she'd checked before Dad and Mom did. Yes, she was fairly sure it was Micky. But the number he'd left where he could be reached wasn't clear. At least he'd called. That was enough.

Feeling better just thinking about a boy calling her, she hurried downstairs. She opened the refrigerator and found a jar of peanut butter. She spread a small amount on two long stalks of celery and ate them both. She'd broken her fast, but the snack might curb her appetite for supper.

She headed downstairs to the family room, only to discover Kevin lifting weights in the corner of the room. "I'm next," she told him.

Kevin spouted back. "Since when do you just waltz in here and demand to be next?"

"Since right now."

He was silent. She'd made him angry. Not a good thing for either their working relationship or their brother-sister rapport. Neither one.

She waited her turn, wishing somehow they could clear the air between them. She wanted to improve their skating relationship especially. Fact was, she'd never forgiven him for dropping her.

"Did you get your phone message?" he asked when he was finally finished. On his way past her.

"Maybe."

He shook his head and left the room.

Eyeing the exercise equipment, she set the timer for one hour. Instead of doing homework, she was going to lift arm and leg weights for a solid sixty minutes. Since Mom was probably at the grocery store, she figured she would be fine with this. Nobody had to know.

She turned on the contemporary Christian station—one in Colorado Springs—that made its way to Alpine Lake. She was glad they got the station, because the town was too small to support its own major stations.

So she worked out, hard as she could, the upbeat music and her own thoughts filling her mind.

Photo Perfect
Chapter Fourteen

On Monday, two days before the modeling agency came to town, Heather asked her mother if she could go and "try out."

"How are you going to fit everything into your life?" Mom asked.

She was ready for that question. "I can do it," she said. "I'll work even harder if I have to."

"Well, how do we know these folks are legitimate?"

"Call Natalie Johnston. Do you think Natalie would advertise something that wasn't on the level?"

Mom glanced toward the ceiling. "Seems to me, your father and I will have to check things out. *If* you go at all."

"Oh please, Mom, won't you come with me? Ask

whatever questions you want to, just let me interview."
She was starting to feel desperate.

Mom sat her down in the living room. "Honey . . .
can you tell me, is this the reason you've quit eating?"

She looked away. "I haven't quit, not completely,"
she said softly.

"Do you want to be a model more than anything
else?" asked Mom.

"Not more than skating, but I *do* want to see if I
have a chance."

Mom touched her hand. "You haven't been yourself
for over a week, Heather. I want to help you."

She remembered hearing her mother's prayer last
week—the night she'd crept to the kitchen for some
crackers and milk. She knew her mother was concerned,
but there was no need. "I don't need help, Mom."

"I think you do. And I've made an appointment with
the doctor." The corners of Mom's eyes were glistening.
"Tomorrow, after lunch, we'll go together."

She knew there was no talking Mom out of this.
She was determined; motivated by what, Heather didn't
know.

"I'm not sick," she said, making an effort. "I don't
need a doctor."

"Well, he can check on your knee, at least." Mom
got up and reached for Heather. "I love you, kiddo.
You're going to be just fine."

Just fine . . .

How did her mother know? Did she have any idea what was going on? Did she?

Before supper, the phone rang. Fortunately, Heather answered on the second ring. "Bock residence."

"Heather . . . is that you?"

Her heart skipped a beat. "Yes, and who's this?"

"It's Micky Waller. Remember, we talked at the mall rink last week?"

Sure, she remembered. How could she forget? "Hi, Micky. How's it going?"

"I called you before, but your voice mail sounded strange."

"It was, but it's fixed now," she told him, not sure what else to say.

"That's cool."

There was a long, awkward pause. Heather didn't know if she should speak first or if Micky should. She felt terribly tense. Was this how it was when a boy called a girl? They hardly knew what to say to each other?

At last, he said, "I saw an ad for a modeling agency at Natalie Johnston's studio."

"Really? I saw it, too."

"So . . . are you going to try out?" he asked.

"I might."

"Hey, really? Well, guess what? I'm going over there,

too." He went on to say that he heard the agency was looking for kids, boys, girls, and older people.

"You're kidding, it's not just for girls?" she asked.

"No, and they offer commercial, runway, and catalog opportunities," he said. "My dad called the phone number listed on the ad. They actually get you set up for a portfolio and slides and everything."

"For how much?"

"I think it's six hundred dollars."

"That much?" she said.

"Seems like a lot, but if you make the final, *final* cut, they'll make appointments with different modeling companies for you. It's great."

She wondered if Micky was planning a future in skating. But she didn't ask. She didn't care, not really. Her interest in Micky was purely shallow. She thought he was nice, of course—and cute—but she didn't have time for a close friendship with a boy. Not at her age.

"Well, thanks for the info," she said, thinking she ought to get going.

"Uh, sure. Can I call you again?"

"You know what? It might be better if we just talk to each other at the rink sometimes. I'm *so* busy with training and my homework." She told him she was homeschooled, too. "We have lots of hours and requirements to meet for the state of Colorado."

"That kind of study is real tough, isn't it?"

"We like it that way. No time wasted, you know."

They said their good-byes, and by the time the conversation was over, Heather felt she knew Micky much better than before. But most of all, she was surprised that the agency was accepting *boys*.

———

Their family doctor seemed almost too pleased to have her visit. "Let's see how that knee's healing," he said, poking and prodding at it. She walked down the hall and up, turned her feet inside and out for him. Even twirled on the carpet to show him how "just fine" her knee was.

But the one-on-one conversation she had with the doctor—Mom outside, in the waiting room—was the most painful. "Your mother tells me you haven't been eating much lately," he began.

She nodded.

"Are you not feeling well these days, Heather?"

"Oh, I'm fine."

"I see." He folded his arms across his chest, studying her through his glasses. "Still have a good appetite?"

"Yes."

"Just aren't eating?"

"Yes."

"And can you tell me why that is?" He tilted his head

the way her father often did when he was probing for answers.

"Well, I want to look skinny . . . uh, thin."

"According to our charts, you're quite slender, just as you are."

"But I want to be thinner."

"Is there any particular reason why?"

She chuckled slightly under her breath. Doc wasn't going to hear about Kevin today. Nobody needed to know how angry she was at him. "I skate lots better when I feel light, that's all."

"Yes, I suppose you do," he replied, getting up and going to the table. He brought back with him a small model of a human skeleton. "Have you ever seen one of these?"

"Only here, in your office."

"Do you understand that there are many aspects to our bodies?" He paused. "Our bones need certain foods in order to maintain health." He continued on, reciting the importance of tissue, muscles, and nerves. "All essential to hold us together." Here, he smiled at her. "We need food to recharge our human machine."

He wasn't telling her anything new.

"Any questions?" he asked.

"No."

"All right, then I'll see you back again next week."

Next week?

"I'm coming back so soon?" She didn't get it.

"Each week, we'll talk . . . okay with you?"

She was still baffled. This was a first. Something Mom had dreamed up, or what?

Before she left, the nurse weighed her and measured her height, recording it in a book.

Very weird, she thought.

Photo Perfect
Chapter Fifteen

By some miracle, Heather's parents consented to allow her to try out with the modeling agency. Mom accompanied her, arriving a half hour before the place actually opened.

They sat in the car, chatting calmly. Mom wasn't pushy, even though she had every right to be. Yet Heather could hardly wait to go through the process of being chosen or not.

By the time the doors opened, at least fifty people had gathered. Even several men and women. But mostly girls her age had come, along with several boys. A few small children were present with their mothers, too.

First thing, she was asked to fill out a questionnaire, asking her vital statistics: chest, waist, and hip measurements. Along with that, her height and weight.

She knew her weight and height precisely because she had been weighed at the doctor's office yesterday. *One hundred and two pounds . . . five feet four inches.* She'd lost three pounds in almost two weeks. Not bad.

When her name was called, two women, beautifully dressed and made up, looked her over, starting with her face. She was also asked to show her hands. "Do you have any scars or tattoos?" one asked her.

"None."

She noticed that most of the girls were at least five feet six inches or taller. She was one of the shortest girls in her age group. Also, one of the thinnest.

"Please have a seat, Miss Heather Bock," one of the women judges said.

Miss Heather Bock. Had a nice ring to it, she decided.

Heather and her mother waited together until the next group of contestants was called. "Do you think I'll make the first cut?" she asked her mother, crossing her legs at the ankles and sliding them under the chair.

"Oh, honey, I'm sure you will." Mom seemed so confident, so poised. Just the way Heather wanted to be. "But if not, please don't take this hard. It's just two women's opinions."

She knew what Mom was getting at. Still, she wanted to be chosen so badly.

"Always remember that what God thinks of you is

what truly counts. You don't have to prove anything to your heavenly Father."

"I know, Mom." Yet Heather fought it. More than anything, she wanted to be accepted here on earth. By friends and family. By her skating partner.

"Promise you won't be upset if you don't make the final cut?" Mom was saying.

"But . . . what if I do? What then?"

"We'll talk about it if that does, indeed, happen."

"So I might be able to do some modeling in my free time?" she asked.

"We'll see."

She had a strange feeling her mother knew something she didn't. But she wasn't bailing out yet. She was going to hold her breath for this.

At long last, the names of girls in her age category were called. The names were called alphabetically. Her name was the fourth on the list!

"What'll I do now?" she whispered.

"Follow instructions, dear." Mom waited while Heather was asked to walk up and down a long aisle, with folding chairs set up on either side.

She felt very much like she did when she was skating. Gliding was more like it. She knew how to put one leg in front of the other, point her feet, and move gracefully.

"Thanks, Miss Bock," the woman said. "Can you and your mother return this evening?"

"Yes, I believe we can."

"At that time, we'll give you additional information about our company, how long we've been in business . . . that sort of thing. We can't guarantee any certain type of job, be it runway or catalog."

"That's fine," she said. "Thank you."

She could hardly keep from dashing back to the area where Mom sat. "I made it! They want me," she said. "Can you believe this is happening?"

Mom smiled and gave her a big hug. "Honey, I know how beautiful you are. No, I'm not a bit surprised."

Joanne and Tommy were surprised, though. And impressed. They trotted around behind her at home all afternoon. "Make way for Queen Heather," Joanne kept saying.

"I'll hold the edge of your royal robe," Tommy said.

"And *I'll* make her crown!" declared Joanne.

"Will you two cut it out," Heather said. "Mom, make them stop!"

Mom did her best, but when they were supposed to be working on social studies at the table, Joanne kept whispering, "Your Majesty . . ."

"Quit it," she whispered back. "I can't concentrate on my work."

Kevin sat at the opposite end of the table. "You've got it coming, Heather," he said.

"Meaning what?" she demanded.

"You know." But he refused to explain.

Heather told herself she really didn't care at all. Let him say what he wanted. Truth was, *he* was the problem.

———

"Are we going back tonight?" Heather asked before supper.

"Maybe you and I will go together," Mom said. "You know how Dad feels about skipping church on Wednesday nights."

"Oh, that's right." She hadn't even remembered.

"How do you feel about being chosen?" Mom asked.

"Fine, if Joanne and Tommy would settle down about it."

Mom nodded, turning to open the cupboard, reaching for five plates. "I think you should have a long talk with Kevin before you decide about modeling, though."

"Why?"

"Kevin's future is on the line if you become distracted with something other than skating."

She'd gotten so caught up in her own interests, she hadn't even thought of Kevin. Or how any of this would affect him. "Do I *have* to talk to him?"

"Kevin's the other half of your ice-dancing partnership," Mom said. "You'll have to deal with him first."

She took a deep breath, not looking forward to discussing things with her older brother. "I'll be in my room," she told Mom.

"Heather?" Mom called after her.

She turned to see Mom standing with her apron on, holding the dishes and the paper napkins. "Have you prayed about any of this?"

"Not really."

"Well, honey, will you?" Mom's last effort.

"Sure," she said. "I'll pray."

What could it hurt?

Photo Perfect
Chapter Sixteen

They want me, she thought, standing at her bedroom window, looking out. She honestly believed that her plan to boycott eating, losing the few extra pounds, was the real reason she had been picked.

"I have the look," she whispered to the sky.

The sun was setting over the mountains, casting a purplish glow over the snow-scattered lawn and trees. She leaned on the windowsill and wondered how things might've turned out if she hadn't gone on the crash diet. Would she have been thin enough?

Mom wants me to pray, she thought. Yet inside, she felt proud of her personal accomplishments. So what if Kevin didn't approve. She could fit everything into her schedule. She knew she could.

What she really wanted to do was phone Livvy, tell

her the good news. But she'd told her mother she was coming to her room to talk to God.

Standing in the window while the sun shed its daytime duties, giving in to the twilight, she began to pray. "Dear Lord, since you know me so well, I'm sure you must know how *really* excited I am right now. It's so amazing to be chosen like this."

She paused, recalling how her dad liked to hear of her achievements, about the events of her day. She continued praying, picturing her heavenly Father listening intently, his eyes on her, wanting to share in her happiness. "I want to be . . ." Stopping, she felt suddenly sad. "I guess I ought to say that I want to be like you, God. But the truth is, I want my own way. I'm stubborn. And Kevin made me so mad when he dropped me and said . . . he said I was too heavy. I know that's not true. How could he say something so stupid?"

She sat down on the floor and cried. "I'm sorry, Lord. I had to do things my way. It was always about me . . . never about you." She brushed the tears away. "Forgive me for being such a jerk to my brother. For . . . depriving myself of food, just because I was so angry, so determined. And so wrong."

Her heart opened wide to God, and she stayed there in the stillness long after she had said "Amen."

———

Kevin seemed surprised to see her when she went downstairs to the family room. Sure enough, he was lifting weights. Probably so he could lift *her* and feel strong and poised on the ice.

"I'll be out of here in a minute," he mumbled.

"That's okay, take your time." She switched on the treadmill, setting it on one of the slowest settings. She would wait him out. Talk to him when he was finished huffing and puffing and stopped perspiring all over the place.

"So . . . when do you start your modeling work?" he asked.

"I'm not."

"But I thought—"

"When you're finished working out, we'll talk." She continued walking at a snail's pace on the treadmill.

Upstairs, something wonderful was simmering on the stove. The smells from the kitchen were wafting down, tantalizing her as she breathed steadily, not overdoing it.

"I'm finished now." Kevin was standing in front of her. "So talk."

She looked at her brother. Almost a mirror image of herself. *My dear brother and partner,* she thought.

"I'm sorry," she blurted. "I was stupid."

"So was I," he said.

"What?"

His face was serious, almost sad. "I think I started this whole mess, didn't I . . . about you not eating?"

"Don't blame yourself," she said quickly.

"Well, I do." He leaned his head against her forehead. "We have to work harder at considering each other's feelings."

"From now on," she promised.

"Me too."

"Race you upstairs?" she said, daring him.

"Bet I can eat more supper than you," Kevin teased.

"Bet you can't."

———

Joanne was setting the table when Heather came into the dining room. "I've been borrowing your body books," the younger girl confessed.

"So you're admitting it . . . you've been hanging out in my room, after all?"

"Just *borrowing,* that's all." Joanne was determined, it seemed, not to be called a liar.

"Why didn't you ask me?" She placed the napkins under the forks on the left.

"Didn't feel like it." Joanne cast an I-dare-you–to-yell-at-me look.

She waited for Joanne to finish with the knives and spoons. "Does this mean you're keeping your nose out of my stuff?"

"Maybe."

"You'd better."

Joanne grinned up at her. "Guess if you can forgive Kevin, you can forgive me, too."

She hugged her bold little sister. "Yeah, I guess so."

———

Mom laughed till she cried when Heather told her the news. "I think I'd rather go to church tonight."

"You're going to skip the modeling meeting?" Joanne said, twirling around in the kitchen.

"I sure am." She couldn't help but smile. And Kevin was grinning right along with her. "Tomorrow, I need to get my hair trimmed at Dottie's Boutique," she said, heading for the dining room.

"How come?" Joanne asked.

"Makes me feel lighter." Getting her hair trimmed up always did that for her. It sure beat starving herself. "Do I have time to make a phone call before supper?" she asked Mom.

"Make it quick."

She hurried to the telephone and dialed Jenna's number. "I've got some good news for you."

"Let me guess," Jenna said. "It's about the modeling agency?"

"Sort of." She wouldn't make Jenna guess anymore. She told her the *real* news. "I won't be poking around at my food anymore. Doc says if I get back up to one hundred and five pounds, I'll be about right for my frame and build."

"You're photo perfect, Heather."

"Thanks," she said, believing it.

"Any time."

"I made the final cut with the modeling agency," she told her. "But I've decided you were right. I want to focus on ice dancing for now. Skating . . . and good health."

Heather wondered what was keeping Mom in the kitchen. She could hardly wait to say good-bye to Jenna and find out.

"The food smells so good," she told Mom.

Her mother smiled and dished up the baked potatoes. "Glad to hear it."

Heather carried the large bowl into the dining room. "Everybody, come and get it," she called, the first to be seated at the table.

After the prayer, Mom announced, "We're *all* going to church tonight."

Dad seemed to catch on without probing. His eyes smiled at the corners as he reached for his napkin.

"But first we're *all* going to eat supper," Heather said, picking up her fork. Her pin-thin days were definitely past.

Star Status

AUTHOR'S NOTE

It was a great honor and thrill for my family to witness (and cheer on!) the Salt Lake 2002 Olympic Torch Relay as it came through our little mountain town, on its way across America. We are now the proud owners of red pennants that read: "I saw the flame."

You can find out more about the 2002 Olympic Games at *www.olympics.com,* as well as the history of the Olympics and other exciting information. Enjoy!

Thanks to the International Ski Federation for vital information, as well as to my husband, Dave, an amazing skier of black diamond slopes.

To
Charlotte Rose Brown,
a true and shining star
to all who know her.

Star Status
Chapter One

Miranda Garcia awakened before dawn, shivering. She reached for her comforter and pulled it up to her chin. Then, lying in the stillness, she listened for the furnace to kick on, straining to hear the soft purr of warm air creeping through the vents and into her room.

She waited for what seemed like hours, and still no heat. The longer she waited, the colder the tip of her nose was getting.

The last time she'd shivered uncontrollably was nearly a year ago. Actually, she had been *much* colder then, thanks to a swift-moving spring snowstorm that hurtled down on her and her ski instructor, Coach Hanson, as they worked the course. They had been speeding down the steep and treacherous Cascade Peak when the freak storm blew in out of nowhere, over the continental divide. There was little either of them could do when the blinding snow and fierce winds caught them off guard. Manda stumbled off course, finding a tree to hug, calling for Coach until the ski patrol finally came and rescued them both. But it was the bone-biting cold that stamped itself on her brain . . . and she wondered, at the time, if she might freeze to death so close to her home, just a few blocks from the base of the mountain.

Manda, as she preferred to be called, had grown up in Alpine Lake, Colorado, a ski-resort town where there was plenty of opportunity for Alpine ski racing—her greatest passion in life. She also took ballet classes, lifted weights, and ran long distance—especially during the summertime "off season"—to keep in shape and build stamina. The exercise also helped her to maintain the "legs of steel" necessary to muscle through high-speed turns, as well as to endure the thrashing of the steep and rugged downhill course. On top of that, Manda tried to squeeze in time for homework, a baby-sitting job after school, and her once-a-week Girls Only club meetings with three other Olympic-crazed friends: Livvy, Jenna, and Heather.

Lately, though, she found herself twiddling her thumbs at club meetings. There were just way too many distractions, it seemed. Her next race was beginning to "close in," which meant that along with grueling and exhausting physical preparation, there was mental groundwork to be laid before the race. March 17, St. Patrick's Day. Ten days away.

Girls Only Club members will understand, she thought. After all, the four of them were head over heels into athletics. Livvy Hudson's dream was to someday skate in the Olympics. Jenna Song's goal was elite-level gymnastics—for the next couple of years. And Heather Bock's main interest was ice dancing with her older brother; the pair were now up for Junior-level international competition.

For Manda, spacing out at the last few club meetings was essential to focus on her next event: the Dressel Hills Downhill Classic. This year, the stakes were exceptionally high. *"VIPs will be watching in the crowd,"* Coach Hanson had said. He felt she was primed and ready to be noticed. She must place high. Snagging first place had become her obsession.

She slipped out of bed and pulled on her robe. Then she hurried down the hall to her mother's bedroom. Mom was sitting on the edge of her bed, wearing a thick, blue terry cloth bathrobe, her crutches propped against the bureau nearby. On one foot, Mom wore a furry white slipper. A full leg cast graced her other foot, due to a bad break on the slopes a month ago.

"It's freezing in here," Manda said, standing in the doorway.

Mom looked up. "The furnace must be on the blink."

"Again?" Manda groaned. "I'll go downstairs and fiddle with the thermostat; maybe that'll trigger something." She really hoped so, because the last time the furnace played hooky was over a year ago, during Christmas break from school. What a disaster *that* was!

She and her mom had gone shopping in Denver for the day, returning home to a burst water pipe. They'd spent days cleaning up the flooded mess, moving furniture, disposing of soggy rugs, having the hardwood floors retreated. Time-consuming stuff right in the middle of Alpine ski racing season . . . a major pain.

In the end, it was Mom's younger brother, Uncle Frank, who'd come to their financial rescue. The kind and cheerful soul had been helping them off and on since Manda's dad had left the family. Yep, it was Uncle Frank who was mainly responsible for Manda's dream-come-true life of downhill racing. He'd supplied first-rate ski instructors since second grade, and extra money for lift tickets, racing gear, and travel to Alpine ski races across the country.

Rich and caring uncles come in handy, Manda thought gratefully, knowing that her hope to gain Olympic status would have been futile otherwise.

Downstairs, she stared at the thermostat, first pushing it all the way back to fifty degrees. She waited a few seconds, then slowly inched the setting up to sixty-eight, right where Mom normally set it during cold months. She stared at the thermostat for several moments, hoping at least the fan might turn on. But nothing happened.

Frustrated, she went to the fireplace and stacked up a few logs. Then she wadded up old newspapers before striking a match. "This'll have to do for now," she muttered. Crouching low, she watched the flame catch the papers, anxious to get the chill off the house before breakfast.

The minute the plumbing and heating company opened, Mom would be phoning for assistance. About now, they could use a bright sunrise and extra-warm chinook winds. So far, March in Colorado's high country had been anything but mild. Winter months were known to be weird and wacky in Alpine Lake. Unpredictable at best.

Manda blew gently on the flame, hoping to get the logs burning good and strong as soon as possible. Anything to keep the water pipes in this old house from exploding again. There was rarely any money left over at the end of the month for emergencies—burst pipes or furnace repairmen. Uncle Frank would probably shell out for a new furnace pretty soon, but knowing Mom, they would try to "make do" until next fall. After all, summer was only a few months away. If they could just make it till warmer weather . . .

"I've got a nice fire going in the fireplace," Manda called up the steps. "Maybe that'll keep the water pipes warm enough." She truly hoped so.

Mom appeared at the top of the stairs. "I'm sure you're right, dear. Now . . . we'll just trust the Lord to take care of things." Slowly, Mom made her way down the stairs, favoring her formerly broken leg. "What're you hungry for?" she asked.

Breakfast? Hmm. Manda hadn't really thought about eating. But today was going to be exceptionally busy, so she opted for eggs, toast, fruit, and a high-energy protein drink made in the blender.

"Oh, before I forget, is it all right if Tarin Greenberg hangs out here after preschool?" Manda asked. Five-year-old Tarin was her baby-sitting charge three times a week. With the Downhill Classic creeping closer, it was becoming more difficult to concentrate on her speed and the race itself. Homework was the only thing, so far, she hadn't chopped out of her demanding schedule. "Would you mind watching him for me?"

Mom agreed to baby-sit. "Just don't forget to notify Mr. Greenberg about Tarin—that *I* will be in charge of him today."

Manda noticed the twinkle in her mother's eye at the mention of Tarin's father. In just two weeks, Mom and Mr. Greenberg had attended a concert in Denver, sipped cappuccino in the nearby village mall, and gone out for dinner twice. Not exactly sure what Manda dared to expect for the future—was a marriage proposal on the horizon? She certainly had high, secret hopes for Mom marrying the handsome, kind, and dashing widower.

A forever kind of love would be nice this time around. Now, there was an interesting concept: a man who actually stayed put in their lives—other than cool Uncle Frank, of course.

At times, Manda struggled with her true motivation for coveting star status on the slopes. Was it a deep-down desire to get her dad's attention—wherever he was on the planet—by making her mark in the world of Alpine ski racing? Was *that* the reason she wanted to succeed as a downhill whiz?

Last week she'd confided in Heather Bock, her best girl friend, about how to draw on every fiber of her being to win . . . win . . . win. "It's ingrained in me. I *have* to win."

"Why? So you feel good about yourself?" Heather asked, frowning.

"I'm a winning machine," Manda declared.

"But what's behind your drive?" her friend asked in the privacy of Manda's bedroom. "Is it about going to the Olympics? Is that it?"

Manda had fallen silent that afternoon. But not for long. Slowly, thoughtfully, Manda opened up even more, revealing her enduring heartache. "We don't even know if my dad's dead or alive," she said softly. "It's been years, and even though Mom's divorce is final, we're not sure where he is."

Heather didn't skip a beat. "But you'd like to know for sure, right?"

Manda bowed her head. "Not anymore," she whispered. "No. I don't even remember him."

Heather reached over and touched Manda's hand. "Why don't you just ski for yourself, Manda," she'd said. "Not to stick out head and shoulders above other superb skiers. Forget about impressing anyone, getting your name in lights or news headlines. Do your sport for *you*."

In that moment, her friend had pierced through a lot of junk, like a good therapist who, after months and months of listening, helps you open the key to your heart in a safe place.

Manda choked back tears, and Heather prayed that God's hand would rest on "my best friend's life—her downhill racing and *everything* she does." Heather's prayer had been a new beginning in many ways. Now Manda was encouraged more than ever to trust the issue of her rejection to her heavenly Father. God's will was *her* goal. With or without Daddy in her life.

"I'll call Mr. Greenberg right after breakfast," Manda told her mom as they sat down to eat. "You're sure you don't mind watching Tarin?"

Mom's dark brown eyes softened at the sound of the little boy's name. "Why would I mind?" she asked. "I enjoy having Tarin around . . . anytime."

"Just checking."

"Tarin's good company," Mom said with a grin.

Excellent, thought Manda, hoping Mom might also *enjoy* having the little boy as a stepson someday. Maybe . . .

Star Status
Chapter Two

The phone rang just as Manda had finished dressing. She was dashing down the stairs when Mom answered. "For you, Manda," Mom called from the kitchen.

She hurried to the portable phone. "Who is it?" she mouthed the words.

"Jenna Song." Mom handed over the telephone, offering an encouraging smile. "Be nice," she whispered.

Yeah, right. Manda remembered how Jenna had been bugging her off and on for the past week. True, she *had* been dragging her feet about all things social, including Girls Only Club meetings, but was that any reason to hound her about it?

"Hey, Jen," she said. "What's up?"

"I was wondering that about *you*." Jenna sighed loudly

into the phone. "Is something wrong? I mean, you're basically spaced out twenty-four/seven, you know?"

"Like I told you weeks ago, the Classic's coming at me fast. I'm thinking of dropping out of everything till it's over." She almost said *everything unnecessary,* but caught herself.

"What about Sunday school and church?" Jenna asked.

Manda wasn't surprised at the question. In fact, she was pretty sure Jen would bring that topic up for discussion. "Well . . . I don't know."

"I do! I've heard you didn't show up last week for youth group. What's with that?"

She's heard? Manda flinched at the interrogation. She wished it didn't bother her. Evidently, her friends were talking behind her back, reporting to Jen and who knows who else about her church attendance—or lack of it.

"Our youth pastor was out of town, so youth group was actually canceled." Which was completely true. Jenna simply hadn't paid close attention to the happenings at Manda's church. Besides, if she'd really been in the know, Jen would've accused Manda of not showing up for the adult service instead.

Manda had no time to argue. Besides, she really wasn't enjoying these conversations with the pompous president of their otherwise way cool club. Jenna could just keep attending her dad's Korean-speaking church and mind her own business. "Look, I've gotta run," Manda said quickly.

"Isn't it a little early to leave for school?" Jenna quizzed her.

"Not school . . . not yet." She was tired of the drilling. Since when was she required to inform her friend of every little move she made, the tiniest details of her life? "I'm going to the gym to work out for an hour before school. See ya."

Manda hung up without waiting for Jen to say good-bye. She carried the phone into the living room, depositing it with flair onto the coffee table.

"Everything okay?" Mom was hovering near the fireplace, an afghan wrapped around her shoulders.

"Sure . . . fine." Manda pulled on her jacket and filled her backpack with her binder and other school essentials.

"Aren't you forgetting something?" Mom asked.

"Oops." She reached for the phone and dialed Mr. Greenberg's cell number. When he answered, she said that her mom was going to baby-sit for Tarin today. "It'll probably be for the next few days," she said, reminding him of the race. "Then things will be back to normal."

Whatever normal is, she thought.

"Sure, Manda. I'll drop Tarin off there. Thanks for

letting me know," Mr. Greenberg said. "Placing in the Downhill Classic is top priority for you, of course."

She could visualize his warm and encouraging smile. "Thanks for understanding."

After she hung up once again, she hurried to the front door. Her hand was on the doorknob when Mom said, "You'll be glad to know that a furnace repairman is on his way."

"Great."

"I phoned while you were in the shower," Mom added.

"Well, stay close to the fire. I don't want you catching cold." She went and kissed Mom on the cheek. "Better give Uncle Frank a call. He'll give you what for if he finds out there's a problem."

They exchanged knowing smiles, then Manda hurried out the door. She caught the city bus to AAG—Alpine Aerial Gymnastics—Jenna's turf. All the while, she thought about the upcoming race, hoping and praying that everything on the home front would be just fine. Soon!

Truth was, she couldn't afford to deal with any more critical issues. Not defunct furnaces, not a wayward father, and certainly not her lack of attendance at church. She was up to here with Jenna's friendly but too-frequent phone reminders. How would Jen like it if Manda did that to *her* before a gymnastics meet? She couldn't imagine poking her nose in Jenna Song's athletic schedule or life. Never.

It wasn't the weight lifting that Manda minded as she worked out at the gym. It was Jenna's voice, ricocheting back and forth in her head, that was unbearable. As hard as she tried, she couldn't shake the memory of her friend's accusing voice. Did Jen actually think Manda was a bad person, staying away from God's house? And just because she'd missed youth group last week. *Get over it!*

Sure, she'd missed last Sunday's service, too. But it wasn't like she'd stayed away without good reason. The day had been well spent, and Mom had approved. Manda and her teammates, along with Coach, had biked long distance to Dressel Hills, the choice ski resort to the north of Alpine Lake. She was working extra hard to catch up, getting fired up to trounce the mountain.

Until recently, one setback after another had occurred, mostly because of her mom's broken leg. To help out, Manda stepped in as instructor last month for the preschool ski class at Alpine Ski Academy where her mom worked.

Manda was that way—always looking out for others—"wearing the pants in the family," her mom often said. Her girl friends thought she'd become so take-charge because her dad wasn't around. But Manda wasn't so sure. All her life, she'd remembered being exceptionally confident, eager, and ready to take on the world.

Now . . . if she could just conquer one more thing: a monster of a mountain!

Can I do it? she asked herself, lifting one leg weight after another, feeling the burn in her muscles. She huffed her breath out one side of her cheek, filling her lungs long and deep, thinking through the downhill course on Eagle's Point in Dressel Hills. Today, after school, she and Coach and her teammates were headed there again for several hours of practice on the beast of a slope. The more she skied the mountain, the more poise—and speed—she could rally. And she would memorize the course, as well. When it came to great skiing, memory played a vital role.

Manda had always had lots of opportunities to ski after Uncle Frank started picking up the monthly tab. The cost of lift tickets was nothing to sneeze at. Growing up in a ski-resort town, she could simply hurry off to the chair lifts and ride up the mountain after schoolwork was finished. Starting with the bunny slopes when she was only a toddler, she'd been fol-lowing her mother down the slopes, getting faster with each run. And there were school trips to Vail and Aspen, where she would ski with her classmates, always competing, no matter the circumstance. She

was hard-wired for ski racing. But could sheer determination, total concentration, and physical prowess
snag her the coveted first place?

Was there more to winning?

Star Status
Chapter Three

For supper that night, Manda helped her mom make oven-baked chicken, potatoes, and glazed carrots. As always, there was a fresh vegetable salad with Mom's own vinegar-and-oil dressing in a garlic-rubbed bowl. The tangy smell of peach cobbler, made with far less sugar than the recipe called for, filled the kitchen. Manda was a fanatic about her sugar intake. Too much was a killer on the slopes when she needed to draw on the stamina and grit that separated the good skiers from a superior dynamo. She didn't call herself Downhill Dynamite for nothing.

"What was I *really* like as a kid?" she asked her mom after dinner as they both settled comfortably into the living room furniture.

The living room—the entire house—was toasty and

warm tonight, thanks to a prompt visit by a local furnace repairman. The logs in the fireplace crackled and snapped, casting flickers of light on the wall. Soft violin music played in the background. The perfect setting and time for a heart-to-heart talk.

Looking up from her magazine, Mom grinned across the room. "Hey, you're *still* a kid, don't forget."

"You know what I mean." Manda sat cross-legged on the couch. "I've got my own memories of who I think I was back then, but I want your spin on it," she said with a sigh. "So . . . what kind of little person was I?"

Mom chuckled softly, then grew more serious. "The truth?"

"The works." Manda settled back against the couch.

"Well, let's see. You were precocious, for starters . . . almost too smart for your britches from day one."

"What else?"

"Everyone who knew you said how determined you were. Even as a baby, you had strong preferences for when and what you wanted. There was no doubt about that."

Manda liked the sound of this. "So, was I a fighter?"

"You were very confident . . . still are. Once, you told me that you had your heart set on winning Olympic gold someday. That was after watching the winter Olympics on TV when you were only five years old."

"I said that?" She couldn't remember the occasion.

"Like I said, you were stubborn about certain things. That's what makes you get out there and ski your best."

"Ski my brains out, right?" replied Manda.

Mom laughed again. "I think a few brain remnants might come in handy at the race, if you know what I mean."

"Isn't that the truth," she whispered, thinking of the powerful skiers she and her teammates would be up against.

———

Much later in the evening, Mom brought up the topic of Tarin Greenberg. "He wasn't quite himself today."

"Probably missed his number one sitter." Manda felt smug and good, missing the little boy.

Mom was thoughtful for a moment, then she said, "I can't really say what struck me differently, but he certainly wasn't his usual cheerful self."

Manda wondered about that. Tarin was the ultimate precocious kid, filling up his free time with excursions through dictionaries and sometimes even online encyclopedias. The little boy could turn on articulate expression with a capital A!

She thought back to her first encounter with him. A few short weeks ago, she had interviewed for an after-school baby-sitting job with Tarin and his father. Exasperating, to say the least. Tarin was a boy with an exceptionally high IQ—a five-year-old genius—who knew three languages, and initially had preferred his attention-getting routine, designed to wow every adult he came in contact with. Absolutely obnoxious, that was Tarin Greenberg. Yet, somehow, she'd won the kid over, partly with the help of her harmonica. She could whip out her tiny mouth organ and play a melody or two, and Tarin calmed right down. Amazing! Who would believe it?

"Do you think Tarin's upset about something?" Manda asked her mother.

"Like what?"

Manda shrugged. "Oh, I don't know."

"Well, you must have something in mind," Mom replied.

Sure, she had something whirling around in her head. But to bring it up with Mom might be just a tad touchy. No . . . she didn't think tonight was a good time to discuss Mom's growing friendship with Tarin's father.

"Manda?" Mom pressed for more.

She knows me too well, thought Manda, fidgeting.

"Okay," she said. She uncrossed her legs and looked her mom square in the face. "I'll level with you."

"Cool," Mom said, the word slipping out so easily.

"Not cool . . . *please* don't say that, Mom. It just doesn't fit someone your age—not to be mean or anything, it's just that—"

"So *I'm* not cool—too old to be cool, right?"

Oh boy, here we go . . . "Back to Tarin," Manda said quickly.

"I'm all ears."

Taking a deep breath, Manda continued. "Tarin's got his hopes up . . . you know, about you and Mr. Greenberg. The future and all that."

Mom fell silent.

"And, well, I guess Tarin and I are in the same boat."

"You're hoping that his dad and I end up together?" Mom asked.

Manda wondered, *Do I dare say it?*

"Is that what you meant to say?" Mom probed.

"Not just together as in dating or engaged, but *married.*" There, the word—the all-important topic—was out in the wide open for Mom to toss around in her brain and in her heart. Manda was all for Mr. Greenberg courting and marrying her mother. The sooner, the better.

Mom closed her magazine and leaned forward,

sliding it on top of several others on the coffee table. She touched the artificial floral centerpiece momentarily. Her face was solemn now, and she seemed to be mulling things over. At last, she said, "Mr. Greenberg— Matthew—and I have been praying quite seriously about our friendship. And yes, I must say that things are moving along rather nicely."

Rather nicely. Whatever that meant. "Do you mean he's interested in courting you?"

"It's a bit soon for that, dear," Mom said, obviously struggling to keep her smile muscles under control. "But you'll be the first to know."

"You mean . . . you might be getting close to an exclusive dating relationship?" She had to know, had to hear the promise of the future—*their* future—from her mother's lips.

"Honey, let's not rush things, okay? After all, I've only known the man a short time."

"But you've been seeing each other a lot lately. Doesn't that count for something?"

Mom couldn't suppress her smile any longer. "For goodness' sake, girl, you must want Mr. Greenberg for your father in the worst way."

"In the *best* way . . ." *If Mom only knew,* she thought.

"Oh, honey, let's do this in God's timing," Mom said.

"Okay," Manda was quick to answer. "But a little

help from some of God's friends won't hurt anything, right?"

Mom stood up then, said she was tired and ready for a bedtime snack, and did Manda want to join her in the kitchen? In other words, it was time to bring this particular discussion to a polite but swift end.

Manda was smart enough to let the Matthew Greenberg issue drop. For now.

Star Status
Chapter Four

Manda awoke in the night, trying to get a grip on the dream that had startled her awake. The dream had been sad; there was still a lumpy feeling in her throat, like instant mashed potatoes that someone had made with too little hot water or milk. The feeling was all globbed up . . . stuck to her throat.

Her room was dimly lit by only the hallway night-light. She could see the outline of several posters featuring downhill ski champs on her wall, including American-born Picabo Street, German skier Katja Seizinger, and Austrian powerhouse Hermann Maier.

Manda rubbed her temples, trying to recall her dream. At least it hadn't been a nightmare. But it *had* been sad, and she didn't know why. Things were all mixed up in her head now. Confused and overwhelmed, she cried softly, using her pillow as a buffer, hoping she wouldn't awaken her mother. There was no need for Adelina Garcia's peaceful sleep to be disturbed, for her to come running to comfort Manda as she often had done in the past. No need for soothing whispers. Those days of sadness and despair were past. At least, she wanted her mom to think so.

Manda was tough enough to handle whatever junk was lodged in her subconscious. "Tough and tumble," Mom liked to call her, referring to Manda's approach to speed and daring on the slopes. So why couldn't she conquer the treacherous slopes of her daily life?

There was, of course, the complication of Manda's father, the fact that he'd never been heard from after leaving Alpine Lake when she was just two years old. A few rumors had filtered around here and there as to his whereabouts, but no one seemed to have any rock-solid info. Mom was perfectly entitled to remarry, having been granted a divorce due to abandonment several years ago. But the gaping hole in the whole scenario bothered Manda. If not consciously, then it was buried deep in her heart.

She knew she was taking on way too much these days. At just twelve years old, what *could* she do, really? Manda knew she'd have to lighten up if she was going to impress the socks off any VIPs hanging out on the slopes of Eagle's Point at the Dressel Hills Downhill Classic.

Just cool it, she told herself. Yeah, right. Like *that* was all it took to make things better, talking to yourself in the middle of the night. Having a one-way conversation in your head.

———

"Are you coming to ballet tomorrow?" Livvy asked her at their lockers the next morning.

"I'll think about it," Manda said.

"What about Girls Only Club?"

She paused. "Yeah, maybe."

Livvy was kind. She said no more. But looking at her, Manda could sense the wheels whirring in her friend's pretty head. No question, Livvy was probably thinking that one of their club members wasn't pulling her weight anymore. Which, in a lot of ways, was true.

At least Livvy didn't shoot her mouth off like Jenna would have—in fact, the way Jenna had yesterday on the phone. Livvy smiled her sweetest smile, turned to the locker she shared with Jenna, and began pulling textbooks down from the top shelf, stuffing her backpack for the day.

"*You're* not mad at me, are you?" Manda said, opening her own locker.

"Why should I be?"

"But someone else is . . . right?" Manda was thinking of Jenna.

Livvy nodded her head, her auburn hair swirling about her shoulders. "The prez is threatening to call a special meeting . . . uh, about, well . . ." Livvy's pretty face grew more serious. "To tell you the truth, Jenna thinks maybe you're just too distracted, as a club member."

"Aren't *all* of us preoccupied with our sports?" Manda shot back. "Isn't that what the club's support system is all about?"

"You know what . . . if you'd just talk to Jenna, that might help. Level with her," suggested Livvy. "Tell her you actually *like* coming to club meetings, that you aren't just using your upcoming race as—"

"As what?" Manda cut in.

Livvy hoisted her backpack up over one petite shoulder. "Well, as an excuse, I guess . . . to space out during Girls Only."

"Is that honestly what you think?"

"We think you're in way over your head," was Livvy's reply.

"Excuse me? What's this *we think* stuff?" She couldn't believe what she was hearing. What did Livvy know, anyway? She thought back to her very private conversation with Heather. Yep, she'd leveled with Heather about some personal things. So . . . what was all this stuff Livvy was saying? Had Heather actually broken a confidence and blabbed to Jenna and Livvy about Manda's obsession with her father's whereabouts?

How could she? Manda thought, wishing Heather were here at school instead of being schooled at home.

Livvy pressed her lips together, then said, "I'd better not say any more. I've probably said too much already."

If the bell hadn't rung just then, Manda might've gone off on Livvy, telling her what she thought of Jenna and Heather both.

Really, she was relieved to hear the bell signaling first period. Time to get on with her life . . . her school life. Forget social life. Jenna, Livvy, and Heather could have their precious meetings without her if that's what they wanted. And they could kick her out of the club, too, for all she cared. Why were they picking on her, anyway?

Manda tried hard to put an end to the negative notions flying around in her head. The more she stewed over Jenna and Girls Only, the worse she would continue to feel all day. And the poorer she would perform today after school when she hit the slopes.

I don't need this! She closed her locker and hurried down the hallway to class. She thought of her beloved harmonica, wishing it were nestled deep in her school bag. About now, she could use some calming down.

Star Status
Chapter Five

Manda gazed at the hazardous downhill course. Like a slumbering white bear, the mountain towered above the town of Alpine Lake, its precipitous slope lying in wait for her. Today, the vertical drop looked unusually steep. She could see the first gate—two poles with a red rectangular panel between them. Fewer gates were placed on the course for downhill races than in the slalom, giant slalom, and Super G, or super giant slalom. The gates on the downhill course basically provided a safety precaution to keep skiers from going too fast. And to keep skiers away from particularly treacherous areas.

I'm a winning machine, Manda told herself. She had been trying to pump herself up mentally and emotionally. But today had been difficult for her. Heather, her all-time best friend, had possibly broken a confidence, blabbing important, private info to Jenna and Livvy.

Bummed, she crouched low at the starting gate, waiting for the signal. Rocking back and forth on her best skis, she could see the valley below. Narrow streets neatly lined up, mapped out in rows with mostly Victorian houses on either side.

Livvy Hudson's old house was one of the many gray-and-white three-story residences on Main Street. She lived there with her widowed father—an artist with a studio high in the eaves—and her fussy grandmother, a gourmet cook.

Jenna Song and her Korean-American family lived in a large, older house, too. Jenna's attic bedroom was not only huge, it was the incredible retreat for the Friday Girls Only Club meetings. Complete with a barre placed in front of floor-to-ceiling mirrors, the place was spacious and airy. The ideal spot for Jen, Livvy, Heather, and Manda to meet once a week, as well as to practice ballet to some of their favorite music. They'd even presented several full-scale musicals for their families featuring dance and drama.

Heather Bock and her cute older brother, Kevin— also her ice-dancing partner—along with their parents and younger brother and sister, lived not far from both Livvy and Jenna. In fact, all of Manda's closest friends lived within walking distance.

But now, high on Falcon Ridge, Manda turned her attention away from the valley to the job at hand. Fortunately, there was hardly any wind today. A nice change after a week of blowing and drifting snow causing white-out conditions, not conducive to skiing. At least the run was free of excessive ice buildup today. It was Manda's pet peeve, and if not handled correctly, a skier's handicap. A picture-postcard day—the sky was a perfect blue and the mountains were amassed with snow on all sides.

Ski, baby, ski, she thought as the signal came. She was revved up and ready to face the fear factor.

Swoosh! She shot out of the starting gate. The snow was too fresh and slowed her down. She wished she might've been third or fourth on the team to ski today. By then, the others would have pushed the snow off the course a bit. But Coach had them draw numbers for this practice, the way it would be in Dressel Hills at the *real* racing event.

Eager to push her speed to the limit, her raw nerve was on the line. But her wits were out of focus. Hard as she tried, she could not still the echo of words from Livvy's lips. *The prez is threatening to call . . .*

She tried to corral the destructive thought, gather it up in a basket in her mind and hurl it over the abyss to her left on this steep and dangerous course.

The margin for error was small on a slope like this. It was much too precarious for her not to focus.

Swish! Past the first gate, she felt herself losing control in the air. Struggling to right herself, she used her ski pole to balance as she was airborne. Then, *wham,* her skis pounded the packed surface with her landing.

"Ski for yourself," Heather had encouraged her. *"Forget about impressing anyone."*

Zooming down the course, she felt herself shifting too far to the left. She fought hard, but she was helpless. The pull of gravity dragged her down, and she wiped out, sprawled like a butterfly in the snow. *Where's my dynamite?* she wondered, staring up at the blue of the sky. She got up, thoroughly disgusted with the run.

I can't let Jen and Livvy get to me. I won't derail my chances!

Yet she'd have to wait her turn, her chance at a second run. The next skier would be shooting out of the gate at the top within minutes. She'd blown her first run of the day. Her supposed *friends* had whacked her a good one.

Maybe it was a good thing she'd made no effort to settle things with the proud prez of the club. She could've told Livvy she would drop by Jenna's tomorrow, if only for a few minutes to say "hi," show some interest in the club. No problem. But thinking about it now, she felt secretly good about ignoring the girls' continual pleas for her company. Good *and* glad. There was no chance she'd make it to any ridiculous special meetings, either. She had too much to accomplish by the race.

Rubbing her sore leg where she'd fallen, Manda winced, though not so much from physical pain. She was almost sure Jenna would see to it that the three remaining members would vote out the one delinquent member—her.

So what, she thought. *Let them kick me out!*

The ride home from practice in Mom's car took longer than Manda had hoped. Tons of homework awaited her attention. Besides that, she wanted to talk to Heather before it got too late. Wanted to give her dearest friend a call and find out what was going on—who told whom what . . . and why.

Mom stopped off at the grocery store, then made a pit stop at the home of a church friend who was altering a skirt for her. "I'll be just a minute," she said, getting out of the car and hurrying across the street.

Meanwhile, Manda wished she'd brought along some homework, to get a jump on math especially. She was still kicking herself mentally for her lousy run on the slopes. Even though the first attempt was a total wash, the second and third were nothing to brag about, either.

Her speed was as slow as a turtle compared to her time on *better* days. Any good skier could've beat her out today. And *all* her teammates had done so.

"You're not losing your fire, are you?" Coach had asked at the base of the mountain.

"Nope," she'd said, disappointed in herself.

Coach frowned slightly, then said, "First thing tomorrow, you and me . . . we're back out here."

"Sure," she'd replied, tears stinging her eyes. "I'll be here at dawn."

"Good. We'll see if you've got what it takes to place—if you can pull out on demand, when it's just the two of us."

Bummer. Manda wanted—*needed*—the competition and fervor her teammates offered. Their encouragement, too. Something that was sorely lacking in her non-skiing circle of friends.

———

Still waiting in the car—impatiently now—for Mom's return, Manda leaned back on the headrest and tried to relax. If only she were a little older, she could drive herself home. If they had more than one car, that is . . .

Someday, if Matthew Greenberg married her mother, they might finally become a two-car family or more. She'd seen his collection of dust-jacketed clothbound books, rows and rows of them. And there was expensive

414

state-of-the-art electronic equipment in his home office, a big-screen TV in the family room, and a new Porsche in the garage. So, her guess—he was probably rolling in it. For one thing, he didn't skimp on dinner dates with Mom. He also took her to posh places like the local dinner theater and the expensive Broadway-style production in downtown Denver. Yep, she was almost positive the guy was loaded. How else could he afford to send his young son to a private preschool, as well as to after-school instruction at the village's elite ski academy? Only rich kids hung out there.

Quite by accident, she had put herself in that category. Of course, she and Mom knew the truth about their meager finances. Suddenly, she realized time was running out, and she hadn't even invited Uncle Frank to the race.

What am I thinking? she wondered. Her mom's brother, above all people, deserved an invitation to the competition in Dressel Hills. Tonight, she would offer a formal invite by phone. Mom wouldn't mind if she made it quick.

Thinking about Uncle Frank, she caught herself staring over at the steering wheel. She surveyed the dusty dashboard and upholstered seats. Mom's car was nothing to look at or brag about. But when it came to reliability, that's where this old coupe shone. It started up and purred on the severest winter days, when newer cars in the neighborhood choked and sputtered, merely sitting.

I don't want a stepdad just so we have more money, she thought. And that was certainly not what motivated her growing interest in Mr. Greenberg's dating relationship with Mom. No, there was much more to it. Mom's radiant smile and genuinely cheerful countenance counted for a lot. Her mom enjoyed her job as ski instructor, adored her daughter, and savored every tiny slice of living. She was an all-around pleasant, fun-loving person.

But this . . . Mom's ongoing sunny disposition was something very special. Her mother just might be falling in love, and Manda couldn't be happier, at least about that one aspect of their lives.

———

"Coach ordered me to the slopes first thing tomorrow," she said when Mom returned to the car at last.

"Extra practice can only help," Mom said. She started the car and pulled away from the curb.

If she only knew . . . Manda wondered how long she should wait before describing her horrendous afternoon on the mountain.

Slowly, they passed through the small residential area of Alpine Lake. Large aspen trees, bare and stark against painted clapboard houses, lined the streets on both sides. And there was an occasional pedestrian, bundled up against the cold.

A storm front had been forecast for later tonight—more snow on the way. Would she have to battle new powder on the slopes again tomorrow? Still, she had been trained to deliver speed and agility no matter the slope conditions. Powder or packed powder, she couldn't blame today's miserable performance on the weather. Yet Manda was looking for *something* to sink her concentration into. Anything but the hard, cold facts.

Star Status
Chapter Six

"Are Mr. Greenberg and Tarin coming to the race?" Manda asked her mom as they cooked supper together.

"I'm sure they'll want to," Mom said.

"Did you invite them yet?"

Mom pointed to the telephone. "Why don't you do the honors."

Manda nodded. "Sure. After supper."

She and her mother kept busy cooking spaghetti with vegetarian sauce, green beans, and steamed carrots and onions. Mom made a delicious tossed green salad while Manda set the table and poured hot herbal tea into mugs. "I guess I thought you'd already invited them," Manda pushed as they sat down to eat.

Mom's eyes took on a curious expression. "Is something bothering you, honey?"

Groaning inwardly, she didn't want Mom to discourage anyone from showing up. She needed all the moral support she could get. But she was struggling. The important race was coming at her so fast she felt dizzy sometimes. "I . . . I don't think I can get ready in time," she confessed. "And I'm not kidding."

Mom's head popped up, and her fork hovered there in midair. "But you want to win more than anything, don't you?"

"Sure, I want it. That's all I think about every minute of every day. But there's so much garbage in my head." She couldn't possibly get into it.

"Manda, for goodness' sake, what's happening?"

She shrugged. "Coach is a little worried. That's all."

"How worried?"

Reaching for her water glass, Manda took a deep breath. "To tell you the truth, I think he's really freaked. Enough to try to pull something out of me tomorrow real early."

Mom nodded. "Why's he freaked?"

"He thinks my passion is fizzling," she said.

"Well, is it?" Mom was freaked now, too.

"Maybe . . . or maybe I'm just so fuzzy right now."

"I don't like what I'm hearing," Mom said.

She knew her mother would say something like that. But Manda didn't want to wallow in the problem.

Much more than her enthusiasm had nose-dived lately. But this wasn't the time to dissect any of that.

"Manda, honey, this isn't like you." A disappointed look crossed Mom's face. She was beginning to wonder if Mom had already told her friends that her daughter was going to place high. Higher than ever. *You just wait and see about my Manda. Mark my words, she's a shoe-in for first place.* Knowing Mom, she'd probably announced this all over town!

"It's not about skiing or winning. Sure, I want both." Manda sighed. Could she make Mom, an expert skier, understand? "This is about me."

Mom nodded her head. "Of course it is, sweetie. Getting in shape and gearing up for a race is *all* about you, me, or anyone who's competing. You know that."

"Right." She couldn't believe her mom was going on like this. Had she already talked with Coach? Eyeing her mom, Manda suspected Coach Hanson of having called on his cell phone—maybe from the slopes—right after her infamous wipe-out.

Mom pressed on. "Top-notch skiing is far less about talent and strength than about a clear head."

"Any ideas how I empty out the junk?"

"Just plain focus," Mom replied. "Push out everything else."

"I'm going to lose friends over my amazing ability to concentrate. It's a full-circle nightmare. I focus on the race and ignore my friends, which helps me ski well but stinks socially. Then, because I'm a self-imposed loner—at the moment—I hear about it from all sides. It's eating me up."

Mom scooted her chair out and rose to pour more tea. Across from the table, a small writing desk was set back in a cozy nook complete with overhead lattice-work. A recent flea market find stood nearby, a tall linen cupboard painted a lighthearted blue. All her life, Mom had longed for a cottage-style kitchen. So when they first rented the house, Manda and her mother set to work painting the walls a buttercup yellow, and the woodwork a dazzling white. A whimsical Mary Engelbreit look, minus the clutter. The curtains over the back door and the large window were bright and pretty in poppy flowers. *"Eye-popping poppies,"* Mom had said of the floral fabric found at the discount mill outlet.

When Mom sat down again, her elbows promptly found the tabletop. "You're coming up so close to this race," she said, leaning near. Reaching across the table, she patted Manda's hand. "I hate to see you like this. Your attitude isn't healthy, hon."

"Yeah, and I'm worried, too." There. She'd admitted to being fearful. *More than anything, I want to win. I just don't know how,* thought Manda.

Mom excused her from helping clean up the kitchen.

"Go start your homework," she said. "We'll talk to-morrow, after your early-morning date with the moun-tain."

For a second, Manda was almost sure her mom was going to volunteer to go along. To observe the private ski session with Coach. But Mom opened the dishwasher and began loading their supper plates and silverware. No tagging along tomorrow—that wasn't Mom's style, anyway.

From the time Manda turned eleven, her mother was one to let Manda do her thing on the slopes. Plenty of faith rested on Coach's expert assistance. And Manda appreciated the fact Mom trusted her instincts. There was never any second-guessing when it came to Manda's skiing abilities. Sure, there were hair-raising moments because of the risk factor. But Mom didn't put the brakes on Manda's willpower and raw nerves. Or talent.

She headed upstairs to her room. The carpet had been vacuumed while she was at school. Looking at her bureau and nightstand, she saw that Mom must've dusted, too. *She does too much for me,* Manda thought, hop-ing that someday they could afford someone to help with housecleaning. If Mr. Greenberg married Mom, they might.

She dialed the Greenberg residence. Because she was the regular sitter for Tarin, she had memorized the phone number. When Tarin's father answered, she reminded him of the downhill race on St. Patrick's Day. "I hope you and Tarin can come," Manda said.

"Of course we'll be there," he said. "The wearing of the green, right?"

She had to smile at that. "Tarin won't pinch me if I wear my purple ski outfit, will he? Since I'm not Irish, I'll probably skip the green thing."

"Do as you wish." He chuckled softly. "I'm sure Tarin will be on his best behavior. By the way, would you and your mother like to ride with us to Dressel Hills?"

"Sure, thanks." She was secretly delighted. Yet another opportunity for the four of them to be together. Like a real, complete family.

———

Sitting at her desk, Manda zipped through the long math assignment as quickly as possible. Several times in the course of forty minutes, she was tempted to call Heather. But she made herself finish all the problems first, then double-checked them. That completed, she picked up the portable phone and beeped it on. Today on the slopes had shown her it was past time to clear the air with her best friend. With the other club members, too. This stuff with Jenna, and now Livvy . . . well, she couldn't afford to let any of it interfere with her skiing goals. Not if she was going to redirect her thoughts toward the race, get herself back on the winning track.

Dialing the number for the Bock residence, she waited, counting the rings. At last, on the fourth ring, Heather answered. "Hello?"

"Hey, Heather."

"What's up?"

Manda sighed. "You tell me."

"You don't sound so good. How come?" asked Heather.

Manda felt her throat closing up. Then, slowly, she began to talk, starting with Livvy's threat of Manda's near expulsion from the club, to the bossy way Jenna was acting lately.

"Trust me, everything will be cool," Heather said when Manda finished.

Everything? She felt awkward. Terribly curious, too. "So . . . what's going on with a Girls Only special meeting? Anything I should know about?"

"Why don't you come Saturday and see for yourself?"

"You know I can't," said Manda. "So fill me in."

"Just the usual, you know." Heather seemed guarded.

"Like what?"

"No one's mad at you, if that's what you think."

"Really? I guess I find that hard to believe."

"Are you doubting me?" Heather sounded edgy. Not herself.

"Maybe." Manda felt lousy. "Look, Heather, I'm going to level with you."

"That would help."

She wanted to say this just right. She didn't want Heather to hang up before she finished. "I've been wondering if you told Jenna and Livvy . . . well, you know, about my messed-up way of thinking."

"Messed up about what?"

She sighed. "Did you tell them what I said about my dad? The private things I shared with you?"

Heather answered softly, "I'd never do that, Manda. You should know I'm a better friend than that."

"I just thought—"

"You should have asked me earlier."

"That was my mistake." Manda could hardly talk. She'd blown it badly with her best friend. Thought the worst about her.

They talked awhile longer, flitting from one topic to another. Heather shared the next skating event coming up. Manda talked about getting back to off-ski season, after the race was over.

Later in the conversation, Heather asked point-blank, "Why are you so upset at Jenna?"

Manda was silent.

"You know what?" Heather said before Manda could answer. "Sometimes, I can see Jen's side of things, too.

She really doesn't get why you're so . . . well, distant at club meetings. She's kinda ticked off about it."

Manda had to speak up, had to make a point. "Do you remember last December, when Jen had her gymnastics meet in Colorado Springs? She was so spacey, super obsessed about doing her best . . . and, hey, I didn't mind. I totally understood. We all did."

"Are you saying Jenna should cut you some slack? Is that what you want?"

"It's her choice." She wanted to get off the phone. "I'm too busy for any of this."

Heather was quiet for a while. Then she said, "We all know how stubborn Jenna can be. But it sounds like the club doesn't matter that much to you. So why should I try to fix anything?"

"Okay, then, just forget it," Manda snapped.

Heather paused a second, then asked, "Will I see you at church on Sunday?"

Manda swallowed hard. "I'll see." She had hoped to avoid the issue of church attendance. Her plans for this Sunday did not include Sunday school and church. She wanted to attack the course at Dressel Hills again. If she could get Mom to approve.

"Try to squeeze some time in for God," Heather said unexpectedly.

Then they said good-bye and hung up.

Manda was glad they hadn't plunged too deeply

into talking about church on top of everything else. After all, why should Heather tell her how to spend her weekends?

Manda didn't take time to read her devotional book or her Bible after she hung up. Instead, she got permission from Mom to call Uncle Frank long-distance. "I'm skiing in the Dressel Hills Downhill Classic on St. Patty's Day," she told him the minute he answered. "Want to come and watch?"

Uncle Frank chuckled softly. "Whose uncle do you think I am?" he teased. "Would I miss seeing you race? No way. I'll catch a flight out on Friday afternoon."

"Great," she said, "but I better warn you. I might not be such good company—the day-before syndrome, you know." She paused a moment. She really didn't want to get into it with her uncle about her lack of focus. He'd start in on some lengthy pep talk, and she didn't need that. Not tonight.

"Don't worry about entertaining me," he said before she could continue. "I can hang my hat most anywhere."

"Mom will probably offer to give up her room, like always."

"Tell her I'll crash on the couch," he said. "Don't let her go to any trouble, especially with her leg on the mend. Promise?"

She smiled. Good old Uncle Frank. He had a cool

way of making you want to move heaven and earth for him whenever he came to visit. Even if you didn't have a fancy-tancy guest suite and private bath for him. Just having him stay with them would raise her spirits. But she couldn't wait that long to get pumped up. She had to get in gear now, get with the program. Fast!

In spite of good intentions, Manda slipped into bed, completely forgetting to talk to God. Instead, she played her harmonica softly until there was no breath left for more songs. And she gave in to deep sleep.

Star Status
Chapter Seven

I'm back! Manda thought as she and her coach took the chair lift to the loftiest region of Falcon Ridge. She repeated her thought aloud for Coach. "I'm back," she said, "in a big way."

"That's the grit I like to see." Coach was obviously pleased. "It's a brand-new day." He smiled broadly. "Reach for it and grab a new beginning with all your might." Coach Hanson was very big on the new-beginning-forget-the-mistakes-of-the-past sort of talk. He knew how to push her ahead, past the doldrums and toward a victory. "Can you taste the win, Manda? Can you?"

She smiled. *Here we go.* "I'm tasting, eating, breathing, and sleeping it."

He grinned at her, his face reflecting the deep red

of his ski jacket. "You've been training harder than ever. The Dressel Hills race is your zenith this year—it's the culmination of everything you know. Everything you are."

Everything you are . . .

She was reminded of Heather's pep talk. *"Ski for yourself . . . do your sport for you, Manda."*

"You're very strong," Coach said as they approached mid-point in the ride to the top. "You take a backseat to no one . . . remember?"

Oh, she remembered. Every race she had under her belt told her that. How could she forget the thrill of a successful run, of winning? Claiming the prize, the surge of joy pumping through her veins—knowing she'd beat out the competition. Every single skier on the face of the rugged mountain having placed second or lower than her time.

Just then, something snapped in her head. She knew, without a doubt, this was her breakthrough day. Her new beginning, just like Coach had said. *Erase the slate. You're on!*

There was a Bible verse from Lamentations that Uncle Frank liked to quote: *"[God's mercies] are new every morning."* Mom had advised her to *"push out everything and focus."* Now Coach was saying some of the same stuff. Everyone was in agreement.

Her gaze was set firmly on the course below. She

could do it. *You want it badly—more than anyone else,* she told herself.

Time for the first run of the day. *I'll be a threat in Dressel Hills . . . no question!* she promised herself.

So what if it had snowed ten inches up here last night. She could ski as swiftly as the wind blew and faster—on new snow, old snow, or crusted snow. Even on ice. Nothing could throw her today.

She was nuts about speed in all forms. The downhill race was the king of all Alpine ski races. There were fewer turns to make, but they were high-speed turns. And the course was steep, a vertical drop of between five hundred and eight hundred meters.

Out the starting gate, she had a super clean, fast start. She flew like an eagle, balancing perfectly, then . . . *pham!* a solid landing. Skimming around each of the gates at top speed was easy today. Adrenaline rushed to every cell of her body.

Downhill Dynamite, she thought, glad for the upbeat music coming through her headphones to her brain. Yep, she was pumped. At the steepest section, she literally flew down the searing straightaway at nearly seventy miles an hour. A slight shift to the left, and she was heading with all her might toward the narrow chute. Tight as a Tootsie Roll, she skied. A week from tomorrow, her fans and other spectators, some with iron cowbells to distract and annoy the skiers, would line the sides, cheering her on. Mom, Uncle Frank, Mr. Greenberg, and Tarin.

As for Heather, Jenna, or Livvy, Manda sure wasn't counting on them showing up. Not if Jenna had her way. Besides, maybe Heather was right about things. Maybe Manda didn't care much about the club anymore. If they came, they came. End of story.

Benny, the young man who was the timer, skied to her at the bottom of the slope. He glanced at his stopwatch. Even before knowing her time, she was thrilled with her speed on this run. Her new and improved mind-set had boosted her to a near-record time. Just under one minute and 37.19 seconds.

Every micro-second counts, she thought.

Later, after she and Coach Hanson had a chance to talk, she rested for a short time, then was eager for another run. She visualized the slope at Eagle's Point, wishing she were there right now. But a super successful morning on Falcon Ridge was something to be jazzed about.

In the end, she beat out her own time by a few hundredths of a second. Trimming off every fraction of a second was cause for glee. "Yes, I *am* back!" she shouted, cuffing the air with her fists.

———

Determination and focus-power characterized the rest of the day. She and Mom talked after Manda showered and dressed for school. "I can't believe the difference today made," she admitted.

"I'm seeing the fight in you again, Manda. You're pulling it out." Mom watched her with keen interest.

"Cool." She liked what she was hearing. "Like Picabo Street says—'It's time to let my tiger surface.' " Over the years, Manda had been spellbound by the Olympic gold medalist from Idaho. In some ways, she was similar in temperament to the popular skier with a fiery temper. With Picabo as the ideal skier to match, Manda knew nothing could get her off course now. She would remain focused no matter what.

Hurrying off to school, she purposely avoided Jenna and Livvy. She got her books out of her locker in record time, then headed off to first period. She took good, solid notes during science, participated in lively discussion in history, rounding up her books and depositing old ones between classes. But she steered clear of eating lunch in the cafeteria. She was deep in thought while she ate at the snack bar, near the gymnasium. Secluded from the rest of the world—right where she wanted to be. Well, at least from certain people in *her* world.

Here came Livvy, the apparent scapegoat. Manda didn't know for sure, but she assumed Jenna had put Livvy up to this mission. Of course, Livvy didn't— *couldn't*—follow through with damaging Manda's ego. But she gave her a good tongue-lashing. Well, as good a tongue-lashing as petite and sweet Livvy Hudson could possibly pull off. "Just between the two of us, I'm not mad at you, okay?" Livvy began.

"Oh, really?"

Livvy glanced at the ceiling, then she looked back at Manda. "Well, I guess I'm a *little* mad."

"No kidding," Manda said.

"I'm stuck in the middle."

"Like how?"

Livvy tugged on her auburn hair. "Jenna wants me to relay messages, you know, to you . . . and I'm really getting tired of it."

"So tell Jen to do her own legwork," Manda said. "This is nuts. I mean, what's this about, really?"

Livvy sat down across from Manda. She leaned forward, eyes zeroed in on Manda. "Look, if you want to know the truth, all of this is Jen's idea. She wants to find out what's going on with you. What's *really* bugging you."

"I'm skiing in a race soon—my most important ever. I told her that." She sighed audibly, frustrated as never before. "You know what? I really can't be bothered with club meetings and other stuff right now."

The second the words flew out, Manda realized she'd made a huge mistake.

Livvy flinched at the insensitive remark. "Are you saying Girls Only is a pain? Are we, your friends, just in the way?" asked Liv. She looked absolutely crushed, like what Manda had just said was ripping apart something dear to her.

Coming from Livvy Hudson, this was startling. Here was a girl—the club's vice-president—who was typically soft-spoken and shy. And so thoughtful. Livvy didn't let people put words in her mouth and just spit them back out. She had a mind of her own. She was careful to evaluate a problem before jumping whole hog into a sticky situation. Like the present one.

Jenna, on the other hand, was an extremely outgoing gymnast. She was hard-driven and proud to be at the top of her sport, at least in Alpine Lake. Her dad was a pastor of a small Korean church in the village, and she and her parents had welcomed an adopted baby boy into their home just before Christmas last year.

All four of them—Jen, Livvy, Heather, and Manda—were caught up, one hundred percent, in athletic goals. But when it came to Jen, there was something extra intense about her. Something that went beyond her strong-willed and outspoken nature. On occasion, Manda had noticed, especially at club meetings, Jen seemed to crave the upper hand. She had to have her way about certain decisions. Maybe that's why she'd ended up as club president in the first place. But it bugged Manda. Big time.

So, here was Jenna's messenger—Livvy—sitting

across from her in the booth at the snack bar. What could Manda say or do that wouldn't create more conflict? Or cause more distraction for her before the most important race of her life so far?

Star Status
Chapter Eight

By the time the bell rang for afternoon classes, Manda and Livvy had come to a small understanding. "I just can't let *anything* keep me from doing my best on the slopes," Manda said.

"So . . . is that your bottom line?" Livvy asked, wearing a severe frown. "Your friends come in a distant second?"

Manda hadn't wanted to admit her priorities quite that way. But sometimes she did feel that skiing was all she needed in life to make her happy. That her friends didn't matter all that much.

"If I tell Jenna this, it won't be a pretty sight," Livvy said. "She bends over backward to juggle *her* social life, you know."

"That's Jenna . . . not me."

Their conversation ended abruptly then. Thanks to the bell.

———

Mom and Tarin greeted Manda at the door after school. "Here's our way cool downhill skier," Mom said.

Tarin agreed, his face shining with eagerness. He wore jean overalls with a red shirt, and his blond hair was combed back away from his face. "I thought you'd never come," he said, pulling on her jacket.

"Hold on," she said playfully.

"I *am* holding on." He continued to hang on her.

"Tarin," she said, smiling at the blue-eyed youngster, "want a snack?"

"Only if you're having one."

So they headed off to the kitchen, where Manda spread some peanut butter on several long sticks of celery. "I can't hang around too long," she told him.

"Are you off to the mountain?" His jaw drooped a bit.

"For a few hours. Your dad will come to pick you up before I get back."

"I'll miss you," he said in a whisper, eyes shining.

"Hey, don't be silly. I'll see you next week . . . on Monday, when I get home from school."

Tarin shook his head sadly. "You don't understand." He began to cry.

"What is it?" She went over and knelt beside him. "What's wrong?"

He sniffled and wiped his nose on his sleeve before he spoke. "I like you, Manda, and your mom, too."

She nodded. "Oh, Tarin, we like you, too. A lot."

More tears. "I don't want to go . . . away."

Manda frowned, not sure what he was trying to say. "Well, why would you *have* to, Tarin?"

His lower lip quivered. Short sobs made it hard for him to continue. "My dad's company is sending him to Utah. I . . . I don't want to leave here."

Reluctantly, Manda stood up and pulled out a chair. She could scarcely believe what the boy had said. His father was being transferred? How could this be?

She thought back to Wednesday evening, when Mom had mentioned that Tarin hadn't been himself that afternoon. Well, no wonder! Did Mom suspect anything? Did she know about the transfer?

The sudden news blew the wind out of her sails. How could she get it together mentally for today's practice run? She must not wipe out again due to lack of concentration. No, she must reject her fears. She would ski just fine. Like Mom said, the fight was deep within her. She was going to pull it out and hit the slopes running.

Still, the bombshell Tarin had just dropped on her in the stillness of the kitchen set her back. If only she hadn't let her fantasies about Mr. Greenberg marrying her mother go so far. If she'd just been reasonable, more practical about Mom's friendship with him.

Manda tried to comfort poor little Tarin. She hugged him for a moment, then hurried upstairs. In her room, she changed clothes, preparing for her afternoon run and session with Coach and her teammates. She knew what she had to do. She must suppress the knowledge, forget that Tarin had revealed anything. She must move ahead with her plan of action for the rest of the day. Sure, the news had jolted her, but it made her want to battle the mountain even more. She was angry. She didn't want to think the obvious, that every man who came into her and Mom's life simply walked away. She refused to think that of Matthew Greenberg. Even though that's how it looked.

Her head swirled with the shocker. Glancing at her watch, she knew that Jenna, Livvy, and Heather—right about now—were laughing and having a good time at Girls Only. . . .

———————

Manda skied well enough, though Coach Hanson asked her if everything was all right at home. She knew if she opened up and shared she would expose too much of herself. Sure, she felt defenseless to change the course of things. And yes, Mom's short-lived happiness was at stake and Manda's own hopes and dreams for a complete family had been shattered. That was no reason to get herself eliminated from the team by skiing poorly. Was it? She was going to Dressel Hills on St. Patrick's Day to win a race.

If anything, she was more committed to skiing her best than ever before. She planned to go into isolation for the next few days. Maybe all next week, too. She'd have to get Mom to sign off on the idea, of course. If missing a few days of school was a problem, then she'd just have to plead with her mother to see the light. Somehow, she was going to make it happen.

There would be no more petty encounters with either Jenna or Livvy. No more opening herself up to distractions of any kind. Nope, she'd had it. Even if Jenna *did* decide to "cut her some slack," as Livvy had put it, well . . . she would have to shelve the friendship for now. Because nobody . . . *nothing* was going to push back the tiger within her. The race was hers for the taking!

Star Status
Chapter Nine

She avoided bumping into Mom on Saturday morning. Manda got up long before dawn and slipped out of the house. She caught the one and only city bus.

The freebie transportation rumbled around through the village, then to the outskirts of town. She was headed for Alpine Ski Academy, hoping to run into Tarin's dad during the early-morning hours.

She knew Tarin's schedule for ski instruction from memory. Saturdays were free-ski days when the preschool-age skiers could hang out on the bunny slope without their regular instructors. Certified assistants hovered near, of course. But the idea was to give little skiers—who'd had a few weeks of training—a chance to try their wings.

Manda was sure Tarin would show up for the

hour-long session. And she wanted to be there—make it look like she was helping out—when Mr. Greenberg dropped off his son.

———————

Clean shaven and casually dressed in khaki pants and a blue knit sweater, Matthew Greenberg walked Tarin to the entrance. Manda watched the two from the window in the lobby area. The place was surprisingly hopping for so early on a weekend, but not so crowded that she couldn't go to them as they came in the door. "Well, hello there, Manda!" Tarin's father said, all smiles.

Tarin ran to her. "Want to watch me ski?" he asked, eyes pleading.

"Sure, for a little while. Then I have to hit the slopes myself." She glanced up at Mr. Greenberg, still taken with his good-natured grin and the way his slate gray eyes held your gaze.

Tarin ran off to hang up his jacket and find his skis. With him momentarily gone, Manda could comfortably bring up the subject of the Greenbergs' possible move to Utah. "I know it's probably not my place to ask, but Tarin said something yesterday . . ."

"About my transfer?" Mr. Greenberg said.

She nodded.

"I'm not surprised," he said. "Tarin's very attached to

both you and your mother. He's not at all happy about leaving Alpine Lake, or either of you."

Well, then ask Mom to marry you and take us with you, she thought.

"Tarin struggles with making new friends. He doesn't easily fit in with other kids."

"Because he's highly intelligent," she said softly.

"For that reason, I'm concerned about moving," Mr. Greenberg said.

Then don't, she thought, wanting to speak up but didn't.

"Does my mom . . . know anything yet?" she asked cautiously.

"I plan to tell her tonight."

Oh great. Manda didn't care to discuss this further. And she didn't want to keep an adorable little boy waiting. "I better catch up with Tarin."

"Okay. Have fun." With that, Mr. Greenberg waved good-bye.

She tried not to think how it would be on the day she and Mom said their final farewells. Thank goodness she still had her mom, the most important person in her life. She would direct her thoughts toward the one terrific parent God had given her. Yep, she'd do that during her practice runs today. No matter what life issues came her way, she knew she was a downhiller. Fearlessly, she pushed the limits of speed and daring.

I was born for this, she thought, heading off to the bunny slope to find Tarin.

————

At the end of another day of training, Manda was beat. But she'd agreed to watch Tarin while Mom went out for dessert with Mr. Greenberg. She wondered how Mom would react to the moving news. Would she be heartbroken? Or indifferent?

"Come play a game with me," Tarin called from the family room. He enjoyed the interactive computer games he'd brought along from home.

Wanting to be a good baby-sitter and provide an entertaining evening, Manda picked up the controls and played along, even though she really didn't care much for the game. And besides, she knew Tarin would end up winning. He was just so smart.

"How's it feel getting beat by a five-year-old?" he often said, eyes wide with glee.

She ignored him or shushed him jokingly, always wishing he might be her little stepbrother someday. Even as super intelligent—and smart-alecky—as he was. Being the only kid in the house could be a lonely state of affairs. *Having a younger sibling would be very cool,* she thought.

Tarin clicked pause, stopping the game for a second,

and turned to look at her. "Do you think your mom will talk my dad out of moving?" he asked innocently.

"Will she . . . or do you mean *can* she?" Manda replied.

"If she *can*, then she's important to my dad," Tarin smiled at that. "I hope she tries, at least."

Manda wasn't so sure. Mom was not the type to push a relationship too quickly. She trusted God wholeheartedly with everything in her life. "You know, I have a feeling something good just might happen tonight," she said.

"What do you mean, Manda?"

She wouldn't go so far as to say that Tarin's dad might hint of a marriage proposal. But she could hope. After all, both Mr. Greenberg and Mom were strong Christians, and they had plenty of things in common. Mom had said that their backgrounds were similar, the way they were raised and all that. It seemed like good, solid stuff to build on for a future of wedded bliss. But Mom wasn't running the show, Manda knew that. Her mother had made it quite clear that she wanted God's timing and His will.

So . . . who was Manda to try to push things through? And what if Mom and Mr. Greenberg weren't supposed to end up together, after all? Maybe the company move was God's way of dealing with that.

———

When the phone rang, Manda hurried to check the caller ID. When she saw Livvy's phone number, she purposely walked away from the phone, not answering. Enough unsettling news for one day.

"Aren't you going to answer your phone?" Tarin asked, eyes blinking.

"Not now."

"What if my dad's calling?"

"It's not your dad. Trust me."

He nodded and turned back to his game. She joined him, sitting down at the computer—doing her part to play well. She enjoyed Tarin's laughter and she was glad she could make him happy. At least for now. When he was gone from her life, maybe the two of them could correspond by email. Or . . . maybe little Tarin and his father would simply fade into the planet, like someone else she'd known.

Manda was actually surprised that Livvy—or one of the other club members—didn't try to call again that evening. In some ways, she was relieved. She didn't want to deal with whatever the club had decided about her at the snooty "special" meeting today. Besides, she was better off without them.

When Mr. Greenberg drove up in front of the house and parked at the curb, Manda and Tarin ran to the living room windows. Peering out, Tarin whispered, "Don't let them see us."

"Are we spying?" Manda asked, standing near.

Tarin grinned up at her. "I guess we are. We're love detectives."

"Oh, you're silly," she said. But she wondered if Mr. Greenberg had even held Mom's hand yet. She didn't suspect them of having even kissed "good-bye" yet. Mom was very cautious, as always.

They stood there silently staring out at the car, watching Tarin's dad come around to open the car on Mom's side. There was no pausing to exchange smiles or speak to each other on the steps as they approached the front porch. No endearing glances. The couple came immediately to the house.

Just before the door opened, Manda grabbed Tarin's hand, and they scurried away to the kitchen like two harmless mice.

———

After Tarin and his dad left, Manda settled down in her room for the night. She figured that if there was some big news Mom wanted to share, she'd come in search of Manda. It shouldn't be the other way around. She didn't want to put any pressure on her mom. She really didn't *have* to know about the romantic or not-so-romantic details of her mother's life. It was best to wait things out.

She curled up in bed, reading her collection of books featuring Olympic stars. Alpine ski racers, of course. As she read, she found herself visualizing the run at Eagle's Point. She could almost see the snow fences lining the most hazardous spots, the bumps, the turns, and the long, narrow path to the finish line.

Wait a minute! She'd forgotten to ask Mom about tomorrow. How could she have spaced *that* out? Coach was expecting her and the other skiers to work the Dressel Hills course. She'd be missing church and Sunday school again. But only if Mom agreed.

Closing her book, she jumped out of bed and hurried down the hall to Mom's room. She knocked on the door and waited, hoping Mom wouldn't think she was prying about the date with Mr. Greenberg.

Waiting longer than usual for a response, she knocked again. "You okay in there, Mom?" she called.

Still no answer.

Assuming her mother hadn't come upstairs yet, she turned and dashed down the steps. There in the living room, she found Mom on her knees, praying.

Wow, something big must have happened, she thought. Feeling awkward standing there, she tiptoed back upstairs. She would be patient and wait to ask her mother's permission later.

Meanwhile, she undressed for bed and picked up her Bible. But she didn't open it to read it. Instead, she sat staring at the leather-bound cover and traced the words *Holy Bible* with her finger. *Why,* she wondered, *do I feel so far from God . . . when Mom is so connected?* She didn't have the answer.

Later, when her mom came up the steps, Manda opened the bedroom door and peeked out. "Coach wants me to practice the run at Dressel Hills tomorrow. Okay with you?"

Mom grimaced a little. "You're missing church too much lately. What do *you* think?"

"I can't let the team down." *Not myself, either,* she thought.

Mom's eyes had that all-too-knowing look. But she didn't say Manda couldn't go.

So Manda took Mom's response as a "yes." A vague sort of answer. Mom wasn't entirely in agreement. First Jenna, Livvy, and Heather . . . and now Mom. God too?

Star Status
Chapter Ten

Sunday's training went better than Coach or anyone had anticipated. Except for one thing. The team's top-ranking male skier lost control and crashed through the snow fence near the top of the course. He ripped his knee up so badly that he had to be taken away to the hospital. Even with extensive rehab therapy, there was no way he could ski in the Downhill. Not with less than a week before the actual race.

As for Manda's performance, Coach seemed pleased. "Looks to me like you've memorized the course." He patted her on the back.

"I know every bump and turn," she replied. "And I plan to replay it in my head a thousand times before Saturday."

"That's the stuff," Coach said, both thumbs up. "You've got a better than good chance at this one."

She was thrilled with his words. It was the payoff for giving her attention to the job at hand. Thoughts of Mom and Mr. Greenberg had not even crossed her mind as she flew down the slope, her headphones cranked way up. She had been absolutely focused. Maybe more than if she *hadn't* had to deliberately block the disappointing news out of her mind.

———

After the ride back from Dressel Hills, she chose to walk from the ski academy to her house, only a few blocks away. She'd thought of catching the bus but needed time to ponder life. *Her* life. Present and future.

The crisp, still air was a welcome reprieve from the lashing winds of the mountain slope. She'd worn her helmet, all her safety ski gear, up there on the blustery slopes. But now, bareheaded—no hat or scarf—the cold slowly crept through to her scalp. She liked the feeling of her hair loose against her jacket and the icy-fresh smell of wintry air all around.

As she walked, she wondered, *What was Mom praying about last night?* For her mother, praying was part of the nightly ritual. But last night Mom had knelt in the living room, beside the sofa, as if she'd fallen to her knees in a hurry. Whatever was on her mind was obviously urgent. It simply couldn't wait for her to pray in the privacy of her bedroom. She'd stopped to ask God for guidance right on the spot. Was that the reason? If so, then Mr. Greenberg must have brought up a serious topic. What else could it be?

Carefully, she picked her way over snow-packed streets toward home. Through a tangle of mature aspen trees, Manda stared at the sky. Crystal blue, the heavens seemed almost within reach. A few flat clouds scattered over the expanse of space. Even though the trees weren't close to budding—it would be at least another month—she liked the way a multitude of branches webbed together above her. Some were so enormous they stretched out over a good portion of the street, like an incomplete awning, of sorts.

What would it be like to leave my hometown and live somewhere else? She thought it would be both strange and wonderful all at once. But, of course, it was silly to think this way, not knowing anything definite.

The city bus passed by just then, stopping at the intersection ahead. She waved back to the bus driver—Ian Kaplan, a native of New York. He'd lived in downtown Manhattan during his growing-up years. But he'd decided long ago to find a small town surrounded by mountains. There, he could go "unplugged," without television and later the Web. "Things got too frantic for me . . . all that technical stuff." And here he'd stayed, in Alpine Lake.

She smiled, thinking of Ian. How long had she known him? For as long as she could remember, he had been driving the town bus. Ian was just one of the "village people" she'd miss if ever she and Mom were to move away.

Coach Hanson was a big part of her life, too. So were her friends at church and school. And at the gym, where she often worked out. And . . . there was Jenna, Livvy, and Heather. But she didn't want to think about the thorny threesome. Not now.

———

The next few days—Monday, Tuesday, and Wednesday—slid by without any additional distractions. Manda decided not to ask her mom about taking off time from school. That could wait for the right moment. She attended school all day, returning home promptly to do homework. Then she hurried off to ski.

She managed to avoid her friends. Occasionally, she ran into one or two of them, but never all three at once. And they were no longer bugging her like before. Were they respecting her need for space at last? Maybe Livvy had gotten through to Jenna that Manda needed her distance. For the purpose of concentrating on the race, of course.

After supper on Wednesday, Manda revealed that she wanted to miss two days of school. "So I can ski all day," she told her mom. "Really get in shape."

Mom frowned. "What about homework?"

Manda had figured her mother would put her foot down. But she'd thought it through—had a plan of attack. "Would you mind sending a note to the principal? Explain everything? See if he'll excuse me . . . I could take it to him first thing in the morning."

"I wonder how this will go over with your teachers," Mom argued.

Manda tried to paint a picture of how things would be. How she would work extra hard on her schoolwork, even get up earlier than usual. Then, off to ski the whole rest of the day. "It's the best plan, Mom. Really, it is."

Then, surprise, surprise, after thinking carefully about it, Mom said it was fine with her. With one condition: Manda had to visit each teacher and get all homework assignments—any extra work, as well—in advance.

She was going to have school at home for a couple of days. *Like Heather and her brothers and sister do every day,* she thought, liking the idea. Maybe someday she would be homeschooled full time. Then she could spend more time in training and on the slopes.

Lots of advanced skiers got their education that way. Why not her, too?

———

Early Thursday morning, long before the bell, Manda took Mom's note to the principal's office. After her note was okayed, she began the process of gathering her assignments. Her history teacher removed his glasses and seemed surprised when she told him. "This is highly unusual," he said.

But when she explained what she was doing—representing Alpine Lake at the Downhill Classic—he smiled and seemed to understand. He also offered his enthusiastic support "for an exceptional run."

"Hopefully, a win," she said.

"That too."

She invited the principal and each of her teachers to watch the race. Most of them said they'd come and cheer her on. "We want our hometown girl to take first place," her English teacher said.

Hometown girl . . . There was a nice sound to that. Yep, she was the village girl, all right. Their star skier and their best hope for winning.

Nothing's going to stop me now, she thought.

As she headed home, her backpack seemed much lighter than she'd expected. Most of her teachers had gone easy on the homework. Especially when they heard she would be racing some of Colorado's best skiers.

Back home, she set to work on her school assignments. She knew the sooner she was finished—to Mom's satisfaction—the sooner she could hit the slopes again. She hoped to be done by early afternoon so she could spend the rest of the day skiing Falcon Ridge, working out with Coach, and maintaining her strength, stamina, and overall fitness. Same thing tomorrow.

Youth service night came and went, and so did ballet class. She hadn't gotten a call from a single friend all week. And she didn't pick up the phone to call anyone, either. Her thoughts were only on the prize. She was a society dropout. An outcast, probably, in Jenna's eyes.

But Manda didn't care. Winning was heavy on her mind.

Star Status
Chapter Eleven

The day before the race, Manda was so psyched she could hardly eat breakfast. But Mom had cooked a hearty and healthy breakfast for the two of them. She even set the table with a tablecloth, flowers, and cloth napkins.

"I've been doing a lot of praying lately," Mom said midway through breakfast.

"Hmm. You pray all the time." Manda grinned across the table.

Mom nodded sweetly. "There's something you should know, honey . . ." She paused. "I've thought a lot about this, and I don't think this will derail your efforts tomorrow. If I thought it would cause you a distraction, I'd save this chat until after the race."

Mom's absolutely radiant, Manda observed, watching

her with interest. "Do you have some big news, Mom?" she asked.

"Not such big news, no. But Matthew—uh, Mr. Greenberg—has asked me to join him in prayer for God's leading. For the two of us."

"So he didn't say anything about marriage yet?"

Mom's eyes blinked a little too fast. "Not in so many words." Her smile gave her away. "I guess you could say we're coming into the courtship phase."

"Way cool. Courtship leads to the wedding altar." She was thrilled.

"Don't get your hopes too high, Manda. We truly want God's will for our lives."

"Sounds to me like you've found it." She waited for another one of Mom's casual comebacks, but none followed.

After another long pause, Manda asked, "Is Mr. Greenberg going to take the company transfer . . . move away?"

Mom said thoughtfully, "That's all part of the pact we've made." Then, with eyes more serious, she said, "Would you like to join in our prayer adventure?"

Manda was taken off guard. She didn't want to admit that she hadn't been talking to God lately. She didn't have the right to ask the Lord to help her mom make an important decision, did she? Not if she wasn't thanking Him for the blessings she'd already received. "If

I'm going to pray, it better be about only one thing," she said.

Mom gave her a sideways glance. "Winning is everything for you right now." The words sounded peculiar—the tone Mom used—like she wanted to make a point and had. In a roundabout way.

"I eat, sleep, breathe, and taste victory," replied Manda. Coach Hanson and others had fostered this attitude in her. Her mother had, too. Mom had been a downhill racer herself, years before Manda was born. Sure, Mom knew the kind of pressure she was feeling . . . one day away.

"Will you miss Tarin if, well, if you and Mr. Greenberg don't—"

"Honey, let's not get into all this. Not today." Mom got up and went over and kissed the top of Manda's head. "There will be plenty of time to talk."

"After tomorrow."

"Right," Mom said.

"I'm going to make you proud," Manda replied.

Her mom went to the calendar hanging on the wall. She pointed to tomorrow's date: March 17. "After St. Patrick's Day, we'll have lots of time to talk. Okay?"

"It's a deal." Manda pushed away from the table. She helped her mom clean up the kitchen. And nothing more was said about tomorrow's race or Mr. Greenberg.

———

By mid-morning, strong westerly winds began blowing heavy gray clouds into the area of Falcon Ridge. By noon, Coach had to call off practice, sending Manda and the other skiers home early. Disappointed and worried about the status for tomorrow's race, Manda stood watching the blizzard from the living room window. She groaned. "Can you believe this?"

Mom encouraged her to hold steady, not to jump to any conclusions. "We'll wait out the storm. This mess could blow out in a few hours."

But the longer they waited for conditions to improve, the worse things got. Reports of the surrounding ski areas made Manda wilt. Dressel Hills was being buried alive!

In another hour, all incoming flights to the Aspen airport were grounded. Then, on top of everything else, Uncle Frank called to say his flight was canceled.

The snowing and blowing continued the rest of the day and into the evening. *The blizzard of the decade,* one TV announcer called the white tempest. Life in general came to a halt in Alpine Lake. But nearby Dressel Hills was hit hardest. The Downhill Classic was postponed until next Tuesday.

Manda couldn't remember ever having experienced such intense disappointment. The rescheduled race put her into a tailspin—set her back so far she had no idea how she could psyche herself up again.

She was ready to conquer a mountain. But now the mountain was out of reach.

———

When the storm subsided late Saturday afternoon, the roads were cleared in short order and village life returned to normal. Manda hurried off to the slopes on Sunday for another day of practice. By Monday, the day before the rescheduled race, she forced her speed and focused her attention on the course—and winning. After another long day, she was pumped up and ready to go.

That evening, Uncle Frank arrived an hour before supper. Mom did her usual song and dance about how terrific it was that he'd still come after the blizzard.

"Tomorrow's the big day, kiddo." He squeezed her so hard she thought she might break apart.

"Sure is!"

"Are any celebrities turning out for my niece's win?" he teased, laughing.

"There won't be any heads of state, if that's what you mean," Manda said.

"Oh, but the town mayor will be there," Mom spoke up.

"Doesn't that count for something?" She loved to banter with Uncle Frank.

"I'll bet some Hollywood types will trickle over from Aspen." He looked at Mom. "Don't you think so, sis?"

"All I can tell you is it's big—*the* racing event," Mom replied.

"Yep, and if I win this one, I'm off and running toward the next level—Coach Hanson says so." Manda was thrilled to give Uncle Frank this kind of report.

He nodded his head, sitting on one end of the sofa. "Which reminds me, I want to take your coach out for coffee while I'm here."

Manda had no idea what *that* meant. But knowing Uncle Frank, she wasn't worried. He had her future at heart. Winning or placing high tomorrow would put her over the top. In every way.

It was no longer could she do it, but when.

She felt so jittery sitting there in the living room talking about the race. She wanted to get out there and run it, especially after the unexpected delay. Of course, she had to sleep well tonight, get her full nine hours in. But how could she with so many things twirling in her head?

The race loomed. But not as enormous as the Dressel

Hills mountain itself. Brushing her hair before bed, she knew the win was hers for the taking. Tomorrow was all about snatching her dream.

The sweet taste of victory was within reach!

Star Status
Chapter Twelve

From the finish line, Manda and her teammates looked like flecks perched on the summit. Distant specks in the vastness of snow and ice.

She waited near the starting gate, high atop Eagle's Point, ready to roll. She was to be the third skier on the schedule. Mom and Uncle Frank and the Greenbergs were in the crowd of spectators somewhere. Exactly where on the course, she didn't know. She liked it that way. Better not to know.

Hard-driving contemporary Christian music pumped through her headphones. In the past, at other races, music had helped give her the edge she needed. If all went as planned, she would be totally jazzed and ready by the time it was her turn.

Manda knew she was fast. But watching the first

skier leap out of the gate and soar like a bird of prey through the air, she knew she was up against some fierce competition.

The fiercer, the better, she thought, thinking of the tiger she was about to let loose within her.

One by one, each skier would go hurtling down the hill. Some at speeds even her mom's car had trouble achieving. But the part that counted most was racing against a clock that evaluated each downhill racer in hundredths of a second.

To top things off, each skier got only one chance. A single run, and the race was over. Manda tingled with excitement. The surge of anticipation crept down her spine, into her rock-solid legs. *I'm so ready,* she thought.

Standing at the top, she looked below. The challenge of layers of new snow and ice lay before her. Red snow fences lined each side of the course. No matter what, she must avoid crashing into them. They were a killer.

Closing her eyes, she could see the memorized course clearly now. Everything she was up against. The vertical drop, the technical things, the corkscrew section, the finish . . . This was a speed course, first and foremost.

And then, she was next to ski.

When the signal came, Manda lunged forward.

Crouching into her racing tuck, she felt the thrill of the contest.

Ski, baby, ski . . .

She popped over the slope at the top of the hill. Then she began to wind her way down the steep course.

Squeezing into a tight ball, she let her legs absorb every bump and dip in the course. She took the turns as narrowly as possible, pushing . . . pushing with every nerve, every cell of her body at attention.

Now the halfway point. She wrung out every bit of speed during the middle section of the course. Anyone watching the race—anyone at all—would be able to see the race clock. They'd have an idea of how well she was doing. Mom . . . Mr. Greenberg . . . Tarin . . . Uncle Frank. Her history teacher, the principal. Half of Alpine Lake had turned out for the well-publicized race.

Is Daddy watching? she wondered. Does he even know? Does he care?

She cut her wind resistance even more by pulling tighter into her Tootsie Roll tuck. She had to win this race.

At the end of the middle section, the Corkscrews came into view. She felt herself losing her balance as she made first a hard right, then a hard left. But by sheer force and determination, she righted herself. She was cautious not to overcorrect and go flying, head over heels, into the snow fence. She'd seen too many skiers wipe out "sprawled eagle" in midair. Not her. Not this time.

She pushed back thoughts of Daddy. This race wasn't for him at all. This day was all about Miranda Garcia. Her dazzling, bright future.

"Ski for yourself . . . ski for you." Heather's words thrust her onward.

She zoomed toward the steepest section of the race—a stretch that would boggle the mind of the most advanced recreational skier.

There were two big jumps in the midpoint just before the narrow chute that made up the finish.

First, one landing—she was hot. Thoughts of her father staring at a TV somewhere, watching his girl do her best intruded her thoughts, but only momentarily. Downhill racing was *her* thing. Who cared if her long-lost father knew how good she was? Or how much she wanted to succeed—shoot for the Olympics someday.

The second landing came so quickly. She was speeding nearly out of control. She almost didn't have time to brace herself for the jump. Poles thrashing in the air, she resisted losing control. *Ka-bam!* She came in harder than usual on the landing.

Finish line . . . in sight. She must get between here

and there in under two seconds. Way under, if she wanted first place.

Dropping into her tightest racing tuck ever, she shot through the tapered chute to the cheer of hundreds of downhill fans. When she zipped past the finish line, she turned and looked up at her time. One minute and 37.14—her fastest yet.

Who on the Alpine Lake team could beat it? Could anyone?

———

The next skier was up. And the next.

When the race was finally over, every single skier had raced as if their future depended on it. But only Manda had snagged first place. She was number one!

A dazzling round medal was placed over her head. Breathing fast, she stroked the long ribbon. *Can this be real?* she thought. *Can this really be happening to me?*

Lifting the coolest prize ever to her lips, she kissed the emblem—a snowflake and the initials DHDC. This year's Dressel Hills Downhill Classic belonged to her and her alone.

Time to celebrate!

She spied Mom and Mr. Greenberg—Tarin too— waving pennants and motioning for her to come over to them. "Oh, honey, you did it!" Mom said, hugging her.

Uncle Frank was cool as always. He gave her a quick hug and several high fives. He said she was "looking good—better than ever!"

She brushed away happy tears. She had done what she'd set out to do.

Mr. Greenberg and Tarin were grinning, and Tarin grabbed her arm. "You're a star," he said softly. "I want your autograph."

"Sure."

"I mean right now." His eyes were wide with expectancy.

Mr. Greenberg turned to Tarin. "You'll see Manda several times next week," he said. "The autograph can wait."

Tarin was less than happy about that. But soon the media began to swarm them. Manda was the skier everyone wanted to interview. Media personnel galore. There were cameramen and women and news journalists vying for her attention. Even the mayors of Alpine Lake and Dressel Hills stood in line to congratulate her.

Her teammates hugged her and patted her on the back. "Way to go, Garcia," said one of the guys.

"You took the bull by the horns," said another.

"Hey, I'm no matador," she said. That brought a round of laughter.

"Well, you're the best, Manda," said one of the girls. "You deserve to win."

"Downhill Dynamite!" said Coach Hanson, giving her an enormous hug.

Manda spotted her principal and her teachers milling around. *They're waiting to talk to me,* she thought. And when, at last, she had a slight break in the crowd, they hurried to see her. "Congrats on a great race," her principal said.

"Thanks," she replied.

School acquaintances, even friends from church who'd known her before today, seemed to look at her differently. As if she'd changed somehow. They stared at her . . . amazed at her performance and speed, sure, but what was that look in their eyes? Admiration? Envy?

"I've been talking with the teachers here," her principal continued. "We've decided to have a Miranda Garcia Day at school." His face was red from the blustery cold, but his eyes shone. "This Thursday."

She was taken aback. "I . . . uh, thank you," she managed to say.

"Yes, we'd love to honor you at school," her history teacher said.

Honor you . . .

All this hoopla made her dizzy. She wasn't used to so many people paying so much attention to her. "You're at the top of your sport now," Uncle Frank said when he and Mom found her again.

"My girl's a champ," Mom added.

"We're very proud of you, Manda," said Mr. Greenberg, following close behind.

"Star status," said Tarin. "Very cool."

———

The thing Manda had been living for—sleeping, breathing, and all that—she wore proudly around her neck. First place! Had she actually skied so fast? Faster than every skier in the competition? Faster than she herself had ever skied down that or any mountain? Yep, she knew she had.

She was top dog. Until the next race, of course. But, for now, she could enjoy the win.

Turning to walk toward the lodge, she glanced over her shoulder once more. Her closest friends were nowhere in sight. Jenna, Livvy, and Heather hadn't shown up. They'd stayed home, probably on purpose. Who could blame them?

Thinking back, she realized she had not prayed about this race. Not even once. She hadn't even whispered a prayer for protection or for God's will in any aspect of this day. Not in the preparation of it, either.

This wasn't the way she had done things in the past. No, she had wanted to do it on her own. And she had.

But now suddenly . . . why was there this miserable, empty feeling in the pit of her stomach? Why didn't she *feel* the way she thought she would? Wasn't she supposed to be jumping for joy, laughing, and celebrating nonstop?

She couldn't fool herself. Something was very wrong.

Star Status
Chapter Thirteen

"I'm in the middle of my fifteen minutes of fame and glory," she told Uncle Frank that night. He had treated all of them, even Mr. Greenberg and Tarin, to a nice dinner out on the town. They'd gone to Alpine Lake's grandest restaurant. And Tarin had gotten his napkin autographed by her.

"Have you informed your face of that?" asked Uncle Frank. "You don't look like you just won the Downhill Classic."

She grimaced. "I guess not."

"So what's the problem?" His face was serious. "Why aren't you eating up all the attention? You certainly worked hard for this moment."

She was glad Mom was upstairs and they were down in the living room. Most likely, Mom couldn't hear any part of this weird conversation. "It's hard to explain," she said, choking back tears. "You'll never understand."

"Try me."

Looking at her uncle, she knew there was no getting past him. Not without a good, long chat. Sooner or later, he'd want to know what was bugging her. And sooner or later, she'd open up and tell him. And be glad she did.

"I've been a jerk," she said softly.

"Now, *that's* hard to believe," he said.

"No, really . . . I have been." She paused, thinking of Heather's helpful comments weeks ago, Jenna's observations of her at Girls Only meetings, and Livvy's phone calls checking in on her. And then, there was nothing. And it was all her fault. She'd shut her friends out. No long talks at lockers or after school. No hanging out in the dressing room after ballet class. No sitting together at youth group at church. No nothing.

They'd given up on her. They'd simply quit trying. And now she couldn't even share her excitement with her dearest friends. "I reached my goal today. But my friends weren't there to see it."

"Did you invite them?" her uncle asked, leaning his elbows on his knees.

"No."

She thought he might chuckle or something. He was silent. "Why not, Manda?"

"Long story."

"Well, in case you've forgotten, you're stuck with me for a couple of days. So shoot. I'm all ears."

She shifted her position on the sofa, pulling her legs up under her. Did she dare bore him with the unpleasant details? There was no need to rehash everything, was there?

"Manda . . ." His voice was more gentle now. "I'm here for you."

He's always been here for both Mom and me, she thought. An amazing feat her own father hadn't managed to pull off.

"Okay, here goes." She began to tell her uncle the whole story. How she'd snubbed her best friends, acted aloof at club meetings—skipped out on one—dropped out of too much just to win the race. "Instead of going to church, I skied. I even missed two days of school. But worst of all, I quit talking to God."

She'd almost expected to get a raised eyebrow over the final comment. But Uncle Frank sat calmly and quietly. He had never raised his voice to her in the past. Why would he now?

"Manda, you aimed your sights on a goal. In the process, you turned your back on your friends."

It sounded downright disgusting. But Uncle Frank's evaluation was completely true.

He continued. "Something deeper is troubling you,

kiddo. Something that's been bothering you for a very long time. Am I right?"

What's he saying? she wondered. How could he possibly know what was eating away at her heart?

"Yeah," she whispered. "Every day of my life."

"Your dad's gone, honey. Good or bad, he's not coming back."

"I know."

Then they began to talk, sharing the good memories Uncle Frank had of her dad. Some of the not-so-happy ones, too.

"My friend Heather Bock says I'm trying to get my dad's attention by winning on the slopes," Manda confided. "Sometimes, I think Heather might be right."

Uncle Frank frowned. "Well, *is* she?"

"I thought I was over this. It's been too long." Her eyes blurred with tears.

Uncle Frank moved to her side and put his arm around her shoulders. "God sees how you're feeling right now, and how you've felt all these years," he said.

She knew that. "God could've made Daddy stay with us, couldn't He?"

"We can't blame God for the decisions your dad made. Sure, God could have sent fireballs and lightning to stop him from leaving, but that's not the way our Lord usually works."

She had to laugh a little at the image of her father dodging heavenly bolts of electricity as he tried to leave the house that last day. Uncle Frank was absolutely right.

Then he said something that startled her. "Have you ever thought of forgiving him, Manda?"

"Forgive . . . Daddy?"

Her uncle nodded.

"I don't get it. Why should I?"

Uncle Frank sat up for a moment, then continued. "It's real important, kiddo. If you ever want to be free of this noose around your neck, you must forgive your dad. The Bible teaches that 'if you forgive men when they sin against you, your heavenly Father will also forgive you.' "

Manda took shallow little breaths. She'd read that verse many times. So many she'd memorized it. Why hadn't she taken the verse to heart? Was she that angry at her dad?

"I'll have to think about it," was all she could say.

"Try praying about it, too." Uncle Frank got up from the sofa. "See you in the morning," he said.

She looked up. Their chat shouldn't end like this. Things felt strained between them. "Um . . . do you want a bedtime snack?" she asked.

He grinned at her. "Thought you'd never ask."

Manda breathed a sigh of relief. The last thing she

wanted was to offend her uncle. They headed out to the kitchen, where she dished up a hefty bowl of chocolate-chip ice cream for him.

"Aren't you having some?" He pulled out a chair at the table.

She surveyed the ice cream.

"It's okay," he said. "Your next race isn't till the fall."

So she gave herself a medium-sized helping. "I've deprived myself for eight weeks," she said.

"Then it's time to celebrate."

Thank goodness for cool relatives like Uncle Frank. She even felt like smiling now.

Sitting down, she picked up her spoon. "You're right . . . about everything," she said.

He grinned back at her. "I'll take that as a compliment."

They enjoyed their ice cream without saying more.

Later, Manda asked, "Any ideas how I can make up with my friends?"

"Are you going to youth group tomorrow night?"

"Sure. You coming to church with Mom?"

"Wouldn't miss it." He looked at her, a quizzical expression on his face.

"What should I do when I see them?"

"Sit with them, for starters," he suggested.

"Are you kidding? Just go up to them—barge in on them?"

"No . . . not that." He chuckled. "C'mon, Manda, you're not shy. What's the problem?"

It was getting late. And the ice cream tasted so good. She really didn't want to get into this now. Truth was, she hadn't told Uncle Frank everything. She'd skimmed over the part about how demanding Jenna had become. Other stuff, too . . .

There was no way she could waltz into the youth service and act like nothing had happened. Far as she knew, Girls Only had already voted her out on her ear last Saturday.

Star Status
Chapter Fourteen

On the way into the church the next evening, several people stopped Manda to congratulate her. The youth pastor and his wife came up to her first. "Nice win, Manda," they said, but not before greeting her with, "Hey, stranger, long time no see."

Inside the church foyer, the head usher stopped to get an autograph. The organist and several friends of her mom's offered their congratulations. All of them had seen the article in the morning paper, it seemed.

She'd read the paper, too. She had scanned it carefully for the story on her win. But she'd found only a scissor-made hole where the article had been. Mom had jumped the gun and cut up the front page of the Lifestyle section too quickly. "It's for our family scrapbook," she'd said as an explanation to both Uncle Frank and Manda. This slash-and-snip session had occurred well *before* either of them had made it into the kitchen for breakfast.

"Aw, sis," Uncle Frank had said as he swigged down his morning coffee. "Leave the paper intact for others to read, *then* chop it up." There was more than just a hint of sarcasm in his voice.

Manda had found all of this banter amusing. But not her first encounter with Jenna Song in the downstairs hallway of the church. "Hey," Manda said, forcing a smile when she spied the award-winning gymnast.

Jenna replied, "Hey." But she kept walking.

So much for sitting together, Manda thought. Actually, she was glad Jenna wasn't all warm and sociable. There was too much to work out between them for a fast and fakey comeback. Fact was, Manda wanted a chance to show Jenna what a good friend she could be. A reliable one. A friend who cared about relationship as much or more than claiming first place on the slopes.

But how? What could she do to get Jen's attention?

Just then, Livvy and Heather came walking toward her. *Here we go,* she thought. How would *they* treat her?

"What's up?" Manda said.

Heather slowed her pace a bit, smiling cautiously. Then she stopped, as though she might not mind talking a little. Livvy, on the other hand, seemed a bit distracted and kept going. It wasn't until Heather called to Livvy that she wandered back to them. Then she turned to Manda and said, "Congratulations on your win, Manda."

"Thanks," Manda replied.

"Yeah, you were really great out there," Livvy spoke up.

Great? How'd Livvy know?

"You looked awesome," Heather piped up. "Especially when you came barreling down the final stretch. Man, it made the hairs on my arm stand straight up."

"How would you know that?" Livvy asked, laughing. "You had all kinds of layers on under your jacket."

Heather seemed to be jiving Livvy. "C'mon, you know what goose bumps feel like, even under two sweaters and a parka." Weird. Heather was humoring Livvy, for some odd reason.

But Manda was surprised at what she was hearing. "Were you two . . . uh, did you actually come to see the race?" she asked softly.

Heather nodded. "Sure. Did you think we wouldn't show up?"

"To see our star skier?" Livvy added quickly.

Our star skier . . .

Now Manda really felt lousy. She didn't say she'd looked for them, hoping they'd come. She didn't want them to know how much it meant to her. Besides, she hadn't offered them an invitation. Yet they had come anyway. Wow.

"We're friends, Manda," Heather said. "We didn't want to miss seeing you."

"Yeah," Livvy said. "You cheer for us at our local events."

Manda was starting to feel better about things. "So . . . then you haven't kicked me out of the club?"

Livvy frowned. "Well, nobody said *that.*"

Whoa. She was really confused now.

"Guess you'd better talk things over with the club prez," Heather said, squeezing Manda's arm. "It's time the two of you had it out, anyway."

Manda wasn't so sure. She didn't like the sound of this. But she followed them off to youth group and sat with Heather. Livvy went and sat with another one of her friends in the last row.

Waiting for the worship leader to get things rolling, Manda felt awkward. Like she knew she ought to tell Heather she was sorry. Anything to smooth things over with her best friend.

She was starting to lean over to say something, when Heather whispered, "Jen said there's going to be a Manda Garcia Day at your school or something."

Manda cringed. "Yeah . . . tomorrow."

"It's all over Alpine Lake . . . about you." Heather seemed terribly excited. "The whole town's jazzed."

She wanted to say she didn't care about the whole town, not even the special recognition day. She only cared about one thing. Where did she truly stand with Heather, Livvy, and Jenna . . . and Girls Only?

———

On Thursday, the walls at school were cluttered with banners and streamers. There was even a blown-up picture of her mounted near the school office.

Miranda Garcia . . . Ski Star, one poster read.

You go, girl! another boasted.

Kids she hardly knew came up to her in the hallway. "How'd you do it?" they asked. "How'd you ski so fast?"

When she finally made it through the crowd to her locker, Livvy was waiting. "Uh, Manda, hey . . . can I talk to you?"

Manda felt a lump in her throat. "Sure, what's up?"

"I was a jerk about—"

"No, *I* was," Manda interrupted. "And I'm sorry."

"Then, you're not mad at me . . . at all of us?"

"You and Heather—why should I be?" she replied.

"We just thought, well, we wondered if your sport was going to your head." Livvy glanced at the ceiling, then she looked right at Manda. "You know what? I get that problem sometimes, too. But is anything really worth losing your friends?"

Manda smiled. "Coming from you, that means a lot."

"Super cool." Livvy hurried to her own locker. "Hey, my locker partner is on her way," she said, glancing over her shoulder. "Better nail Jenna now."

This wasn't like shy, soft-spoken Livvy. *Better nail Jenna?* What did Livvy mean? Was she so eager for Manda and Jenna to patch things up?

Squaring her shoulders, Manda took a deep breath. Yep, she was ready to be friends with Jenna again. Whatever it took.

———

Later, Manda sat in English class while the teacher talked about "Miranda Garcia Day." She blushed at the teacher's words. "One of our own students is on her way to Olympic fame. We have a terrific skier in our school . . . in this very classroom."

Enough already, thought Manda, wishing they could just get started on correcting homework. She had years of training ahead of her—and continuous wins, too—before she could even come close to making the cut for the Olympics. Sure, it was her ultimate goal, her dream. But today she wasn't in the mood to have her future broadcast to a roomful of kids.

Her mind was elsewhere. On Jenna's strange reaction this morning.

Manda had followed Livvy's suggestion and attempted to talk to Jenna. But Jen seemed to be in a big hurry, never even making eye contact with Manda. So much for smoothing things over. Nope, Manda was beginning to see just what a mess she'd created. In time, she might be able to prove herself. Maybe. If Jenna gave her half a chance.

Meanwhile, she felt lonely at the top of the ladder. Sure, everyone was asking her how it felt "up there." And yes, it was great to be a winner. The VIPs at the race were wowed by her speed and poise. She was the hot new young skier in the west. And Uncle Frank had taken Coach to lunch to talk over her bright future before he left town.

But once all the excitement died down, what was left? The memory, sure. Her awesome first-place medal. But what about her friends?

Star Status
Chapter Fifteen

The next day after school, Manda and her mom drove to Kansas to visit Manda's grandparents for the upcoming Easter weekend.

Meanwhile, Girls Only Club members were presenting the spring play to their parents, complete with ballet encore. Manda wondered if Jenna might think the Kansas trip was an excuse for Manda *not* to be in the play.

———

On Monday, after returning to Alpine Lake, Manda found out exactly what Jenna thought of her.

Livvy seemed to scowl when Manda ran into her at their lockers between classes. "Guess I'd better warn you," she began. "Jenna says if you're a no-show at the regular meeting this coming Friday, the remaining members will have to do some serious talking."

"That's not fair!" Manda blurted. "Any other member would—" She stopped. She did not want to battle with Jenna Song's best friend. But the way Livvy's solemn face had turned to an absolute frown—a sad frown— Manda wasn't sure whose side Livvy was on anymore. Was she just passing along info to a soon-to-be-defunct club member?

Their president's attitude was really the pits. Manda decided then and there, she'd had it with Jen's pushy attitude about attendance at club meetings. The four of them had taken time to write bylaws for exactly this reason. Wasn't there a rule that addressed this very issue? Livvy and Heather, after all, were just as involved in skating and ice-dancing events as Jenna was in gymnastics. No one would ever think of harassing *them* for missing club meetings either before, during, or after a major competition. This was absolutely insane!

"It may not be fair, that's true," Livvy said, softening a bit. "But Jenna's really ticked."

"That's her problem." And with that, Manda walked away.

———

Things slowed to a crawl at the ski academy the week following Easter. The days were consistently sunny, warmer now. Less snow. The ski season was fast coming to a close.

Manda deliberately skipped Girls Only that Friday, in spite of Jenna's warning. She *was* lonely, but didn't want to admit it to herself. She had actually walked over to Jenna's house and stood sadly on the opposite side of the street, watching Heather and Livvy go inside. They hadn't seen her, of course. Even if they had, she felt she was a member *not* in good standing. She didn't deserve their friendship.

With Uncle Frank long gone, there was no one to dump on. Mom wasn't a good choice, not with her so caught up in Mr. Greenberg's move. Kind woman that she was, Mom was helping the Greenbergs organize and pack for Utah.

It's crazy, thought Manda. Especially because Mom would never see Matthew Greenberg again. Wasn't that how things always went?

She was sure Mom cared deeply for the man. She'd seen it in her mother's eyes, heard the softness in her voice when she spoke his name. So why was Mom helping them pack? It made no sense.

Nothing did.

———

The weekend came and went. No one called to complain that she'd missed Girls Only again. Saturday, while she was probably being voted out of the club, she hit the slopes one last time. When she arrived home, not a single message awaited her on Mom's answering machine. So, Jenna had worked her magic with both Heather and Lizzy. Against Manda.

Monday morning, before school started, Manda went to the gym. She noticed Jenna working out on the rings, but Manda kept her distance. No need to confront anyone so early in the morning.

Busying herself with leg presses, she wondered what she might say to her former friend, the way she always tried to think through every detail of a ski run. Maybe she wouldn't have the chance to talk to Jenna today. But . . . she could hope.

She didn't know how long she'd been doing that— thinking. But when she changed her position and looked up, there was Jenna standing nearby. "Hey," Jen said. "Need a break yet?"

"Sure."

They walked to the fruit juice vending machines without saying a word. Before Jenna could pay for her own, Manda quickly pulled out a bunch of quarters. "Here, let me buy yours this time."

"Thanks," Jenna said, looking a little startled.

They waited for the machine to eat the quarters and

cough out the boxed juices. Both girls stuck the plastic straw inside the hole and sipped.

When Manda could stand it no longer, she said, "I'm sorry about . . . so many things, Jenna." Her words came flying out. "I was wrong to shut you and Livvy and Heather out." She paused to breathe. "I don't expect any special privileges or anything."

Jenna looked puzzled. "What do you mean?"

"About Girls Only. You don't have to let me back in the club. I just want to be friends. That's all that matters to me."

"You were never kicked out," Jenna said, her eyes squinting nearly shut.

Manda jerked her head and looked at Jen. "What? Are you kidding me?"

"Sure, I used some tricky tactics to try to get you to show up. But if you're wondering about the extra meeting we had . . . well, it wasn't about voting you out."

"What, then?"

"Actually, we met to pray for you." Jenna was smiling now.

"You what?"

"We asked God to wake you up . . . bring you to your senses."

Here she'd snubbed her nose at them, and they'd

prayed. Wow. "Looks like God answered quick," she said.

"So . . . are you ever coming to Girls Only again?" Jenna asked.

"Sure am." Manda was happy, as happy as the day she'd won the race.

———

The next day Manda and her mom said good-bye to Mr. Greenberg and Tarin. The moment had the potential for disaster. But their farewells were actually bittersweet.

Tarin seemed much more content with the move now. "I'll never forget you, Manda," he told her with a smile.

"Don't worry," she said, reminding him that they could "talk" by email. "And you'll have to come back to Alpine Lake and visit us."

Mr. Greenberg cut in. "I'll make sure that Tarin sees both of you again."

Manda looked curiously at her mom. This sounded like the promise of something special. Something more serious than just dating.

He continued. "We'll need some time to get settled, of course."

Mom's eyes twinkled so brightly, Manda knew something was going on.

Then later, after the moving van had pulled away from the curb, Mom filled her in. "Matthew and I believe the Lord is preparing us for a life together. If all goes well, we plan to be married by late summer."

"Mom, is this for real?" She was overjoyed. "I've been hoping for this, you know . . . ever since I met Mr. Greenberg."

"Then . . . you're not upset? I mean, about possibly having to move?"

Manda didn't know why she wasn't. Maybe she was just so eager to see her mother happy for the rest of her life. "Don't worry about me, Mom. This is so exciting for you. For *both* of us. Tarin too."

"The Lord willing, we'll probably move before school starts in the fall."

A brand-new school and a new set of friends next year . . .

She was still for a moment. "I'll miss my girl friends a lot." *I just got them back!* "But there's no reason why they can't come visit us, right?" She was thinking how cool it would be to have her very own, very wonderful, stepdad. She could show him off to Jenna, Livvy, and Heather. They would be so happy for her.

"Matthew wants to build a big house in Utah. So I don't see why your friends couldn't come see us. Even Coach Hanson and his wife could visit."

Mom was talking some interesting stuff.

"How hard will it be for me to get a new coach?" She knew firsthand that Utah had some of the all-time best downhill skiing and ski instructors in the country. It was still ski-racing country, after all.

"Between you and me, I think our move will give you even greater opportunities," Mom said.

Manda was getting antsy. She headed for the steps. "Do you mind if we talk more later?" she asked.

"Why, honey?" Mom followed her to the steps. "Are you upset?"

Manda shook her head. Upset was the last thing she was today. "I just need to talk to someone else for a little while, that's all."

Mom seemed to understand. "Well, when you're finished praying, I'll be here."

She knows me inside and out, Manda thought, hurrying up the stairs to her room. Kneeling beside her bed, she prayed, "Dear Lord, thanks for letting me ski well enough to win first place at Dressel Hills. I know I didn't do it in my own strength. I know you were right there with me." She paused. "I need forgiveness, Lord. For ignoring you for so long. And for the way I treated my friends . . . and everyone else."

A warm and gentle peace filled her heart. "Uncle Frank says I must forgive Dad," she continued. "Well, now might be the time. I don't know how you'll help me do it, but at least you know I'm ready. One more thing: Please bless my mom and Mr. Greenberg in their marriage. Make it an extra-long-lasting one, a forever kind of love. In Jesus' name, Amen."

Star Status
Chapter Sixteen

At the next meeting of Girls Only, Manda shared her moving news. "Mom says all of you can come see us anytime. And there's always the phone or email," she said, trying to soften the blow. "I know it won't be the same. Not even close."

Heather started to cry, and Livvy got quieter than she usually was. Jenna, though, came over and hugged Manda. And then they were all hugging her and one another.

"This isn't the end, not really," Manda said. "We're just moving ahead with life . . . wherever God wants us to be."

"That doesn't make it hurt any less," Heather said, brushing away tears.

Livvy nodded. "I remember how I felt when Dad

and I first moved here. It was so hard. But then it got easier when I made friends with all of you."

Jenna suddenly snapped her fingers. "Hey, maybe Manda could start up another Girls Only Club—like a sister branch, you know."

Manda hadn't thought of that, but Jen's idea was fantastic. "Maybe someday there will be a bunch of clubs like ours all over the country. Who knows?"

"That *would* be cool," said Heather. "Like if my family moved away, too. Maybe to Lake Placid in New York or somewhere. I could start a Girls Only Club there."

Manda, Livvy, and Jenna turned and stared at Heather. "What?" they said in unison.

Heather backed away from them, holding out her hands, palms out. "Uh, I didn't say we're moving tomorrow or anything," she said.

"But are you actually thinking of moving?" Jenna asked, eyes blinking rapidly.

Heather shrugged. "My parents have talked about it. Kevin and I would have better skating opportunities if we did."

"So it's just a *might* happen?" Manda asked.

Heather nodded slowly. "Who knows."

Jenna paced the floor, back and forth two times. "So . . . is anyone *else* leaving town?"

The room was still.

"Hey, it's not the end for us," Manda said softly. "In some ways, it's just the beginning."

"Right, for our athletic dreams," added Heather.

"Our friendship is solid now," Manda said. "We just found out how strong."

"And don't forget, we can pray for each other, wherever we are," Livvy said in a near whisper.

"Oh yeah, we'll pray, all right," Jenna said, chuckling. "We'll ask God to keep Manda and Heather right here in Alpine Lake!"

That brought a flurry of laughter. Manda knew Jenna meant well. Jen had a good heart. Always had. Nothing—not moving away or starting over with new friends in a different town—was going to change how Manda felt about her cool friends here in Colorado.

In God's eyes, each of them were stars, talented in various ways. Each girl gifted uniquely.

Manda also knew in her heart that she would take seriously the short time she had left in Alpine Lake. Because, just as in sports competition, when it comes to friendship, every precious second counts.